I0728263

Eric Wilder

Blink of An Eye

Gondwana Press
Edmond, Oklahoma

Other books by Eric Wilder

Ghost of a Chance
Murder Etouffee
Name of the Game
A Gathering of Diamonds
Over the Rainbow
Big Easy
Just East of Eden
Lily's Little Cajun Cookbook
Of Love and Magic
Bones of Skeleton Creek
City of Spirits
Primal Creatures
Black Magic Woman
River Road

This book is a work of fiction. Names, characters, place, and incidents either are products of the author's imagination or used fictitiously. Any resemblance to actual events or locales or persons, living or dead, is entirely coincidental.

© 2017 by Gary Pittenger

All rights reserved, including the right of reproduction, in whole or in part in any form.

First Printing

Gondwana Press LLC
1802 Canyon Park Cir. Ste C
Edmond, OK 73013

For information on books by Eric Wilder
www.ericwilder.com

Front Cover by Andrés Grau
http://andresgrau.tumblr.com/

ISBN: 978-1-946576-00-2

Acknowledgments

I wish to thank Donald Yaw for helping me edit Blink of an Eye, and providing valuable input involving timeline and character development. Thanks, also, to Don, George Rodman, Lee Kastor, Shane Bohl, Kelly Novakowski, and Raymond Berlioz for answering some of the many questions encountered while writing this book.

For Marilyn

Blink of an Eye

A novel by
Eric Wilder

Chapter 1

Late for dinner and a movie with his steady girlfriend Lynn, Buck McDivit raced down I-35. Almost sundown, snowflakes from a spring cold front dusted his windshield. As sunset began turning the sky red, an old pickup appeared over the rise in the northbound lane.

Almost out of control, the driver flashed his headlights when he saw Buck's truck. In less than a moment, he realized why the old pickup was in such a hurry. A black truck doing ninety or more crested the rise behind it. The speeding vehicle slammed into the pickup's rear bumper, swerving it.

"What the hell?" he said.

Tapping his brakes, he slowed just enough to cross the grassy median in a sliding skid. When he hit the pavement, he floored the gas pedal in an attempt to catch the two speeding vehicles. The big V8 in his Navigator responded with a revving engine and squeal of burning rubber.

The speedometer reached a hundred as he crested a rolling hill and caught up with the two vehicles in front of him. The truck kept banging the old pickup, finally spinning it and sending it into the ditch. It flipped in the air doing a slow-motion tumble before hitting a sandstone outcrop. Buck dialed 911.

"Got a bad wreck on I-35. Need an ambulance, and quick."

The black truck slowed just enough to give Buck time to read its license tag. The personalized plate said BladeRunner-1. With other things more pressing on his mind, he watched as it disappeared over a rolling hill.

Slamming the brakes, he slid to within thirty feet as the truck caught fire and started to burn. Without bothering to shut his door, he raced to the burning vehicle. The truck lay on its side; the hood popped and dark smoke billowing from the engine. Jumping on the running board, he grabbed the door handle and yanked.

An old man lay crumpled behind the wheel, his eyes closed. He felt light as a feather as Buck wrestled him from the cab. Dragging him, he tried to get as far away from the burning truck as he could. They almost made it.

When the truck exploded, the concussion knocked Buck off his feet. Slamming into the pavement, he skidded on knees and elbows, his face scraping asphalt. Hot air warmed his neck as it blasted over his head. The old man opened his eyes when he patted his face.

"I knew it was you when I saw your truck," he said in a whispered voice.

"Do I know you?"

The old man's eyes closed and he grew silent without answering the question.

Scant minutes had passed before sirens began screaming. An emergency vehicle from the Guthrie fire department skidded to a halt behind them. Two EMT's that Buck recognized raced to help.

Clint was short, had a pug nose and a fireplug body. His partner Bones McGee was twice as tall and half as wide.

"Ain't got much pulse," Clint said, slipping an oxygen mask over his face. "You okay?"

"Don't worry about me," he said. "How'd you get here so quick?"

"Just down the road when the call came in. Lucky for you."

The two EMT's loaded the old man into the back of the ambulance and then returned to check on Buck.

"You look like hell," Bones said.

"Where you taking him?" Buck asked.

"Guthrie Hospital," Clint said. "Come with us. You got burned hands and blood all over you."

"Meet you there," Buck said. "Can't leave my truck on the side of the road."

"Okay, tough guy. Just don't pass out on the way there."

Traffic had begun stacking up on I-35, police vehicles, and rubberneckers slowing traffic. At least until a semi racing toward Wichita crested the rise. By the time he saw the congestion, it was too late. The big truck careened full throttle into Buck's Navigator.

Both vehicles ended up in the ditch as firefighters rushed to check on the driver. Buck would have helped but the collision had knocked him smooth out. Ammonia beneath his nose opened his eyes.

"Your truck's toast. Ain't going no place except the junkyard," Clint said."

Buck was in no position to argue. After assisting him to the ambulance, they raced away in a blast of sirens and screech of burning rubber. He recovered enough to touch the shoulder of the old man on the gurney as Bones adjusted the IV in his veins.

"How's he doing?" Buck asked.

"Don't look so good," Bones said. "You got a hell of a knot on your head. Hang on, and I'll clean the blood off your arms and face."

"Just take care of the chief," Buck said. "I'll be fine till we get to the hospital."

The old man's bone structure and hooked nose pegged him as a Native American. He opened his eyes and smiled when he saw Buck.

"I knew I'd find you," he said.

"You know me?" Buck asked.

"Esme sent me. She said to give you this."

He fumbled with something in the pocket of his faded shirt. Buck took the object, turning it in his hand.

"What is it?" he asked.

The old man didn't answer, his eyes closing again.

"We're losing him," Bones said, pumping his chest.

The faint blink of a dark Indian eye showed them he was still alive.

"Hang in there, Chief," Buck said.

A wisp of a smile appeared on the wizened face of the old Indian as he grasped Buck's hand and squeezed. When his hand relaxed, Buck knew he was dead. Bones checked his pulse, and then covered his face with the sheet.

"You knew him?" he asked.

"Never saw him before tonight," Buck said.

"Who is Esme, and what did he give you?"

"A beautiful woman I once knew. Don't have a clue what this thing is," he said.

"Looks like some Indian relic to me," Bones said. "What happened back there?"

"Driver of a black truck ran him off the road. I got his tag number."

"Give it to me. I'll call it in," Bones said.

"BladeRunner-1. Oklahoma vanity tag."

Buck glanced at his skinned elbows and blisters on his palms. After wiping the blood from his face with his blue bandanna, he wrapped it around his right hand. Bones didn't let him finish, moving around the cot to check him out.

"Where does it hurt?" he asked.

"All over," Buck said.

"Least you're alive," Bones said, glancing at the body of the old man covered with the sheet. "More than I can say for the chief."

Chapter 2

Hours passed before doctor and nurses allowed Buck to leave the emergency room. His foster mother, Carol Hagen was in the waiting area and ran to meet him when he exited the swinging doors. The first thing she did after hugging him was to check out his bandages.

"They wouldn't tell us at the window how you were. Jim and I have been sick with worry."

"HIPA," he said, referring to the strict Federal privacy law. "Gotta love it."

Carol was a stunner, even for someone in her mid-fifties. A former homecoming queen, she'd married the captain of the football team. Her supple frame carried not an extra pound. She kept it that way by riding horses and helping husband Jim work their farm. At least when he wasn't busy doing Logan County sheriff work.

"Are you okay?"

"Skinned up, and a few burns here and there. Nothing serious."

Carol grabbed his elbow and pulled him to the door. "Jim and the dogs are in the car. We've been taking turns here in the waiting room."

Buck kissed her forehead. "Thanks, my truck's history. I was wondering how I was going to get home."

He smiled when she said, "You knew we'd be here."

Rain had replaced patchy snowfall as muted moonlight cast reflections off pools of water. A white Suburban moved toward them, two dogs squirming to get out of the half-open window in back. When Carol opened the door, they both came running.

"Boys," she said as they jumped up on Buck.

Buck squatted to show them some love. "It's okay," he said.

Pard was a black and white border collie Buck had rescued from the streets. They were inseparable, and he went everywhere with the young P.I.

Coco was Carol's Chihuahua. Jim's bloodhound Snuffy had died of old age the previous summer.

"Too much pain to deal with when you lose your best friend. I'll never have another dog," Jim had avowed.

Despite himself, he'd grown attached to the little brown dog that wasn't afraid of anything.

Buck was thirty-something, six feet of muscle, dark wavy hair and chiseled good looks. Despite his appearance, he'd never married. As time passed, Carol and Jim wondered if he ever would. Right now, it didn't seem to matter as the two dogs wagged their tails and licked his face.

"Back in the car, boys," Jim said as he exited the Suburban. "You okay?"

"A few bumps and scrapes. I'll be good as new in a day or so."

"Good. Carol was worried about you."

Buck grinned, knowing Sheriff Jim had been just as worried. Two inches shorter, Hagen had cropped black hair and a mustache. A former Army officer, he hated uniforms. The badge on his belt was the only sign he was the most powerful law officer in Logan County.

"It's late. Sorry, you have to take me all the way to Edmond," Buck said.

"Then come home with us. Carol had a tamale casserole in the oven. It smelled wonderful," Jim said.

"You haven't eaten?"

"No, and I bet you haven't either," Carol said.

"I can drop you off tomorrow on my way to work," Jim said.

"Sounds great," Buck said as Pard jumped in his lap and licked his face.

The Hagens lived on a farm east of Guthrie in a bucolic log house that was both spacious and comfortable. Coco and Pard were the first ones out the door. After a friendly argument over a dog biscuit left on the front steps, they cuddled up together on the porch. They were still there when Carol, Buck, and Jim finished eating and joined them.

"You haven't lost your touch, Carol," Buck said. "I've never had tamale casserole. It tasted wonderful."

"You'd say that if I'd cooked an old shoe," she said.

Buck sat on the steps as Jim retrieved a couple of cold Coors from an ice chest he always kept on the front porch. Carol was drinking hot tea. She held the warm cup under her nose, savoring the aroma. Frogs and crickets played a concert as the horn of an eighteen-wheeler faded in the distance. Jim joined him on the steps.

"This is the most peaceful place on earth," Buck said.

"No arguments from me," Jim said. "What happened out there on the interstate?"

"I was on my way to OKC to take in dinner and a movie with Lynn. Her birthday."

"Was she upset when she found out you were

in an accident?" Carol asked.

"She was so busy screaming at me when I called she never gave me a chance to explain why I stood her up."

"She won't stay mad when she realizes what happened."

"Not so sure about that."

"Buck, I'm so sorry," Carol said.

"Don't worry about it. I haven't had much luck with women. Some things never seem to change. I saw an old red pickup heading north. When I passed it going the other direction, the driver flashed his lights."

"You knew him?" Jim asked.

"No. He was driving fast, almost out of control. Someone in a black truck was chasing him, trying to run him off the road. I cut across the median and followed them."

"I tried running the car tag the EMT's called in," Jim said.

"Tried?"

"The Caddo Nation issued the tag. They refuse to share information with anyone outside their tribe."

"They can do that?" Buck asked.

"Unfortunately, yes," Jim said.

"I'm sure they'll cooperate in a murder investigation," Carol said.

"You'd think, but I have no authority to compel them."

Coco and Pard opened their eyes and perked their ears when a distant coyote howled at the moon. They were soon asleep again in Coco's plush dog bed.

"What about the old man?" Buck asked. "Were you able to identify him?"

"Pascal LeFlore, a full-blooded Mississippi Choctaw. He lived alone in the mountains of southeastern Oklahoma. Did he say anything to you?"

Carol's hand went to her mouth when Buck answered. "He said Esme had sent him to find me."

"You have to be kidding," she said, leaning forward in the old rocking chair.

"No one has seen or heard from Esme in a couple of years," Jim said. "You think she's still alive?"

"If I told you, you wouldn't believe me."

"Don't be like that, Buck McDivit," Carol said.

Jim grabbed two more beers from the ice chest, tossing one to Buck.

"You know something you haven't told us?"

"I'm not sure Esme was ever alive, at least in the truest sense."

"What kind of gibberish are you spouting?" Jim asked.

"Esme was a Mississippian Indian. That tribe is long extinct. To me, she was somehow more than human."

"Not human?" Carol said. "What then?"

Buck glanced up as the shadow of a cloud covered the moon. "Maybe a deity."

"Get the hell out of here," Jim said. "What kind of painkillers did they give you at the hospital?"

"I said you wouldn't believe me."

Carol was sitting on the edge of her rocker. "If this is true, why haven't you told us about it before now?"

"Because I knew you wouldn't believe me. I've wrestled with the concept. I have no other explanation."

"Then what was she doing here?" Jim asked.

"She had a plan, part of which was for me to father a child."

"They drugged you," Jim said.

"And tricked me."

"Don't be bitter," Carol said. "Little Adam is a beautiful boy. You should be proud."

"I am, except that Clayton, KK, and Lana are raising him. I have no input. I can't even tell him that I'm his real father."

"Because that's what you agreed to," Jim said.

Buck finished his beer, smashing the can on the porch. "Since I'm working for Clayton now, and see the boy almost every day it's hard to get it out of my mind. He's my son. Hell, for all practical purposes he's your grandson."

"Believe me," Jim said. "Carol and I have talked about that exact thing."

"You had a strange relationship with Esme and Kristy. I know you miss them. Someone else will come along for you," Carol said.

"Not like those two," Buck said.

"Why didn't you go to Austin to see Kristy?" Jim asked.

Buck grinned as he fished another beer out of the ice chest.

"I did. She'd married, had a kid of her own and another on the way."

"Enough," Jim said. "If what you say is true, then why did Esme send the old man to find you?"

Buck reached in his shirt pocket, removing something that fit in his palm.

"To give me this," he said.

Carol got out of the rocker, standing over him for a better view of the object he held.

"What is it?" she asked.

"A piece of black pottery shaped like a cup," he said.

"Let me see it?" Jim said.

"Looks like Indian pottery," Carol said.

"Old Indian pottery," Jim said. "What do you make of it?"

"It's a clue to a mystery. If I knew, I'd have the answer. I don't."

"Not much of a clue," Jim said.

"Depends. I just need someone to tell me what

it is, and where it's from."

"Ned Hartner," Carol said.

Buck glanced over his shoulder. "Who?"

"Deals in Indian art. Has a shop in Guthrie," Jim said. "He also has a collection of Indian artifacts."

"Maybe he can tell you what it is," Carol said.

"I'll look him up tomorrow," Buck said as the coyote howled again.

This time, Pard and Coco didn't awaken.

Chapter 3

Buck's cell phone rang the next morning as he exited I-35 on his way to downtown Guthrie. It was his boss, Clayton O'Meara.

"Heard you had a bad wreck last night. You okay?"

"Banged up a bit. I'll be all right. More than I can say for your Navigator."

"I got insurance. Don't worry about it."

"Figured you did. What's up?"

"We need to talk. Where you at?"

"Coming into Guthrie. I have to pay someone a visit first, and then I'll head your way."

"See you when you get here," Clayton said.

Buck sat the phone on the dash of his old pickup and then reached over and rubbed Pard's head.

"This is what I was driving when I first met you. Remember?"

Pard barked and wagged his tail. Guthrie was the territorial capital of Oklahoma and one of the first towns in the state. Brick-paved streets, and buildings made of native stone dominated its oldest section. All were preserved or restored to their original facades. He waved to someone he knew when he passed the bar that Tom Mix, the cowboy movie star of silent films had once owned.

Tourists taking pictures and enjoying the ambiance strolled along the sidewalks. Buck had something else on his mind as he parked the truck. Ned Hartner's storefront sat between a restaurant and an old hotel.

"Guard the truck," he said. "I got business inside. I won't be long."

Pard barked, and climbed to the open window to watch as Buck entered the little shop. Its sign said Hartner's Indian Art & Antiquities. Bells tinkled when he opened the heavy door, a man appearing from the back to see who was there.

"Help you?" he said.

Dressed in blue jeans and a flowered shirt, he mopped sweat from his brow with a wadded handkerchief. An old ceiling fan moved as slowly as did the balding man. American Indian art lined the walls.

"Buck McDivit. Someone told me you know a few things about Indian antiquities. If I show you something, can you tell me what you think it is?"

"I'm Ned," the man said. "Whatcha got?"

Buck handed him the black object. "Ever see anything like it?"

"No, but I'll give you fifty bucks for it."

"Not for sale. I'm only interested in information."

"Didn't mean to insult you. Make it five hundred bucks."

"Like I said, it's not for sale. You must know something about it if you think it's so valuable."

"Looks like something someone dug up from Spiro Mounds."

"What's that?" Buck asked.

"A prehistoric Indian settlement in eastern Oklahoma, near Spiro. Where'd you get it?"

"Someone gave it to me."

"The state protects artifacts from Spiro. They're illegal to buy and sell."

"You offered to buy it," Buck said.

"Only to return it to the state."

"Uh huh. Thanks for the information," Buck said, heading for the door.

"Wait, I'll give you a thousand dollars, cash money. Right here, right now."

Buck didn't answer as the door closed behind him. He had a surprise when he returned to the truck. A young woman was rubbing Pard's head through the open window. He was admiring her western shirt and the way she filled her faded jeans when she turned and flashed him a smile.

"Love your pooch," she said. "What's his name?"

"Pard," he said.

"Mind if I take his picture?"

"Knock yourself out," he said.

Along with her long blond curls, a digital camera draped her neck. A touch of red lip-gloss was her only concession to makeup, the color highlighting her big green eyes. She was a knockout. He could tell by her body language that she knew it. After taking several pictures, she gave him a card that said, Laura's Fabulous Photos.

"I'm Laura. My shop's just down the street. I'll have prints ready in a couple of days if you'd care to drop by and have a look."

"Buck McDivit. Glad to meet you, Laura. Might do just that."

He whistled to himself as he watched her walk away. "That girl's a looker and she wasn't wearing a wedding ring. You think she was coming on to me?" he asked as he backed out of the parking space.

A bark was his only reply.

Clayton O'Meara's ranch lay north of Guthrie amid the rolling blackjack covered countryside. Most ranches in this part of Oklahoma weren't big. Clayton's was anything but small. Except for a quarter section near the center of his property, he'd bought everything in sight. Unable to buy the land, he'd married the head of the pagan compound. It was a marriage of convenience for both parties.

Lana continued living at the compound with her lover Sara. Clayton lived at his ranch with significant other KK. He'd adopted Lana's son Adam, and the boy split his time between the ranch and the compound. Adam, Buck's real son, had been conceived during a night of drugs and trickery. A complicated situation, to say the least.

Pard's tail was wagging as they passed through the gated entrance to Clayton's ranch. He was soon on the veranda, sitting in Clayton's lap.

"How you doing, Pard boy?" Clayton said. "When you gonna leave this bounder and come live with me?"

"Never," Buck said, smiling as he sat in the rocking chair next to Clayton's.

Clayton was an imposing man. At six foot four, he towered over most people. Though sixty something, he had the demeanor of a much younger man. His hair wasn't gray, it was silver, as was his well-groomed mustache. When he smiled the world smiled with him. As always, a glass of whiskey lay nestled in his hand.

"Morning toddy?" he asked.

"Too early for me," Buck said.

Clayton's long-suffering assistant Maria appeared with coffee, winking as she handed it to Buck.

"I got a problem, and need to take some time off," he said.

"Problem?"

He handed the black artifact to Clayton. "I need to visit eastern Oklahoma to find out about this."

"What is it?"

"Valuable Indian relic. At least by the reaction I got from the slime ball I just showed it to."

"Who you talking about?"

"Ned Hartner. He offered me a thousand bucks for that piece of pottery."

"I heard he's not above fencing stolen art."

"Wonder why Sheriff Hagen doesn't know about it?"

"Such things are hard to track. There's a network of people that launder stolen items for a cut of the pie."

Clayton smiled when Buck said, "How do you know so much about the subject?"

"Lana's the smartest person I ever met. I got more than bed privileges when I married her."

"I see. How does KK feel about that?"

"She usually joins us. That woman is insatiable. Since she's your ex-girl, I'm sure you already knew that."

"You're making me blush," Buck said.

"Don't think so. Where in eastern Oklahoma do you need to go?"

"Spiro. There's a state park there and Hartner seemed to think that's where the pottery came from."

"How long do you plan on staying?"

"Don't know. Can't you spare me for a few days?"

"I can do more than that. I got a little job in eastern Oklahoma I need you to help me with while you're gone."

"Like what?"

"Lana and me own a resort hotel up in the mountains of southeast Oklahoma."

"Oh?"

"Quite a showplace. Bought it last year."

"Didn't know southeast Oklahoma was a tourist destination."

"It's not. We lose money every month. It's never

even been close to full."

"Then why keep it?"

"Because of its location in one of the most beautiful spots on earth. Mountains all around, flowing creeks, waterfalls, and towering vistas. Lana, Sara, KK, and me love the place. You ain't lived till you've sat in a hot tub with three gorgeous women watching the sun set over the Ouachitas."

"I'm impressed," Buck said.

"Lana is astute."

"And you're the recipient of her astuteness."

Clayton grinned. "Among other things," he said.

"What exactly do you want me to do at your lodge?"

"Keep a friend of mine out of trouble."

"Maybe you'd better explain."

"Jacob Huntington is a cryptozoologist."

"And what the hell is that?" Buck asked.

"A pseudoscience with a mighty fancy name. Cryptozoologists search for cryptids."

"What's a cryptid?"

"Sasquatches, Loch Ness monsters, yetis, and such. You get the picture. My friend Jake is the sole heir of the Huntington Oil & Gas fortune. Never done an honest day's work in his life. Doesn't keep him from visiting every continent to try to document cryptids. He arrives at my resort tomorrow to look for a Bigfoot."

"What harm can that do?"

"If he gets hurt at my place, the oil deal I got working with HOG could go down the tubes."

"What makes you think he'll get hurt?" Buck asked.

"Because he don't have the good sense God gave a goose."

"So you want me to nursemaid him?"

"Pretty much," Clayton said.

"Why didn't you tell me about this before

now?”

“I was planning on bird-dogging him myself. Like I said, he’s an old friend of mine. I was with him when he almost drowned us in a mini-sub in Scotland.”

“What changed your mind?” Buck asked.

“A dream I had last night.”

“Oh?”

“Our bedroom opens to the veranda here. A breeze blew the sheet off me. KK always sleeps naked, and I was sorta in the buff myself. I opened my eyes when I got a chill. The sliding door was wide open, the curtain flapping in the breeze.”

“And?”

“Someone was standing at the foot of the bed.”

“Your ranch is like an armed fortress. How did anyone get past your guards?”

“It was more like a dream, the body of the person almost translucent, glowing, moving in and out of focus.”

“A ghost?”

Clayton’s silver hair rippled in the sunlight when he shook his head. ”It was Esme, your Indian shaman girlfriend from the compound at Lycaia.”

“Esme was standing at the foot of your bed?”

Clayton nodded. “KK never woke up. Didn’t matter that I was naked as a jaybird because so was Esme.”

“What’d she say to you?”

“Not a damn thing,” Clayton said. “Maybe I was dreaming. Don’t know because I didn’t remember it until I woke up this morning and heard about your wreck. It caused me to have a thought I couldn’t shake out of my head.”

“Thought?”

“That I needed to send you to bird dog Jake instead of doing it myself. When you said you need to visit eastern Oklahoma, I realized it was more than just a coincidence."

"Bet I'm the only person on earth that believes the story you just told me."

"Then will you help me?"

"You're the boss. You had me at hello."

"Fine, then," he said, his smile returning. "Maria, I need more whiskey."

Maria topped up Clayton's tumbler, shaking her head as she returned to the kitchen.

"Will I have time to do what I need?" Buck asked.

"Jake never does anything fast. He could be at the resort for a month before he decides to go into the mountains. I want you to be with him when he does. Let's go outside. I got something to show you."

Buck followed him through a maze of flowered pathways and arches covered with wisteria. He stopped when they reached the acres of barns and cattle pens. A cowpoke rode past on a horse, its tail swishing flies. In the driveway was a yellow Jeep.

"Called this morning and got you a new ride. This tricked-out little jewel cost me an arm and a leg."

"Kind of bright."

"Beggars can't be choosers," Clayton said. "It's what was available."

"I'm not bitching. I just don't need anything this fancy," Buck said.

"Let me be the judge of that. The hotel has horses and stables. You'll need your pony. The Jeep has a matching horse trailer complete with tack room and everything else you need. You game?"

"Like I said, you're the boss. Anything else I need to know?"

"Just that an Oklahoma oilman raised Jake, so don't trust a word he says."

"Any other instructions?"

"Keep your powder dry until the weekend. Lana, Sara, KK, and me are coming down. I'll be there for a few days to watch your back."

Chapter 4

By the time Buck had loaded his pony into the custom horse hauler and headed east, it was already mid-afternoon. Pard fidgeted in the passenger seat of the new Jeep as the sky behind him began turning red, and then purple. It was twilight when they reached the empty parking lot of the Spiro Mounds Archaeological Center.

"Guess we're a little late," he said, opening the door for Pard.

The little dog waited as he unloaded his pony Lady, so that she could stretch her legs. He was giving her a hug when another Jeep, this one older, smaller and without a top, pulled up behind them. Buck immediately noticed the attractive woman behind the wheel. She wasn't smiling when she stepped from the Jeep and walked toward them.

"You lost?" she asked.

"Late, but not lost," he said. "I was hoping to make it before they shut the doors."

"We're closed today."

"You work here?"

The young woman nodded. "Came in to do some paperwork. I'm Thorn Little Deer."

"Buck McDivit," he said, shaking the petite woman's hand.

Thorn Little Deer's braided pigtails highlighted

her attractive Native American facial structure. Her eyes, light blue as an early spring Oklahoma sky, were her most arresting feature. Her tee shirt said, 'Archaeologists do it in the dirt.' Ankle-length boots and cut-off jeans highlighted her tanned and toned legs. Buck was smitten.

"Beautiful horse," she said. "What's her name?

"Lady. She's a bit skittish," he said as she took a step toward the horse.

Thorn had an apple slice in her shirt pocket. Lady took it, and the two were soon sharing a hug.

"You have a way with horses," he said.

The young woman nodded. "That's what they say. Why are you here?"

"For answers. My only clue led me to Spiro."

There was also a dog biscuit in her pocket, Pard's tail wagging as he took it from her hand.

"Clue? Are you a police officer?" she asked.

"Private investigator, at least on occasion."

"What clue brought you here?"

The soft kiss of Thorn's voice resonated with Buck. Like Pard and his pony, he was already eating out of her hand. He showed her the relic the old man had given him. After a moment, she looked at him, again with suspicious eyes.

"Where did you get this?"

"Last night, I pulled an old man from a burning wreck. He said he knew me, though I'm sure we'd never met. He gave it to me. I found out it came from Spiro Mounds. That's why I'm here."

"It's stolen property," she said.

"I didn't steal it. My foster father is the sheriff of Logan County. He will vouch for me."

Thorn's smile returned. "You have an honest face, Buck McDivit. I believe you, but you need to turn the artifact over to me."

Buck handed it to her. "Can you at least tell me a few things about it?"

"We have a corral in back, a few horses, fresh

water, and lots of hay. Let's put Lady in there, and then I'll answer your questions."

Lady bonded with the other horses in the corral, soon nibbling on a round bale with them. Pard followed Thorn and Buck to the building's entrance. She punched in a code on a keypad, unlocked the door, and turned on the lights.

"This is our control center; the place where most of our real work gets done."

Bones, pottery, and Indian artifacts littered the shelves covering most of the walls. Three metal desks seemed disjointed in the chaotic space. Thorn led him to a less cluttered room where the name on a tidy desk said, Thorn Little Deer, Area Supervisor. A picture caught his attention.

The girl in the photo looked serious as she aimed a bow and arrow at some distant target.

"That you?" he asked.

"I was into archery when I was thirteen. My mom took the picture, framed it, and insisted I keep it on my desk for everyone to see."

"She must be proud of you."

"I hope there are many things that make her proud and not just my expertise at archery."

Buck glanced at the framed degrees on the wall behind her desk. "I'm impressed," he said.

"Don't be. I make less than some of the people working for me. Coffee?"

"I'd rather have a beer."

"Me too, but coffee is all we have."

She heated two cups of cold coffee in a microwave, gave one to Buck and then propped her feet on the desk.

"Well?" he said.

"The Black Cup. Maybe a thousand years old. During ceremonies, tribal elders drank strong tea from it until they threw up. The tea stimulated visions."

Something in Thorn's words caused a bell in

Buck's mind to ring, though he didn't grasp the meaning.

"You said it's stolen property," he said.

"About six months ago. An old man gave it to you?"

"Pascal LeFlore. He died from his injuries. You know him?"

"Pascal worked here for years as the custodian. He was so honest; I can't believe he ever stole anything."

"Someone in another truck was chasing him and ran him off the road. I'm just shooting from the hip here. Maybe they were trying to retrieve the Black Cup from Pascal."

"Any idea who the person was?"

"The truck's vanity tag issued by the Caddo tribe said BladeRunner-1. They don't share tribal information with the rest of the world."

Thorn wrote something on a notepad. "Caddo tribal councils are protective of their people. I think you should understand, considering the historical treatment of Native Americans by the government."

She nodded when he asked, "Are you Caddo?"

"Yes. I have connections with the Tribal Council. I'll see what I can find out."

"Is this the first theft you've experienced?"

"I wish. Recently, it has become an epidemic. The state police and O.S.B.I. are working on it. Why are you involved?"

"Before he died, the old man told me he'd traveled to Guthrie to give me the black cup."

"If you didn't know Pascal, how did he know you?"

"He said that someone I once knew had sent him to find me."

"Who?"

"A Mississippian witchdoctor."

His answer erased her frown, replacing it with

a pretty smile. "Mississippians built the Spiro complex. The tribe no longer exists," she said.

"I know. Esme disappeared two years ago."

"She died?"

Buck glanced at Thorn's degree from the University of Arkansas hanging on the wall behind her.

"You're an educated woman. I'm not sure how much you believe in the spiritual world."

"I'm an Indian. Need you ask?"

"Then maybe you'll understand when I tell you that Esme didn't die. I'm not sure she was ever alive."

"A spirit?"

"Does that sound as outrageous to you as it does to everyone else I tell?"

"Like I said, I'm Indian. The spirit world has great meaning to me. I believe you."

"Thank you. It's getting late. Pard and I haven't eaten all day. Can I buy you dinner and a cold beer?"

She glanced at the clock on the wall before answering. "Only a few places to eat around here, especially this late. Give me thirty minutes, and then I'll take you to a place that's still open."

An hour had passed before Thorn caught up on her paperwork. Pard napped under her feet while Buck browsed the artifacts littering the other rooms. She finally raised her head.

"I'm done. You ready?"

"Starved," he said.

"Sorry I took so long."

"No problem. Do you know how far it is to the Sunset Lodge from here?"

"About fifty miles. You'll never make it tonight if that's your intention."

"Why?" he asked.

"It's on top of a mountain at the end of a winding road that goes on forever. It's hard enough to find in broad daylight. If I were you, I wouldn't try it at night."

"My fancy new Jeep has a GPS," he said.

"GPS? Guess you have no Indian blood."

"Cherokee, and it's gotten me into trouble more times than it's bailed me out."

"I hear that," she said. "Leave Lady in the corral overnight. She'll be fine. I'll take you and Pard to a motel in Spiro. We'll go eat after you get checked in. I'll pick you up tomorrow so you can get Lady. You'll be at the lodge before ten."

"Sounds like a plan," he said. "I wasn't relishing the idea of another two hours on the road."

They were soon tooling toward Spiro on a potholed country road in Thorn's Jeep. The only similarity between her open vehicle and Buck's Jeep was the name. Pard loved it, wagging his tail and barking as the bumpy vehicle blew up dust behind them. Thorn and Pard waited until he'd finished checking into a motel and had stowed his bags.

"Where now?" he asked as he climbed in beside her.

"My surprise. You like Mexican food?"

"Who doesn't?"

Except for a few streetlights and filling station signs, the little town was dark. After Thorn had pulled away from the main highway, Buck began seeing the glow of lights on the horizon.

"What's going on?" he asked.

"Horse arena. Not much to do in Spiro."

As the road opened through the trees, he saw what she meant. Lights on tall poles and a faded wooden bleacher surrounded a large corral. A woman on a horse raced around barrels as a small crowd of enthusiastic people watched. Others were milling around outside the arena near a food truck. The crowd applauded wildly when a man's voice on a loudspeaker called out the woman's time.

"My kind of place," Buck said.

"Thought you'd like it," Thorn said. "And the people that own the food truck make the best tamales and Indian tacos you ever ate."

"My mouth's watering. What about beer?"

"Don't worry. They have plenty."

In muted darkness, they sat at a picnic table near the edge of the parking lot. Buck had brought food for Pard, and he sprawled at Thorn's feet after eating.

"I'm jealous," he said.

"About what?"

"Both my horse and dog seem to like you better that me."

She responded to his comment with only a smile. "How's your taco and tamales?"

"Like you said, the best I've ever tasted. The Coors ain't bad either."

"Glad you're happy," she said.

"Feels like home. You live around here?"

"On a little acreage up in the foothills."

Another racer barreled across the finish line to the applause of the small crowd.

"I like your tee shirt. You an archaeologist?"

She nodded. "Work for the state, don't wear a uniform and pretty much keep whatever hours I please. That's the good news."

"And the bad?"

"I'm the only state archaeologist in southeast Oklahoma. Seems like I move from one site to the next putting out fires. Considering the amount of time I spend on the job, I make about twenty cents an hour."

"You made enough to buy land and a house."

"It's hard to overspend in these parts. What's your story?"

"I was a down on his luck P.I., my old truck

starting to go south on me. When I found Pard, I had just enough money to buy him a can of dog food."

"What happened? From that expensive pussy wagon you're driving, I'd say you aren't down on your luck anymore."

"I solved a problem for a rich rancher. He hired me as his director of security. I haven't worried about money since."

"I'm glad," she said. "I already love your dog and pony."

"And I love your blue eyes. You're Indian. Where'd you get those eyes?"

It was dark. Though unsure, he could have sworn his remark made her blush.

"Ever visit Heavener Runestone Park?"

"Heard about it," he said.

"Vikings may have visited Oklahoma centuries ago. Some say they carved the runes at Heavener. There are lots of blue-eyed Indians in eastern Oklahoma and western Arkansas."

"I don't see a wedding ring. You married?" he asked.

She shook her head. "You?"

"Nope. Got a boyfriend?"

"You're nosy, you know it?"

"P.I.'s ask questions for a living. Bad habit, I guess."

"An Indian brave named Zeke Big Shoe. Dumb as a stump with a heart of gold. You?"

"I was in a relationship until last night when I pulled Pascal LeFlore out of the burning truck. I missed my girlfriend's birthday."

"She wasn't worried about your injuries?"

"Guess not," he said.

"You okay?"

"I'll be fine in a day or two. Will you let me help you find the person or persons robbing the antiquities?"

"Of course. You're the answer to a prayer. I'm getting no feedback from the authorities working on the case."

"Good. I have my other job to do at the Sunset Lodge, though my boss assures me it won't take all my time. When I get situated, I'll drive back down."

She handed him a business card. "I don't usually give these to people I just meet. I wrote my cell number on the back."

Buck gave her one of his. "Mind if I hold your hand?"

"I hardly know you," she said.

"So?"

When he clutched her hand, she didn't pull away.

Chapter 5

The sun was peeking over the horizon when Thorn Little Deer knocked on Buck's motel door. Didn't matter because he was ready to go.

"You're quite the early bird," she said as he lugged his bag out to her Jeep.

"I'm not much for lying in bed," he said. "Unless I have a beautiful woman beside me."

"Dream on, cowpoke," she said. "Hungry?"

"Starved."

"Me too. There's a café on Main Street that serves wonderful omelets."

"With hash browns?"

"And biscuits and gravy, if you want," she said. "Pard will have to wait in the Jeep."

"He'll guard it for you. At least if we bring him a slice of bacon."

"I can handle that," Thorn said. "Sleep well?"

"The mattress had more bumps than your county roads, not to mention the lumpy pillow."

"Poor baby," she said. "You'll feel better after breakfast."

They left Pard to guard the Jeep. Happy to do so, he began working on the anklebone Thorn had brought for him. Conversation and clatter of dishes filled the little café as they sat near a picture window. Buck felt better after his first cup of coffee.

"What can you tell me about the Sunset Lodge?" he asked between bites of his scrambled eggs and bacon.

"A world-class resort that includes hunting, fishing, hiking, sightseeing, and horseback riding. No place around here quite like it," she said. "What are you doing there?"

"My boss's friend is a rich oil man that likes to hunt for mythical creatures. He heard there's a Bigfoot that likes to hang around the lodge. He's there to document it. My job, I'm told, is to protect him from himself."

Thorn didn't smile. "There is a Bigfoot that lives in the mountains near the lodge," she said.

"You kidding me?"

"I've seen it."

"What's it look like?" he asked.

"A big hairy humanoid you'll smell long before you ever see it."

"You're not kidding, are you?"

Thorn winked as she peeked over her coffee cup. "You don't believe me?"

"If you say you saw it, then I believe you," he said.

"I was only twelve, my family on a camping trip in the mountains. I heard something outside of my tent and thought it was a bear. Whatever, it stunk to high heavens. When I finally got the nerve to peek out, I saw it."

"A Bigfoot?"

"I'm not sure I like your disbelieving look," she said.

"I believe you. I know how you feel because I've seen things that people laugh at when I tell them. Were you frightened?"

"When it saw me peeking through the tent flap, it ran into the woods. My father told me I needn't have worried because the creatures are gentle and harmless."

"Wow," he said.

"I know what you're thinking. Why hasn't someone documented a Bigfoot if they are real?"

"What's the answer?" he asked.

"There are bobcats all over Oklahoma. How many people have ever seen one? Doesn't mean they don't exist."

"Can't argue with that," he said. "What now?"

"I have to go to work. Don't know about you."

Thorn returned him to the Archaeological Center, helped him load Lady into his hauler, and then kissed him.

"When you return," she said, "I'll take you on a tour of the mounds, and fill you in on all the thefts we've had."

"Can't wait," he said.

Buck hadn't seen another vehicle since leaving the main highway. He realized as much when a flock of wild turkeys crossed the road in front of him. His winding path grew ever steeper as he neared the top of the ancient mountain range. Towering pines masked his view until he rounded a tight bend in the narrow road. A protruding ledge provided a stunning view of the valley below. Above him, a bald eagle floated motionless in a thermal updraft.

Something had bothered him since leaving Thorn at the Spiro Mounds Archaeological Center. He hadn't told her, although he was sure that someone had broken into his Jeep and horse trailer. He'd found the door unlocked and the vehicle rifled through. He had the feeling the person was looking for the Black Cup.

The road, changing from pavement to broken rock, continued growing narrower. He'd thought the GPS had led him in the wrong direction, at least until he rounded the next bend. When he did, a beautiful resort hotel appeared, replacing vines and bushes with groomed grounds and manicured gardens.

An edifice made of native stone, massive rustic timbers and lots of glass stood before him. Instead of being empty as Clayton had suggested, cars and trucks filled the parking lot. He had little time to gawk as a helicopter descended near the building. A bell captain dressed in beaded shirt and baggy pants motioned him to pull the Jeep in front of the ornate entrance. Opening the door, the man began unloading Buck's bags.

"You Mr. McDivit?" he asked.

"That's me."

"Been expecting you. I'll take care of your Jeep, and get your pony boarded down. Our manager, Mr. Big Shoe wants to visit with you before you head off to your room."

"Can you watch my dog until I get checked in?"

"You got it, Mr. McDivit. I'll take care of him and see he gets fed."

Buck handed him a twenty and then pushed through the revolving door leading into the main lobby. The place was huge, the motif that of a hunting lodge somewhere in the mountains of Colorado. The main showpiece was a circular stone fireplace. Its wood fire crackled even though the air conditioning was cranking full blast. Leather furniture on plank wood surrounded the fireplace, along with one large bearskin rug. He could only imagine how much it had cost to decorate the place. An older man smiled as he awaited him with an outstretched hand.

"I'm Ezekiel Big Shoe, the manager. You must be Mr. McDivit."

Dressed in sandals, white pants, and a bright yellow shirt, Big Shoe shook Buck's hand with a firm grip. He had the regal nose and cheekbones of a Native American, and gray peppered his dark hair.

"Just Buck," he said.

"We were expecting you last night."

"Got a late start and decided to stay in Spiro."

"Good idea," Big Shoe said. "The road to the lodge can get narrow and treacherous after dark."

"I see that. Your name sounds familiar. Have we met?"

"Don't believe I've had the pleasure. Mr. O'Meara wanted me to introduce myself and familiarize you with the operation. You mind?"

"No problem. What's the deal with all the people? From what Clayton told me, I wasn't expecting so many guests."

"Local news stations got wind Cryptid Hunter was coming here to do his show. Reporters and their film crews are crawling all over the place. All the rooms are full; the outlying cabins starting to fill up."

"Huntington has a show?"

"One of the biggest on cable TV. Cryptid Hunter Jake Huntington has more fans than a rock star."

"Guess I don't watch much cable TV," Buck said.

"Then prepare yourself. If it gets any more crowded, we're going to start charging admission just to watch."

"Do they really expect him to find something?"

"You kidding? Half the people around these parts have seen Bigfoot. I even saw it once when I was fly fishing down in the valley."

Buck didn't comment as he followed Ezekiel Big Shoe to his office. Like the lobby, wood floors, expensive furniture, and American Indian art dominated the fancy workplace. Big Shoe went straight to a wet bar and poured himself a glass of Dewar's.

"Something to drink?" he asked.

"Too early for me. Love your office. I'd be too

busy checking out the scenery through your picture window to get any work done."

"Lucky for me I have minions for that. I just rush around looking busy."

"Did an Indian tribe used to own the lodge?"

"We tried to turn it into a gambling casino. Had opposition from other tribes and finally gave up. Miss Lana and Mr. Clayton bailed us out and kept the entire staff intact. I own a small piece, thanks to Lana and Clayton."

"Good people," Buck said.

"The best," Big Shoe said. "We have a luxury suite reserved for you on the top floor."

"You mentioned some cabins. Have anything closer to the stables?"

"You won't have quick access to the bar and all our amenities."

"Doesn't matter," Buck said. "I'd rather be close to my pony."

"Why not?" Big Shoe said. "After last night's little problem, it's probably a good idea."

"Problem?"

"Security breach. What I'm about to tell you is sensitive. Sure you don't want a drink?" Big Shoe asked.

"I'm Clayton's security director. Please feel free to tell me anything. And I think I'll have a whiskey and water."

Big Shoe handed him a drink. "Clay said you like Wild Turkey."

"My favorite, now please tell me about your security problem."

"When you didn't show last night, we let your room go to a reporter with CBS. Someone made a mess of it while he was drinking downstairs in the bar."

"Valuables were stolen?"

"The room was rummaged through as if the person was looking for something. Nothing was stolen.”

“What do your security people think?”

“We’ve never had problems with theft. We have no security people.”

“Maybe it’s something you should look into,” Buck said.

“We’re isolated up here. Might not be so easy finding qualified personnel.”

“Let me know if you need any help,” Buck said. “I’ll be here awhile. I’m sure we’ll see lots of each other.”

“Mr. Huntington will be in the main bar about nine. He asked me to bring you with me.”

“That’ll give me time to rest.”

“And Buck, I’ve asked another person to join us I’m sure you’ll find interesting.”

Chapter 6

The unnamed person joining them at the meeting with Jake Huntington had piqued Buck's curiosity. He wondered why Big Shoe had made such a point of telling him about it. His mind gravitated to other things as he unlocked the door to his assigned quarters.

The lavish cabin was a smaller version of the lodge, complete with its own stone fireplace. The surrounding deck provided a stunning view of the valley below. He found Pard lying in the center of a king-sized bed, his tail wagging.

"I think I could get used to this place." After unpacking, he scratched Pard behind the ear and said, "Let's check on Lady."

As Big Shoe had implied, the stable was a short walk from his cabin. The barn, like everything else at Sunset Lodge, was world-class. They found Lady in an air-conditioned stall munching oats.

"Don't get used to all this luxury," he said. "We have to go home sometime." Satisfied she was safe and happy he gave her rump a pat. "Let's go, Pard. We got business to attend to."

Expensive vehicles crowded the graveled lot behind the lodge. Buck was checking them out, row by row when a man approached him.

"Help you?" he said.

"I'm Buck McDivit. I work for the owners."

"I'm just the lot attendant, though I like to keep my eyes on things. You got a beautiful dog."

"Name's Pard."

"Hey, boy," he said, kneeling to pet him.

Pard's tail wagged, and he was licking the man's face when Buck said, "You sound like a cop."

"Once was," he said.

"What happened?"

"Last in, first out. Lost my job when the economy turned bad. Even my recent degree in Law Enforcement didn't seem to matter."

"What's your name?" Buck asked.

"Don Boone."

Don was forty-something and two inches taller than Buck. Thinning brown hair partially framed his perpetual smile.

"You look a little old to have just graduated college."

"Joined the Army when I was eighteen. Served twenty and decided that I'd had enough. I went to UCO on the G.I. Bill."

"What did you do in the Army?"

"Spent most of my time as an M.P. in Korea."

"You don't look Indian. How'd you get a job here?"

"Guess I was the only one that would work for the money they were offering."

"Married?"

"One beautiful and tolerant wife, and two boys, ages ten and twelve. Looking for something? Maybe I can help."

"Noticed anything unusual, maybe someone driving a late model black truck?"

"No truck, though I did spot someone my M.P. training told me I should keep an eye on."

"Show me," Buck said. Don led him to a

wicked-looking black Corvette. "It's beautiful. Is that what caught your eye?"

"He backed in. A sign of two things: he might need to make a quick exit, and he likely doesn't want anyone to see his tag. Take a gander at the license plate."

The tag said BladeRunner-2.

"Did you get a look at the driver?"

"Husky man built like a professional wrestler. Black Mohawk with a bushy ponytail. Tribal tattoos on his arms, neck, and behind his left ear. He was wearing a heavy gold chain around his neck, a Rolex Commander on his wrist, and a huge diamond pinkie ring. He looked ready to chew nails, and I had no doubt he could."

"You're good. You always check tags?"

"Old habits die hard," Don said.

Got a resume?"

"In the truck. You know someone looking for an ex-M.P.?"

"Maybe," Buck said.

Buck was soon scanning Don's resume. "One of your references, Delmar Jones, used to be Payne County sheriff. How do you know him?"

"Worked for Sheriff Delmar during summer vacation when I was in high school."

Buck reached for his cell phone. "I'm calling him now." He hung up smiling after a short conversation. "I may have a job for you if you're interested."

"You kidding me?"

"Sheriff Jones had only good things to say. From the way Pard took to you, I was already convinced. He doesn't tolerate bad guys."

"Mind if I ask what the job entails?"

"Strange as it sounds, the lodge has no in-house security. There was a break-in last night. I think I convinced the manager to hire someone to fill the position."

Don's shoulders slumped and his smile disappeared. "You already pointed out I'm not Indian. What if he doesn't like me?"

"I'll run interference for you," Buck said, handing him a business card. "I'm in the cabin closest to the stables. Meet me there tomorrow morning. I'll hopefully have good news for you."

"Thanks, Mr. McDivit," he said.

"If you don't want to get fired before you ever start, I'd suggest you call me Buck," he said with a grin.

"Will do, Buck," Don said, saluting.

After checking out the rest of Sunset Lodge, Buck was beat when he returned to the cabin. He'd popped the top on a cold Coors and had joined Pard on the bed when his cell phone began ringing. It was Clayton.

"Met Jake yet?" he asked.

"Your man Big Shoe and I are having drinks with him at nine."

"Everything okay?"

"Not quite."

"What's the problem?" Clayton asked.

"Your world-class lodge has no security. I talked to Big Shoe about it. He promised to assemble a staff. I have someone in mind I'd like to hire."

"Can't help you there," Clayton said. "When Ezekiel took the job as manager, I promised him he'd be in charge of hiring and firing."

"This person already works for the lodge. He has an extensive background in law enforcement."

"Still has to go through Big Shoe. Shouldn't be a problem if he already works for the lodge.

"There's one slight snag."

"Oh?"

"He isn't an Indian."

"Big Shoe's a prideful man," Clayton said. "My

gut feel is he's not going to like you meddling in his business."

"Excellent security for the paying customers is his business. You have to back me up on this."

"I can voice my opinion. Doesn't matter because Big Shoe has the final say. You have some other reason for wanting this hire?"

"I believe the person that ran the old man off the road is here at the lodge."

"What makes you think that?"

"Some inside info, plus a strong hunch."

"You be careful," Clayton said. "You already know he's dangerous."

"The very reason I need someone to watch my back."

"If I know Big Foot, and I do, you may have to settle for me. What else is going on?"

"This place is crawling with reporters. All the cable stations and even the major networks are here. The lodge is full."

"You gotta be kidding."

"I'm not. You didn't bother telling me that Huntington has a reality show."

"Don't you watch TV?" Clayton said.

"Not enough, I guess."

"Jake's showboating. Everyone knows Bigfoot is just a myth."

"Not to those around here. I've already talked with two people that swear they saw it."

"Amazing," Clayton said. "If you think your suspect is at the lodge, why don't you call the cops and have him arrested?"

"Not that easy."

"And why not?"

"There are more people involved. The relic I showed you is priceless. Someone had stolen it from the Spiro Mounds Archaeological Park. The person that ran Pascal LeFlore off the road followed me to Spiro."

"How do you know?"

"Someone broke into the Jeep last night."

"Could have been a coincidence."

"Let me finish."

"Sorry," Clayton said.

"I didn't make it here last night. Stayed in Spiro instead. Someone ransacked the room Big Shoe had reserved for me."

"The same person that went through your Jeep?"

"That's what I think. I checked the vehicles in the parking lot. A Corvette has almost the same tag as the black truck that ran LeFlore off the road. I got a physical description from the man I want to hire."

"What about a name?"

"If he's staying here, I'll find out from the hotel registry."

"You sure about not calling the police?" Clayton said.

"They're already working on multiple thefts of antiquities in eastern Oklahoma. My source says they've made no progress in six months. I'll handle this myself."

"Don't be bullheaded and get yourself killed," Clayton said.

"That's why I need someone I can trust."

"I'll recommend your man. That's all I can do."

"I'll talk to Big Shoe myself after we meet with Huntington. Maybe I can convince him."

"Don't bet on it. Like I said, he's a prideful man," Clayton said.

"Big Shoe's name seems familiar to me for some reason."

"His son Zeke is the quarterback for the Saints. I thought you kept up with pro football."

"That one slipped past me. How did a dumb jock become a pro quarterback?"

"You kidding me? He graduated from Stanford.

He damn sure ain't dumb."

"Someone I know says he is," Buck said.

"They're pulling your leg."

Buck lay on the bed thinking about Clayton's words long after he'd hung up the phone. Pard was pawing one of the bags where he kept the dog food.

"Sorry," he said, pouring some into his dish.

Realizing he hadn't eaten all day, he checked the lodge menu on the nightstand, and was soon feasting on a sandwich brought by a friendly waiter. As he ate, he wondered why Thorn hadn't told him her boyfriend was quarterback of the New Orleans Saints.

Chapter 7

Evening sun lay low on the horizon as Buck headed to his meeting at the lodge. He left Pard at the cabin.

"Guard the place while I'm gone," he'd said.

The woman at the front desk gave him directions to his meeting.

"Sunset Bar and Grill. Upstairs and to the right," she said.

Like most cozy Oklahoma bars, this one featured dim lighting and icy air-conditioning. Pine paneled walls, and a dripping fountain provided the perfect ambiance for selling alcohol. Big Shoe clutched a tumbler of scotch and sat alone near a big picture window.

"You're early," he said.

"Can I join you?"

"Sure," he said, pointing to the leather chair next to him. "Kristen, we need more drinks over here."

A young woman dressed in pink shorts and purple halter-top brought Big Shoe another drink from the bar. Her dark hair was short, highlighting her feather earrings and squash blossom necklace.

"Hi, handsome," she said. "I'm Kristen. Whatcha having?"

Buck had to bite his tongue to keep from

saying something crude.

"I'm Buck, pretty woman. I'll have Wild Turkey and water."

"Wild Turkey man. Think I'm gonna like you."

"That girl's hot," Buck said as he watched her strut back to the bar.

Big Shoe wasn't smiling. "I'd stay away from that one if I was you," he said. "She's bad news."

"Didn't mean to step on any toes," Buck said when he noticed him fidgeting with his wedding ring.

Big Shoe grinned and said, "Whatever."

A throng of people had congregated outside on the deck overlooking the mountains.

"Quite a crowd out there," he said.

"Same thing every evening. Our deck faces west. People come from all over to watch the sunset. It's quite spectacular, and it's what puts this place on the map."

"And how the lodge got its name?" Buck said.

"Yes. Found things to your liking?"

"I would have been happy in an old camper, much less the gorgeous cabin you have me in."

"Big Shoe beamed. "There are no bad rooms at the Sunset Lodge. The people that stay here expect as much."

"Looks like a great bar crowd."

"At least until the sun goes down," Big Shoe said. "After a full day of hiking, fishing, or horseback riding, many of the guests are too tired to spend time in a bar. Most of the people on the deck are beer or wine drinkers. They'll tab out after snapping their pictures and crowing over the beautiful sunset."

"Quite a few reporters here," Buck said. "Never known many news hawks to hit the sack without tippling at least a few first."

"Got that right. They're upstairs at our poolside bar on the roof. They've pretty much closed the place down the past few nights."

"Sweet," Buck said. "Must be helping the bottom line."

"We need it. Winter bookings were way down."

"Considering all the free publicity you're getting, I'd say that's about to change. Where's Huntington?"

"Late," Big Shoe said, glancing at his watch.

Buck sank into his overstuffed chair as the sun disappeared below the piney mountains. As Big Shoe had said, the crowd applauded. Most were clearing their tabs as the sound of a helicopter droned outside the lodge.

"That'll be Huntington's jet-powered chopper."

"Must be nice," Buck said. "Can we talk about something before he gets here?"

"Shoot," Big Shoe said.

"I met a man today with years of experience in law enforcement. He would be perfect for your security position."

"Is he a Caddo Indian?"

"No, but he already works for the lodge."

"Doing what?"

"Parking lot attendant."

Big Shoe laughed. "Why would I want to elevate a parking lot attendant to a position of authority?"

"Because you won't find anyone more qualified than him."

"Is this man a friend of yours?"

"Just met him today," Buck said.

Big Shoe waited a moment before replying. "I'll choose my own security person."

"Won't you at least interview him?"

"The job is going to a Caddo Indian."

"You're missing out on the best person for the position," Buck said.

"You're out of line, McDivit. You have no authority here, so back off."

"I'm not trying to be disrespectful or usurp your authority."

"Then what are you trying to do?"

"Clayton says no one's more qualified to run Sunset Lodge than you. Still, you have no experience in law enforcement. I do."

"Doesn't matter. Everything at the lodge goes through me first."

Big Shoe sat back in his chair, frowning, and arms folded when two men entered the bar as if they owned the place.

"What's wrong, Ezekiel," one of the men said. "You look like you just ate a bad oyster?"

Big Shoe's angry demeanor vanished as he stood to pump his hand.

"I'm good, Jake. You?"

"Me and Colley just had one hell of a chopper ride from Fort Smith. I always forget how treacherous the crosswinds can get in this part of the Ouachitas. Who you got with you?"

Seeing that Big Shoe wasn't going to introduce him, Buck stood and shook his hand.

"Buck McDivit," he said.

"Clayton's security man, of course. I'm Jake Huntington. This wizened old war dog with me is my chopper pilot, Colley Hornbeck."

Except for gray hair cut stylishly long, Huntington had the demeanor of a much younger man. His frameless glasses hinted that he was worldly and intelligent. Wearing snakeskin boots and a safari jacket, he looked as if he'd just returned to camp from a big game hunt. The man beside him was grinning.

"Jake took the controls halfway here. I haven't had a thrill ride like that since the last time I strafed a company of NVA in a raid on Cambodia."

"Colley's a hero; one of the best pilots to come out of Nam."

Colley didn't look old enough to have served in

Southeast Asia during the war in Vietnam. Like Huntington, he had hair long enough to cover the tops of his ears. Unlike the younger man's, his was light brown, as was his trimmed beard and mustache. His cowboy boots were well-worn cowhide that accented his faded jeans, white western shirt, and black leather vest. He also had the good looks of an aging movie star.

Kristen, the pretty waitress, blushed when he caught her staring at his faded blue eyes.

"Honey babe, can you get my boss and me a drink. I'm having straight whiskey with a beer chaser. Boss man here likes Bombay Gin. Kinda goofy if you ask me, but hell, he pays the bills."

Apparently used to Colley's mouth, Huntington took no offense. "With Fentimans Tonic Water, if you have it."

"Baby," she said. "I got most anything you want."

Colley pinched Kristen's bottom when she returned with their drinks. Buck caught Big Shoe's momentary glare from the corner of his eye.

"Clayton was telling me a little about you, Buck. He said you're part Cherokee and as good a tracker as there is. That true?"

"I'm fair, but far from the best."

"I have been chasing Bigfoot for years. I'm convinced I'll not find him until I hook up with a great tracker. The best tracker in Oklahoma, at least according to Ezekiel, is on his way to meet us. I'd love to have you both on the expedition. Can you work with another man?"

"I'm easy," Buck said.

"You don't need another tracker," Big Shoe said. "I'm confused why you need McDivit at all."

Sensing a sudden chill in the air, Colley slugged his whiskey and then raised his hand for another. Huntington leaned forward on the couch.

"Something amiss between you two I need to

know about?" he said.

"Nothing we can't handle," Big Shoe said.

"If you say so," Jake said. "Tell me more about your tracker."

"Haskel Doonkeen is Caddo. A hunting and fishing guide now, he was an Army sniper in Afghanistan. Had more than a hundred confirmed kills. His nickname is Blade because he scalped his victims after killing them."

"Myth or for real?" Jake asked.

"I've seen pictures of him with scalps hanging from his belt," Big Shoe said. "It's real."

"We had a few like him in Nam," Colley said. Most were a tad bent if you know what I mean."

"You wanna find Bigfoot you need a man like Blade."

Buck wondered what was coming next and didn't have long to wait as someone swaggered into the bar. He matched Boone's description, right down to his Rolex and diamond pinkie ring. Jake reached up from the couch and shook his hand.

"You must be Haskel," he said.

"No one except my mama calls me that. To everyone else, I'm Blade."

"Glad to meet you, Blade. I'm Jake. These two are Colley and Buck," he said.

Blade didn't smile, his expression even more ominous when he glanced at Buck.

"Take a load off," Colley said. "Zeke's already told us a little about you. How about filling us in on the rest."

When Kristen arrived with vodka for Blade, Buck realized she knew who he was. From her expression when she handed him the drink, Buck could see she didn't much care for him.

"I'm a guide. I arrange trips all over Oklahoma."

"And you were a sniper in the Army?" Jake

said.

"In an RSTA unit in Afghanistan."

"Which is?" Jake asked.

"Reconnaissance, surveillance, and target acquisition. We worked behind enemy lines for up to three days at a time. My specialty was target acquisition."

"Sounds as if you were pretty successful at it," Colley said.

"I killed my share."

"How did you get your nickname?"

Blade showed the hint of a smile for the first time. "Because I'm the best there is with a knife."

"Enough about Afghanistan," Jake said. "Have you ever seen Bigfoot?"

"If I had, it wouldn't be alive now," he said.

"I'm not talking tall tales here. I just want to find one. Can you help us do that?"

"Lots of expeditions have tried tracking down Bigfoot. None has succeeded. There's a reason," Blade said.

"Which is?"

"The Kiamichis. These mountains aren't high like the Rockies. They're steep, the valleys narrow and entrenched. What the forest don't cover is grown up with vines, briars, creepers, and brush."

"What about all-terrain vehicles?" Jake asked.

"Only if they're running behind a bulldozer," Blade said. "Even then, the terrain is so rough the dozer would have a hard time operating. There are no roads or even footpaths into the heart of the mountain range."

"What else?"

"Bears, coyotes, wild hogs, mountain lions, rattlesnakes, ticks, mosquitoes, wolves. You name it."

"I never heard of wolves in Oklahoma," Colley said.

"Camp out in the Kiamichis, and you'll hear

them howling at the moon," Blade said. "That ain't all. Bigfoot's out there. He survives cause he's king of the jungle."

Jake Huntington still wanted an answer. "So you're saying we're going to have to hike in?"

"Won't work. Bigfoot lives in the middle of the range. With the conditions the way they are, it would take at least three days to hike that far. Other than me, no one else is fit enough."

"Any ideas, Buck?"

"Blade's right. A grown man can only carry about a hundred pounds of food, water, and equipment on his back for any length of time. Even if we made it in, we'd have no food left to make it out."

"Then what?"

All eyes turned to Buck. "Chopper into the center of the range. Repel down ropes and cut a landing zone like they did in Nam. Establish a base camp and have Colley supply us every three days," he said.

Even Big Shoe seemed impressed by Buck's idea. Jake glanced at Colley. "How much space do you need to put that chopper on the ground?" he asked.

"Hell, I've landed in spots so tight the jungle was almost touching the rotors. At least we won't be under fire."

"Now we have a plan," Jake said. "It'll take a few days to put together supplies, and my cameraman hasn't arrived yet. Other than that, is everybody in?"

"I got a question for you, Blade," Colley said. "If the forest is as thick as you say, how are you gonna get a clear picture of Bigfoot, even if you find him?"

"Don't rely on pictures," Blade said. "Kill him on the spot. Everyone has seen pictures. No one believes they're real. Only way to prove it is with the creature's DNA."

"What if you can't get close enough to kill one?"

"I've got a bear trap that'll stop a grizzly in its tracks. My bet is it'll work just as well on Bigfoot."

Sarcasm laced Colley's voice when he asked, "How you gonna pack the carcass out?"

Blade pulled a knife from his belt. "You don't. Kill him, then take his scalp. That'll be DNA enough."

"Out of the question," Jake said. "There'll be no rifles, bear traps, or killing on my expedition."

"Suit yourself," Blade said. "But don't let failure surprise you."

"We won't fail," Jake said.

"Sounds like you're pretty good at taking scalps," Colley said.

Blade didn't like Colley's reply. He threw the knife, impaling it in the wall beside his head. Before anyone could react, he retrieved the weapon and started for the door. No one spoke until it had closed behind him.

Chapter 8

A wry smile crossed Colley's face as he exchanged glances with Jake Huntington.

"That fella's kinda touchy," he said.

"A little nuts, maybe. Don't matter cause you won't find Bigfoot unless he leads you to him. That's my opinion," Big Shoe said.

Though Colley wasn't happy, Jake seemed convinced. "We need someone like him if our base camp is going to be as wild as he says."

The bar was empty, the last customer gone. Big Shoe slugged his drink.

"Gentlemen, we're closing for the night. There's a bar on the roof. Lots of reporters and news people, most likely half smashed already. Join me?"

"I'm game," Colley said. "Maybe one of those pretty female reporters will want to hear some of my war stories."

"Why not?" Jake said.

"Count me out," Buck said. "I have an early appointment tomorrow."

"Kristen's going to close the place, and then join us. I need to speak to her before we leave. Be right back."

Big Shoe's conversation with Kristen was short. He dimmed all the lights as Colley and Jake followed him out the door. Kristen appeared from behind the bar, grabbing Buck's hand before he could go.

"Hey, cowboy, can you help me carry something?"

"Sure," he said. "Like what?"

The door had shut; everyone else had gone. They were alone in the dark.

"Me," she said, embracing him and smothering him with sultry kisses.

The two whiskeys he'd drank and Kristen's perfume were overpowering. He didn't resist when she led him to a leather chair. In a moment, she was sitting in his lap and draped all over him.

"I want you, baby," she said, slipping her hand under his shirt.

Buck didn't protest, untying the straps of her halter top. In the throes of mad foreplay, Kristen's squirming bottom incited his passion. Before the scene could escalate, she began to cry and pushed away.

"I'm so sorry," she said. "I can't do this."

"What's the matter?" he asked.

"My little girl has the mumps. I want to be with her right now."

"Sorry about your daughter. Anything I can do to help?"

Kristen wiped her eyes with a bar napkin. "I'll be okay. Mom's there to take care of her. I wish I had enough money so I didn't have to work late every night."

"I don't see a ring. You a single mom?" Kristen nodded as a tear rolled down her cheek. Buck reached for his money clip, peeled off a hundred dollar bill and gave it to her. "Maybe this will help," he said.

She kissed his forehead. "Ezekiel will be furious if I don't get the bar cleaned up and join him. Will you help me?" she said, retying the straps of her halter-top.

"Sure," he said.

It was getting late when she locked the bar and pecked him on the cheek.

"Thanks, baby, you're a real gentlemen. See you around."

He watched as she scurried off to the bar on the roof. When he reached his cabin, he found the door ajar, Pard waiting for him. The room was a mess. Someone had rolled the place, pawing through the drawers and closets. Buck had little doubt who it was, or for what they were looking.

"You okay, buddy?" he said, rubbing Pard's head. After a walk through to make sure no one was still in the cabin, he locked the doors and windows. "Guess now I know why Kristen was being so friendly," he said. "Let's get some sleep. We'll clean this mess up tomorrow."

<hr>

The sun peeked over eroded mountaintops as Buck and Pard finished their morning walk. He'd almost forgotten about last night's break-in. At least until they entered the cabin and he saw the mess on the floor. A country song on his cell phone interrupted him before he could put things back in order. It was Clayton.

"Did I wake you?" he asked.

"Drank a pot of coffee already, and Pard and me went on a morning walk."

"I had a call from Ezekiel last night. Guess I don't have to tell you that you're not his favorite person."

"And?"

"The lodge won't be hiring your man."

"But Clayton, I need him."

"Big Shoe threatened to quit on the spot and take all his people with him. With all the reporters there, I couldn't afford to call his bluff."

"You might want to reconsider. The situation is

critical."

"Tell me," Clayton said.

"Fill you in this weekend when you come down. I wish you'd rethink your decision."

"Didn't say I wouldn't hire him, just not for the lodge. Lana checked him out through her sources. She found his credentials impeccable and told me if I didn't hire him that she would. He'll have to move to Guthrie when he finishes this job."

"What about pay and benefits?"

"He'll be your second-in-command. There's a company truck waiting for him in the parking lot. His first month's pay is in the briefcase on the front seat. Sure you don't want to tell me what's going on?"

"Have to go to Spiro to check out a few things. I'm running late. I'll fill in Don, your new hire, and have him call you with an update later today."

"Okay," Clayton said. "Any gorgeous women staying at the lodge?"

Buck had to laugh. "You already have more gorgeous women than you can say grace over. Someone's knocking."

"Talk to you later," Clayton said.

Pard was the first out the door to greet Don Boone.

"Speak of the devil," Buck said. "Come in. I was just brewing up a second pot of java."

The aroma of strong coffee wafted through the cabin as Don followed him inside. Clothes and boots still littered the floor."

"I didn't take you for a messy type," Don said.

"Had a break-in last night while I was at the lodge."

"Any clues?"

"I think I know who did it. I had drinks with him last night. Grab a chair. I'll get the coffee."

"I didn't tell my wife Candy about the new job. Didn't want to jinx things."

"Just as well," Buck said. "I have good news and bad news."

Don's head drooped as if he were expecting as much. "Might as well tell me the bad news first," he said.

"You don't have the job with the lodge we talked about."

"And the good news?"

"If you'll move to Guthrie, I got a career for you some people would kill for."

"Candy's from Oklahoma City. She has been trying to get me to move there since I got out of the army. What kind of job?"

"I better give you a little background first. My boss, Clayton O'Meara, is one of the wealthiest men in Oklahoma. He's into oil, cattle; you name it. He owns half of the Sunset Lodge."

"Half?" Don said.

"His wife Lana owns the other half. They're married although they don't live together."

"Separated?"

"They've never lived together, at least full time."

"You're confusing me," Don said.

"I told you it's complicated. Clayton has a large ranch north of Guthrie. There's a settlement called Lycaia right smack in the middle of it. Only females live there."

Don's eyes grew ever larger, steam rolling up from the cup as he sipped his coffee. Pard was beneath the table and licked his hand.

"You're losing me," he said.

"Lycaia runs on sustainable energy. The women raise most of their food. They are artists, scientists, bankers, and so on. Lana, Clayton's wife, is the Chief of Lycaia. She's also head honcho of all their national and international businesses. She's richer and more powerful than Clayton is."

"And they don't live together?"

"No, Lana lives with Sara, her longtime companion. Clayton lives with KK, a former girlfriend of mine."

"My brain's starting to melt," Don said.

"I told you it's complicated. The marriage between Clayton and Lana is a union of convenience. Still, they have a son, take part in many business deals, and even sleep together on occasion."

"The four of them?"

"Kinky, I know. Lana checked you out and liked what she saw. You'll be answering to her and Clayton. If you have a problem with their sexual shenanigans, you better bow out now."

"Hell, Buck, I was an M.P. in Korea. I've seen everything. I'm all in. When do I start?"

"You're already on the payroll. There's a new company truck in the parking lot waiting for you. The briefcase in the front seat details what your duties will be. It also has your first month's paycheck. Better go look.

Don was beaming when he returned with the briefcase. "Candy-apple red Dodge Hemi. Always wanted to drive one of those big boys."

After placing the briefcase on the coffee table, he thumbed through the stack of documents.

"Everything okay?" Buck asked.

"A dream come true. Candy and me are finally gonna be able to get a home of our own."

"Good for you. More coffee?"

"Please, and then you can fill me in on what's going on," Don said.

"I forgot to ask if you take cream and sugar," Buck said as he refilled the cup.

"I like my beer cold and coffee black," he said with a grin. "Other than that, I'm a simple man. You said you know who rolled your room last night."

"The big Indian that owns the Corvette you

showed me. He's the reason I'm here."

"Tell me."

"Three nights ago, someone in a black truck with the vanity tag BladeRunner-1 ran a pickup into the ditch. The driver of the wrecked pickup died, though not before giving me an Indian artifact. It's a relic from Spiro Mounds."

"Took the boys there last summer," Don said. "Interesting place."

"I'm guessing BladeRunner-1 was chasing the old man, trying to retrieve the relic. I'm fairly sure he followed me to Spiro because someone rifled through my truck that night. Seems too much of a coincidence to blame it on random theft."

"Why didn't you just turn the matter over to the police?"

Buck gazed out the picture window. "Because the old man knew me. Before he died, he said someone I know had sent him to find me."

"You knew him?" Don asked.

Buck shook his head. "We'd never met. There was never any doubt I was going to have to solve this mystery myself."

"What's the connection with Sunset Lodge?"

"I guess you've heard the ruckus about Jake Huntington?"

"You kidding? Cryptid Hunter is one of my family's favorites. The boys and me never miss it."

"Huntington is a friend of Clayton's. When I told him about Spiro, he asked me to bird dog Jake Huntington while I was in the area."

"You mean like a bodyguard?"

"Something like that, though my title for his expedition is guide," he said.

"Go on."

"It was late when I finished my business in Spiro, so I spent the night there. Found out yesterday that someone rolled the room they had reserved for me."

"BladeRunner-1?" Don said.

Buck nodded. "His name is Haskel Doonkeen. Seems he's a friend of Ezekiel Big Shoe, the manager of Sunset Lodge. Big Shoe has talked Huntington into hiring him as his guide to find Bigfoot."

"Along with you?"

"Yes."

"Not good."

"Doonkeen's nickname is Blade. When he was a sniper in Afghanistan, he had the habit of scalping his victims."

"Peachy," Don said. "Why does he want to go looking for Bigfoot with Huntington?"

"Don't have a clue. I'm on my way to Spiro. Maybe you can find out for me while I'm gone."

"I'm on it, boss," Don said.

"Turn this cabin into your office. There's a nook with a desk and Internet connection. Use your new laptop and find out anything you can on Haskel Doonkeen."

"I still have contacts in the army that will help."

Buck gave him a fist bump and started for the door.

"Doesn't matter how many people he killed in Afghanistan. If he's responsible for the old man's death, I'm going to see he's tried and convicted of murder."

Chapter 9

Buck's cell phone began ringing as he walked out the door. It was Jake Huntington.

"Clayton gave me your number. What's on your plate today?"

"Business in Spiro."

"Can it wait a couple of hours?"

"Maybe. What's up?"

"Racquetball. You play?"

"Sure."

"I like to check out my associates before I take them on an expedition with me. See how fit they are, and how well they react to stress and pressure. I have a court reserved at the lodge's health facility. Will you join us?"

"I don't have my racquet with me."

"No problem. They have loaners at the club."

"I'll see if I can dig up a pair of gym shorts and tennis shoes."

"Good," Jake said. "We'll be waiting."

Don glanced up from his laptop when Buck reentered the cabin. "Change your mind about going to Spiro?"

"Slight detour. Jake's got a wild hair. Wants me to play racquetball with him to see how I measure up."

With only a shake of his head, Don continued

working.

The lodge's health club featured three courts visible through a Plexiglas wall. Colley, Jake, and Doonkeen were warming up when Buck arrived. Neither Colley nor Jake weighed more than one hundred and sixty pounds. Both looked fit, though neither man seemed particularly athletic. Buck was different: one hundred and ninety-five pounds of toned muscle, perfect coordination, and lightning speed.

Doonkeen was another creature altogether. He had the arms and chest of an Olympic weightlifter. Four inches taller than Buck, he outweighed him by at least fifty pounds. Colorful tribal tattoos decorated his arms, legs, and neck. He looked like an Indian warrior decked out in war paint.

They chose sides, Doonkeen and Jake against Buck and Colley. Doonkeen didn't look happy about having to play racquetball to prove to Jake he deserved a place on the expedition. His angry frown let everyone know it.

Quite the athlete, the big man pounded winner after winner. It wasn't that he was so much better than Buck. He was just lots better than Colley who seemed unable to make even the simplest shot.

"That's it for me," the pilot finally said, walking off the court.

"We can play cutthroat," Buck said.

"You two go at it," Jake said. "Colley and I will grab a beer and watch."

After Colley and Jake had left the court, the structure of the game changed, the balls hit harder and faster. People in the health club grew interested, spectators continuing to grow. Buck winced when Doonkeen nailed him in the small of the back with the rubber ball. The stinging hit almost sent him to his knees. Closing his eyes, he had to catch his breath before continuing.

Doonkeen was an angle master and Buck no

slouch. Both were breathing hard before Doonkeen managed to win the first game. Halfway through the second game, Buck nailed Doonkeen in the back with the ball. His ugly scowl caused Buck to think he was going to drop his racquet and attack him. He didn't.

"Sorry," Buck said.

Doonkeen's hand-to-eye coordination had helped garner him more than a hundred kills as a sniper. Buck was his equal, matching him shot for shot. Doonkeen slammed his racquet into the wall when Buck won the second game.

"Watch your ass this time, Blade. I'm gonna smoke you," Buck said, trash talking.

"Play your best, white boy," Doonkeen said.

The blue ball began whizzing around the little court, spectators vying for a view of the action. They applauded when Doonkeen placed a shot in the corner so low that Buck couldn't dig it out. The set went to Doonkeen, but only by the narrowest margin. Doonkeen bumped Buck, making sure he was the first one out the glass door.

"We'll be in the bar," Jake called from the upstairs bleachers.

A scrawny black cat was on the bench in front of Doonkeen's locker. He brushed it aside before turning to Buck.

"I don't like you one bit, McDivit," he said.

He got so close that Buck could smell his sour breath. "You're not on my favorites list either," he said.

They showered and put on their clothes. The black cat was underfoot when Doonkeen slammed his locker. Without even thinking about it, he kicked it across the floor. The cat screeched and went running. It was more than Buck could take.

Grabbing Doonkeen's shirt, he punched him in the mouth with a roundhouse right hand. The big Indian's knees buckled. He didn't go down.

They were soon exchanging punches, bouncing off lockers and tripping over benches.

Buck was big and strong, Doonkeen bigger and stronger. He had the better of the fight as long as they were standing straight up. Buck had wrestled in college. He knew if he got him on the floor, the big man's height and weight advantage would disappear. Using a wrestling maneuver, he flipped him off his feet.

When Blade hit the cement, Buck dived on top and began pummeling him. Blade covered up as best he could, then somehow grabbed Buck's throat. He was gasping for breath when a security guard smacked Blade in the back of the head with a nightstick. He and another guard were cuffing them when Big Shoe rushed into the locker room. Buck glanced up at him, rubbing a knot on his head.

"Thanks," he said.

"Shut the hell up, McDivit."

One of the security men raised his club, threatening to use it on Buck. Big Shoe stopped him.

"I'll take care of this," he said.

"You sure, boss?"

"You heard me."

The two guards exited the locker room as Buck wiped blood streaming from his nose with the back of his arm. Big Shoe was in their faces.

"What the hell do you two think you're doing?"

"I'm done," Blade said, glaring at Buck. "I think I made my point."

"You?" Big Shoe said.

"Me too," he said.

"Huntington and Hornbeck are waiting in the health club bar. If you have differences, settle them away from the lodge. This television gig is too important for the hotel. I won't have either of you botching it. Understand me?"

Buck and Blade nodded.

The janitor began rearranging benches and lockers as Big Shoe huffed out the door. Neither Buck nor Blade spoke as they washed away blood and dirt from their cuts and scrapes. Their silence continued as they exited the dressing room.

As Big Shoe had said, Jake and Colley were waiting at the little bar in the health club. A white-haired woman sat with them, her wrinkled face making her seem as old as time. Despite the heat outside the club, she wore a bright Indian blanket around her shoulders.

"What the hell happened?" Jake asked.

"Something the matter?" Buck said.

Jake and Colley stared at their swollen jaws, busted lips and scraped elbows.

"You boys had a rougher match than I thought," Colley said.

Still early in the day, Jake was drinking beer. Colley was also drinking beer, though he was using his as a chaser for his whiskey. Seeing that neither Blade nor Buck was going to discuss their scuffle, Jake changed the subject to the impending expedition.

"Thanks for obliging one of my little idiosyncrasies. I like to know how well my fellow researchers are going to perform under pressure."

"You boys put on quite a show out there," Colley said.

"Everyone in the facility was watching the match," Jake said. "Has either of you ever played a professional sport?"

Both Buck and Blade shook their heads. "Well, you could if you wanted to," Colley said.

"I'm buying," Jake said. "What are you drinking?"

"Water," Buck said. "I still have to drive to Spiro."

Blade took notice when Buck announced

where he was going. "Water, no ice for me," he said.

Colley grinned and gave Jake a look. "You boys are way too serious," he said. "One little drink won't hurt you."

"Maybe not," Buck said. "Thanks anyway."

Jake and Colley didn't force the issue. Buck fished a cube of ice from his water and used it to rub on his broken lip.

"I have someone to introduce, though I'm not sure I can pronounce her name."

"You can call me Yellow Paint Woman," she said.

"I'm Buck," he said, offering his hand.

"I know you both," she said.

"When I was asking around about Bigfoot, everyone seemed to give me Yellow Paint Woman's name. She has lived in this area her entire life."

Though wrinkles lined the woman's face, her voice was strong and clear. Despite her American Indian facial features, she had pale blue eyes like Thorn.

"My people know me because I am a witch. They come to me when they are sick or need advice."

"You said you know about Bigfoot," Jake said. "Can you share your insights with us?"

Yellow Paint Woman sat straight in her chair. "Every tribe has a name for Bigfoot. They all describe the creatures as large and hairy. One tribe calls them "People of the night.""

"Are they vicious?" Colley asked.

She shook her head. "They are gentle. I know of no instance where they have harmed anyone."

"Are they real or just figments of someone's wild imagination?" Colley asked.

"They are not ghosts if that is what you mean. I assure you, they are gentle."

"Blade wants to kill one and take its scalp," Buck said.

"That would be an affront to the Great Spirit," she said.

"Bullshit!" Blade said. "They are no more human than a mad skunk. Killing one won't make any difference to anything."

"What if you're wrong?" Buck said. "What if they're human? Wouldn't that be murder?"

Buck's question seemed to distress Jake Huntington. "This conversation is drifting in the wrong direction," he said.

Buck gave him a long gaze. "What's your stance? Blade seems intent on killing a creature and taking his scalp. Is that what we're talking about doing?"

All eyes turned to Blade. He gave Buck an angry glance before looking at Jake.

"I could drop one with my sniper rifle. Then we'll know if it's human or monster. My guess is monster."

"And if it's not?" Jake said. "There'll be no weapons on my expedition."

"What if we encounter a bear or a mountain lion? It's been a long time since I fought a bear with a knife."

"Though I hate to agree with him, Blade's right," Buck said. "We're going someplace wild and dangerous. Someone should carry a weapon."

"You're in charge of this expedition," Blade said. "I'll do whatever you say." He glanced at his Rolex. "Right now, I got business in town and gotta go."

Jake shook his hand. "I've never taken weapons on an expedition. I won't start now."

"Fine," the big Indian said before hurrying out the door.

"Are we done here yet?" Colley said. "I need to go someplace where they mix real drinks."

"Then get lost," Jake said. "I can't believe you think we should bring weapons."

"It's your call," Buck said. "I'm just along for the ride."

"Then it's settled," Jake said. "Thanks for your input. I better go keep tabs on Colley in case we need to fly somewhere."

They left Buck and the old Indian woman alone. "You are going to Spiro," she said. "Can you take me to my house?"

"You bet I can. I just need to drop by my cabin and pick up a few things. If you want to stay out of the heat, I can come back and get you."

She smiled for the first time. "I can walk twenty miles if I have to."

"I'll bet you can," Buck said.

The day was bright, the sky clear as they strolled along the manicured pathway to his cabin. When they reached the door, she pulled something from beneath her blanket. It was the black cat.

"You stood up for this creature at the risk of your life. You must continue seeing for its well being."

Buck hesitated before taking the animal. "I've never owned a cat," he said.

"And you never will. Cats and humans can only coexist."

"I can't take him," he said. "My dog will kill me."

"No," she said. "They will love each other. You will see."

"The cat's feral. He'll just run away."

"He'll be here when you return from Spiro."

Buck left the cat with Don. "What's his name?" he asked.

"Doesn't have a name," Buck said.

"I had a cat that looked like him when I was growing up. My mom loved Shakespeare, so she called him Hamlet."

"Then Hamlet he is," Buck said, watching with interest as the scrawny cat and Pard sniffed each other.

"I know you need to go to Spiro," Don said. "Don't worry about Hamlet. I'll take care of him while you're gone."

As Yellow Paint Woman had said, Pard's tail was wagging.

Chapter 10

Three buzzards took flight as Buck rounded a bend in the steep road from Sunset Lodge. Long past noon, he knew Thorn Little Deer would be wondering why he was late. Pard was enjoying the ride, his tail wagging as his head stuck out the window. Yellow Paint Woman's smile softened her stoic face.

"There's a dirt road almost hidden by the trees up ahead. The only way to my house. I'll warn you when we draw near," she said.

Yellow Paint Woman's road was little more than a wooded trail. Though rough and rutted, Buck's new yellow Jeep had little trouble traversing it. In about a mile, the forest opened into a clearing abutting a rock cliff overlooking the valley below.

A log cabin occupied the center of a fenced enclosure. A faded Indian blanket draped an old rocking chair on the rickety front porch. The deep-throated bark of a lop-eared hound greeted them as they got out of the Jeep.

"You walk up to the lodge to buy your supplies at their general store?" Buck said.

"I got good legs and lungs for an old woman."

"You must. It's at least two miles up the mountain. Maybe you need a horse or a mule."

"I have a mule, but she's too old to make the journey."

Yellow Paint Woman had her own cats, a white one named Squeaky, and calico Chani. They brushed against Buck's leg as he helped the old woman carry groceries into the cabin.

"Mother and daughter," she said. "Chani hasn't left her mother's side since she was born. Though she was grown, she lay with the kittens when Squeaky had a second litter."

A stone fireplace dominated the tiny cabin's rustic interior. Indian rugs covered the wooden floor. The walls were bare.

"Who cuts wood for your fireplace?" Buck asked.

"Sons, grandsons, and great-grandsons. I rarely need anything, except occasional peace and quiet."

Buck could hear chickens scratching outside the open back door. She also had several goats that seemed unafraid when he peeked outside.

"I see no electrical lines," he said.

"Candles and coal oil lanterns are all I need."

"How do you keep your groceries from spoiling?"

"Store them in my icehouse. My family cuts ice from the pond for me in the winter. Insulation in the icehouse keeps the ice frozen all summer. I also have an icebox in my kitchen. Summertime, I cook outside."

"Why do you live up here all alone?"

"Some people call me a witch. I am a shaman and prefer solitude."

"What exactly does a shaman do?"

"Heal people, tell their fortunes, comfort them, and provide advice. Let me put something on your cuts and bruises."

Yellow Paint Woman cleaned Buck's wounds and rubbed them with a healing salve. They had a remarkable effect, the swelling decreasing as he watched.

"Your medicine is powerful. You said you tell fortunes. What's mine?"

"The future isn't easy to read. It requires not only a ceremony but also a belief in the results. There is one thing I can tell you."

"And what is that?"

"The man Blade is dangerous. Before a week has passed, he will try to kill you not once, but three times."

Buck felt his swollen lip. "He tried once today already."

Thorn met Buck and Pard as they pulled into the Spiro Mounds Archaeological Park.

"I was beginning to think you'd stood me up," she said, resting her elbows on his open window.

"Never. I met an old Indian woman and helped her take groceries to her house."

"Yellow Paint Woman?"

"Know her?"

"Everyone calls her a witch. She sells potions and poultices, and some say she performs magic."

"Does she?"

"I'm an Indian, so I'm naturally superstitious. I'm also a Ph.D. and have learned to be skeptical of such things. What happened to your face?"

"Altercation with a business associate."

Thorn didn't ask him to elaborate. "Not much happening and it's a beautiful day for a horseback tour of the park," she said. "Get out of the Jeep and let's go."

It was a gorgeous day, the sky a perfect shade of blue to backdrop two chicken hawks circling overhead. Pard leaped from the open window, running to Thorn and demanding attention. She grinned as she obliged.

"I just love this boy," she said. "You need to let

him come home with me."

"Only if I'm also invited," Buck said.

"Better saddle up Lady while I get my horse," Thorn said, not responding to his remark.

Lady was ready, Buck in the saddle when Thorn came riding around the corner. Her horse was a beauty. The black stallion had a white face and random white splotches on his sides and hindquarters. His rear feet were also white, his gorgeous tail extra long. The little horse stood two hands shorter than Lady did.

"He's a handsome dude," Buck said. "Never seen one like him before."

"Chester is a Spanish Mustang of the Uvero paint variety. He's a wonderful saddle horse. Speaking of which, let's ride. We're burning daylight, cowboy."

Buck and Lady were happy to oblige. Pard chasing after them as Thorn smacked Chester's rear, sending him into a gallop. They couldn't see the river though Buck could smell the water and sensed it was near. The terrain was flat except for a hill up ahead. As they approached, he realized it was a mound made by humans.

"There are twelve mounds on this park's one-hundred-fifty acres," she said. "This one's the closest to our headquarters."

The mound was little more than a flat hill overgrown with grass. "Doesn't look like much," he said.

"It's higher than it looks. I assure you it was quite spectacular a thousand years ago."

"Take your word for it."

They both laughed when Pard barked.

A walking trail intersecting all the mounds wound around the park. They stopped in front of the largest one and dismounted. Something glinting in the sunlight caught Buck's eye. Picking it up, he scraped dirt off it.

"What is it?" Thorn asked.

"Arrowhead."

"Good eyes," she said. "It's a beauty." The perfect point had serrated edges. "There are massive chert bluffs not far from here; the rock most people call flint. The artisans at Spiro crafted thousands of arrow and spear points. Other Native Americans traveled great distances to trade for them."

She shook her head when he said, "Can I keep it?"

"You know better than that," she said.

Taking it from him, she raced to the top of the mound, Buck chasing after her.

"Told you it's taller than it looks," she said.

Plopping on the grass, they removed their cowboy hats and relaxed. The spectacular vista stretched for miles.

"It's beautiful up here. I didn't know we were so close to the river. Guess I never realized how big it is," he said.

"The Arkansas is navigable. Imagine what this view was like before centuries of erosion took its toll."

"Tell me."

Thorn made a sweeping motion with her hand. "This was once the largest and most powerful city in North America."

"Why here?"

"Like you said, it's in the bend of the Arkansas River. Rivers were major trade routes at the time, and this was an important trading center. Indians came here from as far away as Mexico, and maybe even South America to barter with each other."

"What did they have here that someone from Mexico would want?" Buck asked.

"Bois d'arc Osage orange wood, for one thing. The best bow-making wood in North America."

"So this was a major trading hub?"

"The Mississippians that lived here were true artisans. They carved elaborate shell gorgets found in ancient Indian settlements all over the country. They created much sought-after pottery and unique jewelry. This was also a religious center. Visitors from all over took part in the ceremonies."

"So a thousand years ago this was the capital of the new world?" Buck said.

"Maybe it doesn't seem so now, but that's the reality of it," Thorn said.

"I couldn't believe all the intricate objects you showed me in the museum," he said. "I've never seen anything quite like it."

"Nowhere else in the world," she said. "Not to mention the pottery, stone pipes, feather and fabric arts. I'd put the Mississippians right up there with any group on earth when it comes to art."

"What else?" he asked.

"Their art tells a story. Though no Mississippians exist today, it demonstrates that they were an advanced civilization. You can't imagine what I'd give to have a time machine transport me back there."

"I feel your passion," he said. "There's something about this place. It feels like hallowed ground. It's calling to me too, and I'm not exactly sure why."

"A thousand years ago it was the hub of the universe."

"Now I understand why you're so attached to this place."

"The mounds were much larger and shaped like pyramids with flat tops. A palisade built from tall timbers circled them. The chiefs, medicine men, dignitaries and their families lived within the enclosure."

"And outside the palisade?"

"The home to ten thousand people or more."

"I've learned something. I didn't realize there was such a place as this in Oklahoma."

"Most people don't. The chief occupied a house atop the highest platform mound. It was where the elders and tribal council met. The lesser officials lived in houses built on smaller mounds."

"What's the story on this one," Buck said.

"Craig's Mound, also known as the Mortuary Mound. A mining company purchased the rights during the Great Depression. They tunneled into it, extracting a fortune in artifacts that they sold all over the world."

"Doesn't sound good."

"It prompted the state to step in and shut them down. This is the first and still the only archaeological park in Oklahoma."

"Doesn't seem possible there would be enough food to feed ten thousand people. What the heck did they eat?"

"The Mississippians were far more than hunter-gatherers. They raised corn and squash, foraged for grapes, roots, wild nuts, greens, and berries."

"They were vegetarians?" Buck asked.

"Stop being silly. They fished, hunted deer, caught turtles, and gathered mussels from the river. You should see our collection of freshwater pearls in the museum."

They were sitting close, their shoulders touching. When Buck took her hand, she didn't pull away. A gentle breeze blew up from the river, rippling her dark hair. Her eyes seemed even bluer against the cloudless sky.

"What?" she finally said.

"You are gorgeous. I can hardly take my eyes off of you."

"You're so full of shit," she said, wrenching her hand away. "I thought you cared about the prehistoric inhabitants of this river valley."

"I do, but your perfume is distracting me."

Thorn gave his shoulders a push, and he flopped to the ground. When he did, Pard jumped on him and began licking his face.

"Time out," he finally said.

"He's bad, Pard. Don't let him up."

Buck finally managed to get to his feet and brushed himself off. Pard's tail was wagging as he licked Thorn's nose.

"I'm not lying when I say your eyes are haunting," he said.

"How many women have you used that line on?" she asked, hugging Pard. "If you have no more questions about the mounds, then let's go."

"I'll be good," he said. "Tell me about the thefts. Is it just here at this site?"

Thorn shook her head. "What do you know about archaeology in Oklahoma?"

"Not much," he said.

"There were Native Americans all over this state long before the Trail of Tears. Workers at construction sites discover artifacts on almost a daily basis."

"You mean like when they clear a location for an oil well?"

"Yes, or a new shopping center, or housing development. Work has to stop until someone checks it out. Usually, it's nothing more than an arrow point or a few shards of pottery. I get involved when someone uncovers a gravesite or ancient village."

"Some of the objects you find at these locations are valuable?"

"You can only imagine. Consider the historical value of the Black Cup, not to mention that it is perfect and unbroken."

"You're saying someone stole it from a site other than this?" he asked.

Thorn nodded. "We have several digs going on as we speak in eastern Oklahoma. It would surprise you the things we discover."

"Was Pascal LeFlore working on the dig?"

"He was nowhere near. That's why I find it so hard to believe that he had the cup in his possession. Where did he get it?"

"Guess that's the sixty-four dollar question," he said.

"And why I'm glad you're here to help."

"Who participates in these digs?"

"Graduate students, many from OU, OSU, and as far away as the University of Texas."

"Could one of the grad students be responsible for the thefts?"

"Not likely," she said. "There are different teams working different digs. We've had artifacts disappear now from all the digs."

"Theft like that is all but impossible to trace, and someone knows it," he said.

"It's heartbreaking. I feel so helpless."

Buck took her hand again. "I promise I'll find out who's responsible for the thefts and see that they end."

"I'm not exactly sure why I believe you," she said. When he moved to kiss her, she pushed him away and sprang to her feet. "You're hopeless. I'll race you back to the museum."

"Lady's a registered quarter horse. There's no faster breed on earth. Chester's pretty, but I'll be waiting for you before you're halfway back."

"Wanna bet dinner on it? She said.

"You're on, pretty girl."

Thorn gave him another push before turning and hurrying down the hill. Buck ran after her, slipping and tumbling the final ten feet before reaching the ground. She was already in the saddle, racing toward the museum. Doing a flying mount, he gave Lady a slap on the rear, and tore after her.

They'd gone two-hundred yards before Buck realized he was in a hopeless position. Lady was fast, though had no chance against her speedy little stallion. When he and Lady barreled to a stop, Thorn was already dismounted and smiling as she leaned against his Jeep.

"You cheated," he said.

"I didn't need to. I beat you by a country mile."

"A hundred feet maybe," he said. "What kind of horse is Chester?"

"Spanish Mustang," she said. "Now you owe me. After racing you into the ground, I'm starved. I want the biggest T-bone in the county, a bottle of expensive wine and at least two foo foo drinks to top things off."

Chapter 11

Buck didn't like losing. Even after they'd groomed the horses and stowed their tack, he was still pouting.

"Give it up, cowboy. You never had a chance. Everyone around here knows Chester is the fastest horse in the county. I'll buy dinner tonight, and I'm sorry I duped you."

"A bet laid is a bet made," he said. "You won fair and square, and I'm buying. I don't renege on wagers."

"Sure about that?"

"I want a rematch one of these days. Right now, I'm up for the most expensive place around. I'm buying and not taking no for an answer."

"Got room in that expensive hauler of yours for another horse?"

"You bet," he said. "It's a double."

"Then let's take the ponies to my house. It's not far from here, or the restaurant. Pard can stay with my dog Maggie while we eat."

Thorn's house was in the foothills overlooking the river. Buck followed her there from the Archaeological Park. He waited until she'd unlocked the gate and had parked in front of the house, then pulled in behind her.

A porch with a railing surrounded the house.

A stone fireplace protruded from its sloped roof covered in rusted tin. She helped him unload the horses, leading them to a barn, putting them in adjoining stalls.

"I have a large pasture for my donkey Ted, pot-bellied pig Manda, and two llamas, Cheech and Chong," she said. "They keep coyotes and other predators away. Your beautiful horse will be safe and happy while we're gone." A large bird dog came running around the corner to greet them. "This is Maggie. She's my big baby."

Maggie was a beautiful shorthaired bird dog. She and Pard stood nose to nose. Their wagging tails told Buck all he needed to know about how they would get along while he and Thorn were at dinner. Hearing their commotion, Manda came running from around the corner.

"She's the nosiest animal I've ever had, and also the best watchdog, or in her case, watch pig."

Buck rubbed the friendly animal's ears when she walked up to check him over with her big snout.

"Watch it, or you'll never get rid of her."

"I love her," he said. "How much does she weigh?"

"Don't ask. She eats me out of house and home. Let me check their food and water before we go."

Thorn's ranch was a little slice of heaven on earth with an amazing view of the distant river. Buck took in the scenery as he helped her finish her chores

"You ready?" she finally said.

"Can we go like this?"

His question made her laugh. "Everyone will be in boots, jeans, and Stetsons."

They wheeled into the parking lot of the Buffalo Roadhouse about twenty minutes later. The secluded establishment lay at the end of a dusty dirt road on a bluff above the Arkansas River.

Friday night, darkness approached. Motorcycles and shiny pickups filled the gravel parking lot. Country music poured from the front door when a smiling couple exited.

"Think I'm gonna like this place," he said.

"You like to line dance?" she asked.

"Does a bear shit in the woods?" he said.

Music from the dance floor was a little too loud, the aroma drifting from the kitchen intoxicating. A smiling woman led them outside to a deck overlooking the river. In Stetson, red bandana, boots, and faded jeans, she looked the part of a western cowgirl.

Japanese lanterns swayed in the breeze. Fans and misting devices cooled the temperature and kept the mosquitoes away. A waitress dressed like the woman that had greeted them arrived to take their order.

"Mimi," Thorn said, embracing the older woman. "Buck, this is Aunt Mimi."

Mimi was an older version of Thorn, complete with blue eyes.

"Aunt," Buck said. "You look more like sisters."

"I think I like you," Mimi said. "What you drinking, baby?"

"Daiquiri," Thorn said.

"You're bad. I see it in your eyes. I'm going to tell your mother."

"Tell her. See if I care."

"You, sweetie?" Mimi asked, looking at Buck.

"Coors, and save your cold mug for someone that needs it," he said.

"Isn't it wonderful?" Thorn asked when Mimi had left.

"Love it here," he said. "Your aunt can't be much older than you are."

"Nine years. Mom has four sisters and a brother, Mimi the youngest. She used to babysit me."

It was growing dark, birds circling an eddy in the river below them. Mimi returned with their drinks and menus.

"Don't need one," Thorn said. "Bring me your most expensive steak, rare, salad, and baked potato with all the fixings."

"Make it two," Buck said. "And your best bottle of Cabernet."

"You got it," Mimi said as she hurried back to the kitchen.

People began pouring out of the restaurant as the sun dipped toward the horizon.

"You're about to see the Roadhouse's biggest attraction," she said, clutching his hand.

They watched as a spectacular sunset disappeared below the hazy horizon. "Beautiful," he said.

"You'll have more surprises before the night is over. Wait till you try the steak."

Thorn was right again, Buck's T-bone grilled to perfection. When someone opened the swinging doors, loud country music blasted out at them. Glancing around, he noticed someone standing in the half-opened doorway, staring in their direction. Thorn didn't notice and he didn't mention it to her.

When the band took a break, several couples joined them on the deck, some smoking, and others enjoying the clear night. The bottle of wine already gone, Thorn drained her second daiquiri.

"I have to go to the ladies room," she said. "When Mimi returns, order me another drink. Tell her we'd like a table inside closer to the music."

Thorn's Aunt Mimi was happy to oblige and moved him to a dark table near the dance floor.

"I'll tell Thorn where you are," she said.

The band was returning from its break, preparing to start their next set. After ten minutes had passed with Thorn failing to show, he went looking for her.

Swinging doors separated the main dining room from the dance hall. He saw her through the glass. Three diners occupied a table, Thorn chatting with them. One was Ezekiel Big Shoe, the woman beside him likely his wife.

Thorn was in an animated conversation with the third person. The young man he'd seen staring at them while they were sitting on the deck. Neither he nor Thorn was smiling. Buck returned to his table on the dance floor without disturbing them.

Dancers clad in Stetsons, boots and faded denim jammed the dance floor. Thorn joined him, a fresh drink in her hand.

"Everything okay?" he asked.

"Couldn't be better," she said. "Let's dance."

They danced almost every song during the band's set. Thorn was consuming daiquiris at an alarming rate and becoming ever tipsier. When she went to the cowgirl's room and left her keys on the table, he appropriated them.

Ezekiel Big Shoe, his wife and the man to whom Thorn was talking, exited the dining room. When the younger man saw him sitting alone, he strolled over.

"I'm Zeke Big Shoe. And you are?"

"Buck McDivit. Glad to meet you. The Saints are my favorite team, behind the Dallas Cowboys, that is."

Zeke wasn't smiling. He was four inches taller than Buck and had the good looks of a GQ model. His designer jeans hadn't come from a rack in Wal-Mart, and his expensive snakeskin boots were custom-made. He flashed his Super Bowl ring in Buck's face as the older Big Shoe and the woman with him joined them.

"I should have known," Big Shoe said.

"You two know each other," Zeke asked.

"He works for Clayton," Ezekiel said.

When Buck saw the older Big Shoe wasn't going to introduce him to the woman, he stood and shook her hand.

"I'm Buck," he said.

"Madelyn Big Shoe," she said.

Except for a streak of gray in her hair, Madelyn was an older version of Kristen, Big Shoe's girlfriend. Buck felt sure she had no idea why her husband was acting like a complete asshole.

"Pleased to meet you, Ms. Big Shoe," he said.

"Seems my husband doesn't like you," she said.

"We got off on the wrong foot, though we still have time to mend fences."

Big Shoe's wry smile was his only comment as he turned away and headed for the exit.

"Nice meeting you, Buck," Madelyn said before following her husband out the door.

Zeke continued giving Buck the once over. "What's your deal with Thorn?" he asked.

"Deal? We just met yesterday. I'm working with her on something at the Archaeological Park."

"Like what?" Zeke asked.

"Stolen Indian antiquities," Buck said, realizing the conversation had turned cool.

"Thorn's had quite a bit to drink."

"I took her keys," Buck said. "I'll see she gets home in one piece."

"See you around," Zeke said.

Buck followed him out the door. Far away from the nearest city, vivid starlight ruled the cloudless sky. In the fluorescent glow of a parking lot lamp, bats circled, darting for flying insects. A rocking chair beside the door moved in a gentle breeze. He sat in it, watching Zeke open the door to a late-model Cadillac for his mom. Ezekiel wasn't with them.

The Caddie had disappeared over the hill when a black Corvette came around the corner. Instead of following the Caddie back to town, the Vette sped away in the opposite direction. The vanity tag, BigShoe, left no doubt who owned it.

Mimi met him with more drinks when he returned to his table. "Guess you met the Big Shoe's," she said. "What do you think?"

"You tell me," he said. "You know them better than I do."

She glanced around, looking for Thorn, pulling up a chair beside him when she didn't see her.

"Ezekiel Big Shoe is a womanizing prick. He's come on to every woman in the county, including me. I'm afraid Zeke is just like his daddy. Don't know that for a fact. I do know he's broken Thorn's heart. I hope to hell you get rid of him for her."

"Is that what she's trying to do?"

"Don't know, but I'd be careful if I were you. Zeke's the hero of the county. Some of his good-old-boy buddies might not like it if they think you're trying to steal his girl."

"Does she love him?"

Mimi didn't have time to answer as Thorn returned to the table, tapping her aunt's shoulder.

"Trying to steal my new boyfriend, Aunt Mimi?"

"If I was ten years younger and could move on the dance floor like you, I'd give it a try."

"Then you like him?" she asked.

"You kidding me, baby. Every woman in this place has their eyes on this stud muffin. If I were you, I'd get him out of here before they start in on you."

"Mimi, you crack me up," Thorn said. "Did you bring me another daiquiri?"

"I was thinking of calling a cab."

Thorn giggled. "There are no cabs around here. Don't worry about me. I've made it home in lots worse shape than I am now."

When Mimi glanced at Buck, he showed her Thorn's keys. "I'm drinking 3.2 Coors. I've only had a couple, and a glass or two of wine. We'll be fine."

Mimi gave them both a hug. "Okay, baby, one more daiquiri. Don't tell your mama on me."

They had danced through another set before Buck begged off. "You're wearing me out. I need to sit for a spell."

When Mimi returned to the table to chat, he stepped out for some fresh air, and a moment away from the noisy crowd. At least he thought he was alone until someone tapped his shoulder.

He wheeled around in time to duck a roundhouse punch whistling over his head. The person that had taken the swing outweighed him by forty pounds or more. Catching the man's hand, he applied a finger hold he'd learned as a police officer. The attacker yelped in pain and sank to his knees.

"What's your problem, big fella?" he asked.

"Thorn is Zeke Big Shoe's girl. Everyone around here knows that."

"Thorn and Zeke are adults. They don't need your help."

The man moved away without replying when Buck released him. He handed Mimi his credit card when he returned to the table.

Thorn's words were slurred when she said, "I'm not ready to go. There's another set coming up."

"You have a dig early tomorrow," he said. "Remember?"

"Baby, you've had enough," Mimi said, putting her shoulder under her arm and leading her to the door.

Thorn's head bobbed as they helped her into the Jeep. Mimi gave Buck a wink, waving as they drove away down the country road.

Chapter 12

Buck fumbled in the dark with the keys when he reached the front gate of Thorn's property. She was asleep in the passenger seat and hadn't moved since they'd left the Roadhouse. Pard and Maggie were raising a ruckus in the backyard as he unlocked the front door and turned on the porch light.

Thorn was dead weight. He had to wrestle her onto the bed. Maggie and Pard watched, wagging their tails, as he pulled off her boots. Knowing how bad it felt to wake up with a hangover, he thought about removing her jeans and blouse. Instead, he covered her with a quilt, deciding he didn't know her well enough. Turning out the lights, he went into the kitchen.

Maggie and Pard demanded attention. After popping the top on a cold beer he found in the refrigerator, he obliged them. They gobbled up a couple of dog treats, then returned to Maggie's extra large doggie bed by the stove.

Turning off the lights, he went into Thorn's cozy den. Pulling off his boots, he plopped on the old couch that sat in front of her pot-bellied stove.

"Good for you, Pard," he said, glancing at the doggie bed. "At least one of us has a girlfriend to keep them warm tonight."

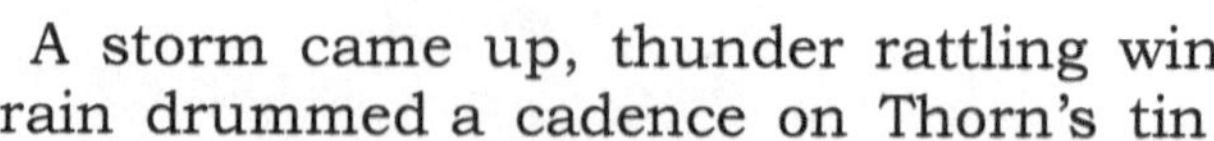

A storm came up, thunder rattling windows as rain drummed a cadence on Thorn's tin roof. Lost in a dream world, Buck didn't awaken. At least until a bright light shining in his eyes caused him to open them. When he did, he sat straight up on the couch, not believing what he saw.

Before him stood a beautiful woman, an aura of blue light radiating from her naked body. He first thought it was Thorn. Instead, it was someone he'd never expected to see again. His heart began racing inside his bare chest.

"Is it you, Esme, or am I dreaming?"

"Come to me and see," she said."

When he pressed against her and began smothering her with kisses, he knew she was real.

Esme was tall and graceful, her long hair and demanding eyes as dark as the storm raging outside the house. As he pressed against her soft breasts, a familiar rush coursed through his body. Just to make sure it was she, he turned her around. As he remembered, a rattlesnake tattoo highlighted the supple curve of her shoulder.

"It's been two long years. Not a day has passed that I didn't think about you," he said. "Why did you go away?"

"I know it hurt you, Buck McDivit. I could not help it because I am from a different place and time."

"What place, and what time?" he said.

"You will see. I will take you there. First, you must become as naked as I am."

Buck's jeans dropped to the floor. "I'm ready," he said. "Where are we going?"

"To a place you've never imagined," she said.

Esme held his hand as they passed through the locked door as if it weren't there. The storm had grown stronger as rain poured down in sheets. Thunder rocked their steps, lightning sizzling across an angry sky.

Sharp stones from the gravel driveway didn't hurt his feet. Though rain gushed off his head and shoulders, he was oblivious to it. Esme led him down the hill, their feet sinking into the mire as they reached a pond overflowing from the deluge. Lightning laced the darkness above them. He hesitated when she stepped into the roiling water.

"Come with me," she said.

He continued to waver. "It's dangerous."

Pulling him toward her, she said, "Trust me."

Neck deep in churning water, they embraced as lightning kissed the pond. It set off a kaleidoscope of radiating colors that made his head spin. When he opened his eyes, darkness was gone. So was the storm. Dancing rays of sunshine radiated through the cloudy sky. Birds soared overhead, and only friendly drops of rain rippled the water's surface.

"We've crossed over," she said.

"That was the wildest ride I've ever taken. What just happened?"

"You did this once before. You just don't remember."

"Did what?" he asked.

"Walked across time," she said. "Brace yourself for culture shock because you are now in my world."

They were in the river. Esme took his hand and led him out of the water to a teepee near its bank. The same teepee Esme lived in when he'd met her near the pagan village of Lykaia. When they pushed through the flap, he saw Beauty, Esme's giant wolf dog. They moved toward one another, meeting in the middle, and were soon rolling on a deerskin rug.

"Where the hell have you been," Buck said, giving her big neck a warm hug.

"She's missed you, and so have I," Esme said.

"You can't imagine how much I've missed both of you."

"Yes I can," she said. "Let's get you dressed. I have much to show you."

Soon, Buck looked like a Mississippian warrior, Esme like a medicine woman. Beauty hadn't left Buck's side until Esme told her to stay and guard the teepee.

"She doesn't like crowds," she said.

Buck gave the large beast another hug and then followed Esme out the door. He could hardly believe the sights that began unfolding around them.

Dozens of canoes occupied the riverbank and more floated in the river. When they crested the natural levee, his jaw dropped. Wooden houses with thatched roofs stretched for as far as he could see. Indian women, naked from the waist up, were working small truck gardens. Men, returning from a hunt, carried a deer and a large turtle.

"They are preparing for the festival," Esme said.

Buck was curious. "Festival?" he said.

"You'll see."

They were both resplendent in colorful paint and feathers. Esme seemed to know everyone and exchanged smiles and greetings as they passed. They soon reached a palisade. Behind the timbered walls, stately mounds, topped by wooden houses, jutted toward the sky. Activity outside the entrance to the palisade was heavy.

"It's festival day," she said. "Some of the people have traveled a thousand miles to be here."

"Tell me about this festival."

"Tomorrow is the first day of summer, the longest day of the year. For my people, it is one of our holiest days. Today is the eve of the summer solstice. Our chief will speak, and there will be a game of chunkey. Following the game, the bonfire is lit, and everyone feasts, chants, and dances until dawn."

Buck had met Esme for the first time during a solstice celebration. He remembered because he'd been the only male present. He and several hundred naked pagan females had danced the night away in a solstice ceremony. When he'd met Esme, she'd been the spiritual leader of the pagan enclave known as Lykaia.

"Are we going to dance like we did when we first met?" he asked.

She shook her head. "I am the medicine woman. I must feast with our chief, the elders, and the emissaries from many other tribes. I have other plans for you."

"What tribes?"

"Mississippians from all over, Aztecs and Mayans from Mexico, and Anasazi from Four Corners."

"You must be kidding."

"I assure you I'm not."

They all wore their festival best. Pearls, shells, and colorful beads adorned the braids in many of the women's long hair. Most of the men had painted faces and shaved heads with only a top knot. Colors of their costumes moved like a kaleidoscope in slow motion.

The palisade was on a hill. From their vantage, they could see the bend in the large river. Hundreds of canoes lined the bank, more still arriving. Everyone, it seemed, was smiling.

"How can so many tribes coexist?"

"Spiro, as you know it, is the religious hub of our universe. There can be no war, strife, or disagreement in this holy place, especially on the eve of the summer solstice. Well, except for chunkey," she said.

The scene reminded him of the open marketplace in Santa Fe. This was similar but ten times larger. A myriad of color, noise and excitement, and jewelry wasn't the only thing for sale.

The aroma of fresh corn, squash, grapes, and a dozen other vegetables floated in a warm breeze. A big black dog that no one seemed to own sniffed his leg before disappearing into the crowd.

"This place is shoulder to shoulder," he said. "Reminds me of the crowds at the state fair, or an OU football game."

"There are many thousands here today," she said.

"Thorn would be in heaven," he said.

"She descended from Mississippians."

"I can't imagine anyone loving their cultural history more than her."

"She is a good person. Maybe too good for the likes of you."

"What about for you?"

Esme's smile disappeared. "We were never meant to be."

"Star-crossed lovers?" he said, squeezing her hand.

"We must live in the moment. I have you now, at least for a short time, and there are many things I need to tell you."

They strolled through the open-air market, marveling at the crafts. There wasn't a cloud in the sky, only a flock of gulls circling to land on a pond created by a bend in the river.

"It's time to enter the palisade," she said.

"I understand every word these people are saying. They can't be speaking English."

"You left your clothes and many other things in Oklahoma. While you are here, you are one of us."

The high-timbered palisade surrounding the enclave was more spectacular than Thorn had described. A moat filled with water surrounded the tall timbers. Guards armed with spears left little doubt that no one entered except by invitation. He and Esme were on the list. They followed a circular maze until it opened into the ancient gated city of Spiro. The panorama blew him away.

"I visited the Archaeological Park yesterday. I had no idea it looked as spectacular as this."

"The new world's version of Camelot," she said. "The chunkey game is starting. Would you like to see?"

In the distance, hundreds of spectators occupied a large arena where two teams were beginning to compete.

"It's a half-mile away. It'll be lunch before we get there," he said.

"We don't have to walk," she said, snapping her fingers.

Four men appeared with a hand carriage, waiting until Esme and Buck had climbed aboard. Hoisting it to their shoulders, they began trekking toward the chunkey game. Rampant noise grew louder as they approached the arena, covered seating awaiting them. Play stopped as the players, and the crowd acknowledged Esme's appearance.

"They treat you like a goddess," Buck said.

She wasn't smiling when she said, "To my people, I am a goddess."

Forty people occupied covered seating opposite them. A man in bright paint sat in a cane throne decorated by wreaths of flowers and feathers. The throne rose high above everyone else in the box.

"He must be a bigwig," he said.

"Walking Wolf is chief of the Mississippians. He's without a doubt the most powerful person in North America."

Walking Wolf's throne was quite a distance away for a good look. Still, the regal old man seemed strangely familiar to Buck.

Chapter 13

Buck had attended many sporting events, both amateur and professional. He'd never seen one quite as loud and raucous as the chunkey match.

Eight contestants and a referee, surrounded by several thousand adoring fans, occupied the football-sized field. Dressed in breechcloths, the competitors had faces painted white with black eyes like raccoons. Both teams wore pillbox hats woven of straw. One of the men stood at least six-six, and towered over the others.

"That's Talako," Esme said. "He's the captain of our team. We have never lost a game."

"Impressive," he said. "Who are they playing?"

"A team from a large Mississippian settlement called Cahokia. They have also never lost."

"One of their dudes is almost as big as Talako," Buck said. "How is the game played?"

"With short spears and a stone roller chiseled from quartz. Talako and the big man from the other team are the spears. They do all the throwing and most of the scoring. Each team has a disc roller and two team members called fronts that run interference. Only the disk rollers can touch the disk, and only the spears can throw them. The fronts use their spears for tripping, and preventing the disk from going through the goal posts. That's five points. You'll get the gist once they start playing."

One of the Cahokians had a six-inch stone disk with a hole in the middle. Taking a stance like a pro bowler, he rolled it toward the opposite goal. The referee waited until the disk had traveled about twenty feet and then waved his hand. Talako and the big man from the Cahokia team launched their spears. When the disk came to a halt, a ref ran onto the field, picked up the closest spear to the disk and held up a finger.

"One point," Esme said. "The first team to reach twelve points wins."

"What's the significance of the hole in the disk?" Buck asked.

"If a spear penetrates the hole, then the game is over. The team that makes the toss is the winner."

"Seems unlikely for that to happen."

"Almost never," she said.

When the ref waved his hand again, eight men ran toward the disk. The melee that followed resembled hand-to-hand combat. Both teams pushed and shoved, the fronts doing their best to break their opponent's legs. A Cahokian retrieved the disk and launched it toward the goal. The scrum continued, both teams fighting for position and scoring a few points. The crowd had grown inflamed.

"There's massive betting going on in the stands," she said. "Much property will change hands because of this match."

"Most everyone's rooting for our team," Buck said.

"Not all. There's a large contingent of Cahokians here to watch the game."

Talako's spear landed within inches of the disk, the crowd standing and yelling. When the ref waved his hand, the two Cahokian fronts took

Talako's legs out from under him. When they did, the big spear kicked him in the side.

"Damn! That looked like a foul to me. Those boys are serious. They don't have a penalty box in this game?"

"Chunkey emulates combat. Bones are often broken. The crowd expects the team to play through their pain."

"Brutal. Sort of like pro football. How long till the ref calls a break?"

Esme shook her head. "They'll battle until they drop, or the game is over. There are no quarters."

"And the reward?" he asked.

"Life, the losers killed and their scalps displayed on the winner's belts."

"You gotta be kidding me," he said.

"If the visiting team wins, our chief will pardon them because this is a religious holiday. If our team loses, they will lose their heads."

"Doesn't look like they're in any danger of that. They're ahead by six points."

"I pray not," Esme said. "Talako is Walking Wolf's only grandson, and the greatest warrior our tribe has."

"Your chief wouldn't allow his own flesh and blood to have his head chopped off."

"Not only allow it, he would proclaim it so. He would have no choice," she said.

"You seem distressed. You okay?"

"These games always frighten me."

"You want to leave?"

"I can't," she said.

"Something you aren't telling me?"

"Walking Wolf and I are time walkers, inherited only when both parents are also walkers. The only other walker in the tribe is Talako."

Buck stared at her anxious expression, trying to decipher what she had just told him.

"So you and Talako are . . . ?"

"Betrothed," she said. "We must marry and have a child."

She squeezed his hand, her eyes begging for understanding.

"I had hoped we were going to do more than just hold hands tonight."

"I am so sorry. That is not possible," she said.

"Do you love him?"

"As much as I love you."

"Then I guess it's okay," he said.

When they returned their attention to the game, they saw that the Spiro team had drawn within a point of winning. The Cahokian roller gave the disk a great heave, the crowd waiting until the referee waved his hand. As he did, Talako and the big Cahokian launched their spears. The disk hit a bump and fell on its side as Talako's spear sailed over it.

When the Cahokian's spear began its descent, every spectator in the arena sensed what was about to happen. As the missile landed in the hole in the disk, the crowd grew deathly silent. The chief came down from his cane throne, motioning Talako to approach him. Esme's face turned bright red as she squeezed Buck's hand.

"I can't believe this," he said.

"If he can break Talako's spear, then it is a sign that the Great Spirit wishes him to die. Walking Wolf will have to take his head."

Buck stood. "I'll stop it," he said.

Esme pulled him back into his seat. "No. If the spear breaks, then it is ordained."

Talako's head hung low as he knelt in front of his grandfather and handed him his spear. Removing a serrated stone dagger from his ceremonial belt, Walking Wolfe drove it into the earth. Then he raised the spear over his head and did a slow turn so that everyone in the stands could see.

Esme let go of Buck's hand, her tears flowing and the veins in her neck bulging. She clinched her hands, almost as if she also had hold of the spear.

Though smaller than his grandson, Walking Wolf looked anything except weak. Buck could see he was preparing to break the spear and had little doubt that he could complete the task. As the rapt crowd watched in silence, his muscles strained, his face turning red. Buck and everyone else expected the spear to snap at any second.

Despite his efforts, the spear never even bowed. Finally, the anger imprinted on his face disappeared, replaced with a smile. He turned again to the crowd.

"This spear is unbreakable. Would anyone care to try?" He walked around the arena, offering it to anybody that might accept it. No one did, not even the contingency from Cahokia. "Then the Great Spirit has spoken," he said. "I deem this contest a draw."

Cheers erupted from the crowd as Chief Walking Wolf returned the spear to Talako. Buck glanced at Esme, her hands still clinched and tears streaming down her face. He took her hands and uncoiled her fingers. Two deep red welts occupied her palms. He began massaging them.

"You saved him, didn't you?" he said.

Her breathing labored, she answered. "It took every ounce of power I have. I couldn't let him die."

People began filing out of the arena as Esme regained her composure.

"What now?" he asked.

"A meeting with Walking Wolf. You are about to learn why we brought you here."

Mesmerized by the game in the arena, Buck hadn't noticed much of the scenery inside the palisade. Now that it was over, he glanced around at the mounds that seemed much larger than when he viewed them with Thorn.

"These structures are magnificent pyramids. They seemed like nothing more than mounds of dirt when I saw them yesterday," he said.

"Withered by centuries of wear and erosion. I am thankful you get to see them in all their glory."

"So am I."

"Like the pyramids of the Mayans and Aztecs, ours predict astrological patterns."

"Like tomorrow's solstice?"

She nodded. "Now, we must meet Chief Walking Wolf in the Great Hall atop the main pyramid," she said.

Buck was breathing hard as they climbed the pyramid. When they reached the top, he could see that the panorama was breathtaking.

"What are they building down there?" he asked.

"A giant bonfire to celebrate the solstice. Chief Walking Wolf will address the masses just before dark. The ceremonial lighting of the bonfire will then occur. You will see."

A massive wooden house occupied the flat top of the pyramid. Esme led him down a long hallway to a darkened room and the chief of the Mississippians soon joined them.

"Oh, my God!" Buck said when he saw him. "You're Pascal LeFlore."

"I am Chief Nashobanowa. That means Walking Wolf in our language. I go by many other names. Like you, Esme, and my grandson, I am a walker. I was the one that handed you the Black Cup."

"But you died," Buck said.

"No, because I was never alive in your time. Walkers cannot alter time. Please, have a seat."

Chief Walking Wolf sat on a colorful blanket situated on the dirt floor. Buck and Esme joined him. The man was much older than they were, though younger than the old man he'd pulled from the burning pickup.

"There is much you don't understand about walking through time," Esme said. "Right now, it is not important. What is important is the reason we brought you here."

"Which is?" he asked.

"We first must drink from the Black Cup," Walking Wolf said.

The cup was similar to the one Pascal LeFlore had given him. This one exuded a distinct glow, its aura pulsating when Walking Wolf shifted it in his hands.

"You have done this before," Esme said. "With the Great Spirit when he took the embodiment of a man."

"I don't remember," Buck said.

"It is okay," Chief Walking Wolf said. "The point is we know you are reverent and that you appreciate this moment."

"The Black Cup is as old as time," Esme said. "The relic is the most valuable, venerated, and holy object our tribe possesses. Every one of us would give their life to protect it."

"And we do," Walking Wolf said. "But there is a problem."

"The Black Cup is in danger of desecration," Esme said. "Though not in our time, and out of our control."

They both nodded when he said, "Haskel Doonkeen?"

"The man who calls himself Blade," the chief said.

"He has gone to great lengths to get the cup," Esme said. "Chief Walking Wolf and I have done everything we can. We are powerless to protect it from him in your world."

"Will you help us?" he asked.

"If it's within my power, I'll stop him," Buck

said.

"I believe you," Walking Wolf said. "But we must drink from the Black Cup to assure that it is so. Are you prepared?"

Buck nodded as a young woman appeared through the door's skin flap. Below the waist, she wore moccasins on her feet and a deerskin skirt. Above the waist, except for red paint, bright feathers, and strings of beads, she was quite naked. She was also attractive.

"This is my daughter, Teawah. She will assist us with the ceremony," he said.

Chief Walking Wolf held the cup as she filled it. He took a deep breath before drinking. Whatever was in the cup was potent because his eyes crossed, and he looked as if he were about to pass out. Esme took the cup from his trembling hand, waiting as Teawah refilled it from her pitcher.

"The tea from the Black Cup induces visions," she said. "It tastes like death, though is life itself. It focuses our mind's patterns and illuminates the future."

She took a drink from the cup, her reaction to tasting the concoction much the same as Walking Wolf's. Buck thought she was about to throw up. She didn't, though her entire body shook as she handed him the empty cup.

"The tea lays bare our fears and desires," Walking Wolf said. "Two things from which we hide. Take it in one drink, or you won't finish it."

Teawah drew close to him, filling the cup with the viscous fluid. He could feel her warmth and smell her lotus perfume as he touched the dark concoction to his lips. The tea was so foul tasting he had the instant urge to spit it from his mouth. He didn't, taking the chief's advice and drinking it in one long swallow.

Buck felt his eyes cross. The room began to spin, Esme, Walking Wolf, and Teawah staring at him, laughing. His body shook and stomach churned as Teawah pulled him toward a door that led outside. He reached it in time to vomit over the railing. With his body twitching and head pounding, he let her lead him back to his seat on the rug.

The hallucinogenic tea affected Walking Wolf and Esme less than Buck. He watched as Teawah refilled the chief's cup. This time, she had to lead him to the back door. Esme soon followed.

Buck's head continued to swim. He'd never felt so drunk. The room had begun to rotate. Explosions of colored lights illuminating dark worlds he'd never imagined. Esme was a snarling jaguar, the chief a giant wolf pacing the floor.

Teawah's smile was sultry as she approached him. Engulfing him in her willowy arms, she kissed him and pressed her soft breasts into his chest. When her intoxicating perfume changed into the fetid breath of a man, he recoiled. It was Haskel Doonkeen. Buck pushed him away.

Blade's features began to change. He morphed into a giant, hairy creature that looked almost human. Buck was trying to scream when someone put the Black Cup to his lips again. It was the last thing he remembered for awhile.

Chapter 14

Buck's brain was trying to kick its way out of his skull when he opened his eyes. The visions were gone, though his stomach continued to churn. It forced him to take yet another trip to the back door.

"We gave you the antidote," Esme said. "You'll feel better in a few minutes. Can you tell us what you saw?"

"Haskel Doonkeen and a giant, monster-like man," he said.

He omitted telling them about his sensuous encounter with Teawah.

Esme took Buck's hand. "Chief Walking Wolf and I are powerless to protect the Black Cup in your world. We need your help against Blade."

"You have my word."

That was all Chief Nashobanowa needed to hear. After giving Buck a solemn nod, he exited the dark room with Teawah. Before disappearing through the deerskin flap, she turned and nodded. It made him wonder if part of the vision had actually been real. Esme gave him no time to ponder.

"Are you okay now?" she asked.

"I'll live," he said. "I wasn't so sure a few minutes ago."

"Do you still have the Black Cup?"

"It's with Thorn at the museum."

"And that's where it should stay," she said.

"How many children and grandchildren does Chief Walking Wolf have?" he asked.

Esme laughed. "Many."

"And Talako is the only time walker?"

"Chief Walking Wolf has many wives. Only one was a walker. Talako's father died in battle; his mother while giving birth to him."

"You said I'm a walker."

"A gift bestowed by the Great Spirit."

"Then why couldn't you and I have a child?"

Esme squeezed his hand. "We come from different times. You can do nothing to affect my world, or I to yours."

She pulled him to his feet and led him to a window covered by a deerskin flap. Opening it, she pointed to the giant bonfire burning in the center of the palisade. Drums were beating, and shouts of revelry echoed across the plain.

"It's dark already," he said. "Have we been here that long?"

"The tea alters your perception of time. The celebration has begun and will continue until dawn. I must join Walking Wolf in the main hall for the meeting with important emissaries from other tribes." He felt her warmth one last time when they embraced. "At the base of the pyramid Beauty awaits. She will lead you back to the pool."

"Will I ever see you again?" he asked.

"I don't know what fate holds for us. I do know you are in grave danger, and that I cannot help you.

"One last kiss?"

She kissed him and said, "I hope not. And Buck, wash the paint off before you return to your world."

Beauty awaited him at the base of the stairs. "I

think you and Lady are the only two females who know me," he said.

A yelp was her acknowledgment that his words were likely true.

She led him through the meandering crowds, and out the door of the palisade. Muted moonlight cast golden ripples on the river. She didn't stop when they passed Esme's teepee. As he began washing off the ceremonial paint, she whined and licked his face. He gave her one last hug before wading into the dark water.

Rain began to fall, and then he heard thunder. Closing his eyes, he knew what was coming. It would change him forever, though he knew it wouldn't heal the pain in his heart.

Buck's head was again pounding when he opened his eyes the next morning. The aroma of brewing coffee caused him to keep them open. The first thing he saw was Thorn smiling at him.

"It's alive," she said.

Pard and Maggie were at her side, their tails wagging a mile a minute.

"Something smells good," he said, ignoring her obvious amusement.

"Hangover food. Homemade biscuits, sausage gravy, hash browns, and sand plum jelly."

"I didn't drink anywhere near as much as you," he said. "Why is it I have a hangover, and you look fresh as a daisy?"

"Genetics, I guess. I've never had a problem with hangovers."

"Lucky you," he said.

Thorn's pink nightie caused him to remember his own nakedness. At least a fleece blanket covered him.

"What happened to my clothes?" he asked.

"In the washer," she said. "There was a storm last night. Thunder and lightning woke me, and I checked on you. You were shivering on the couch, naked and wringing wet. I covered you with a blanket. What were you doing outside in the storm?"

"Walking," he said. "Sleepwalking, I guess. Hope I didn't give you too much of a start."

"I have brothers. I've seen naked males since I was old enough to remember. Believe me when I say I wasn't shocked. What's that on your face?"

Before he could answer, she rubbed his cheek with a dampened paper towel.

"What?" he said.

"Looks like war paint. What exactly were you doing last night?"

"Guess I drank too many Coors. I do remember meaning to tell you that you are the best dancer I've ever had the pleasure to two-step with."

"You're pretty good yourself. Every female in the place had their eyes on you. Why do you feel so bad? You drank nothing but Coors and a glass of wine."

"Lightweight, I guess. I could use a cup of that wonderful coffee I smell."

"What about biscuits and gravy?"

"Twist my arm," he said.

Pulling the blanket around his waist, he followed her into the kitchen. He had a hard time keeping his eyes off her athletic body the nightie did little to hide. She didn't seem to mind when she saw him looking.

"I met your boyfriend last night," he said. "Didn't realize you are dating the crown prince of New Orleans."

"He's a jerk," she said. "I told him to take a hike."

"Sure about that?"

She turned away from the skillet, stood on her tiptoes, and planted a sultry kiss square on his lips.

"Proof enough for you?"

"I could use more evidence."

"Not gonna happen," she said. "Today is the summer solstice, one of our biggest tourist draws of the year. I'm conducting tours until well after dark."

"But it's Saturday. You shouldn't have to work on the weekend."

"Why not? You are. Besides, we can't choose which day the summer solstice falls on. I have to work, and that's that."

"Damn!" he said. "If that's the case, I may have to spend extra time in the shower."

"Whoa!" she said. "Too much information."

"Sorry about that. If you throw a robe over that pretty nightie of yours, I'd be able to think a little straighter."

"My nightie? What about what's beneath it?"

"Fancy wrapping always enhances the package," he said.

She was grinning when she said, "You never give up, do you?" She returned from her bedroom with a tattered terry cloth robe wrapped around her. "This make it any easier for you?"

"Not working. My imagination just kicked in."

She gave his cheek a playful slap. "Have some eggs and biscuits and try to calm yourself."

Buck's thoughts of sex waned as he dug into breakfast. Thorn poured him a large glass of tomato juice, doctoring it with salt, pepper, and Tabasco Sauce. After sopping the last bite of gooey egg yolk, he felt almost human again. Thorn's old robe had cracked open a bit, highlighting her tanned bosom.

"If you quit staring at my tits, I'll tell you something," she said.

"I'm all ears," he said.

"And eyes. I feel like a hunk of meat in a cage with a starving tiger."

"T-bone, rare," he said. "My favorite."

"Get your mind off sex, at least for a moment. Please?"

"I'm having a hard time."

She shook her head and covered her face to keep from laughing aloud.

"I had a friend check out the license tag BladeRunner-1."

"And?"

"A corporation named Forbidden Treasures owns the vehicle."

"Any idea who was the regular driver of the car?"

Thorn nodded. "Someone named Haskel Doonkeen."

"What's his position with Forbidden Treasures?"

"Don't know," she said. "They have a website and sell antiquities from all over. There isn't much corporate information on the site."

"Indian antiquities?"

She nodded again. "Nothing illegal, at least as far as I can tell. Still . . ."

"What?"

"The site advertises that almost any antiquity is available for a price."

"How can they do that?"

"There are hoops to jump through if you want something specific. From what I saw, the corporation is highly secretive."

Thorn was cleaning the table when her house phone rang. She returned to the sink looking distressed.

"What's up?" Buck asked.

"Someone broke into the museum last night."

"A robbery?"

She nodded. "As best as we can tell, there's only one object missing."

"The Black Cup?"

"How did you know?" she asked.

"It's the most sacred object the Mississippians possessed. They used it in religious ceremonies. It was like their Holy Grail."

"How do you know that?" she asked.

"Research."

"I've never seen an article stating the religious value of the Black Cup."

"The thief knows about it."

"Then he must be psychic," she said. "The police told one of our staff members they found little evidence."

"How did the thief get in? I don't recall seeing any windows and few doors. Did they say how they entered the museum?"

"That's what's so strange," she said. "There was no evidence of a break-in. The alarm was still set when Valene opened this morning."

"Then how did she know there was a theft?"

"She found a broken pot on the floor. When she began picking up shards, she noticed the door to the cabinet where we had the Black Cup was open."

"Sounds like an inside job to me," Buck said.

"No way."

"Then how did they get inside without tripping the alarm?"

"All our employees are trustworthy. I'll vouch for it."

"Did you know Haskel Doonkeen is an associate of Ezekiel Big Shoe?"

"You're kidding," she said.

"I'm not. He's staying at the lodge. Big Shoe introduced him to me."

"Tell me again what you're doing at the lodge."

"Ever seen the cable network reality series, Cryptid Hunter?"

"Who hasn't?"

"Jake Huntington, Mr. Cryptid Hunter himself,

is at the lodge. My boss, Clayton O'Meara, is a friend of his."

"What's Bigfoot got to do with Indian artifacts?"

"I'd be ahead of the game if I knew the answer," he said. "Clayton will be there this weekend. He'll ask me that same question."

"Mind if I change the subject to something a bit more pleasant?"

"I'd love it," he said.

"After the last tour tonight, I'll be off for the rest of the weekend," she said, putting her arms around his neck. "I've never stayed at Sunset Lodge. What's a girl have to do to get an invite?"

Chapter 15

Buck was both angry and excited when he left Thorn's little ranch and headed back to Sunset Lodge. Angry he'd failed on his promise to Esme and Walking Wolf to protect the Black Cup. Excited about spending the rest of the weekend with Thorn.

"The last tour is a lecture on the astronomical significance of the mounds. It doesn't end until well after dark. I'll need to return home to shower and change clothes. It might be after midnight before I get to the lodge."

"You're welcome no matter what time you arrive. I'll be waiting with a bottle of champagne," he'd said.

Buck fretted about Thorn and the theft of the Black Cup all the way to Sunset Lodge. When he arrived, he took Lady to the stable, handing her reins to a groom.

"I'll take care of her," he said.

The stable keeper, a man whose nametag said Gus, joined him as the groom led Lady to a stall.

"You have quite an operation here," Buck said.

Like every other employee of the lodge, Gus was an American Indian.

"Mr. Big Shoe won't settle for anything less," he said.

A couple of horses, munching hay from a round bale, were in the big stock pen next to the barn. A large mule was with them.

"You have a mule?"

"Not by choice," Gus said. "We got him thinking he would keep the coyotes and wolves away. Ain't none up here, so we don't need him."

"He for sale?"

"For the past year."

"What do you want for him?"

"How much you got?" Gus said.

Buck counted out four twenties. "Sixty bucks and a twenty for your trouble."

"That'll work."

"Can you keep him till I'm ready?"

"You bet," Gus said, stuffing the money into the pocket of his western shirt. "He's yours. Take him anytime you want."

"What's his name?"

"Ain't got one," Gus said.

"I'll pick him up in a day or so. Entering the barn, he found Lady's stall and patted her neck. He wanted to talk with Don Boone, though he doubted he'd be around on a Saturday. He was wrong.

Don was working at his laptop, Hamlet, the black cat on his lap. He glanced up when Buck opened the door.

"Glad to see you," he said. "I was beginning to think you'd gone back to Oklahoma City and forgotten about me."

"No way. I spent the night in Spiro. Looks like you got a new friend."

"He's a cutie," Don said. "I got him a litter box, kitty bed and plenty of food at the lodge's general store."

"Good man," Buck said.

Don didn't quiz him about why he'd spent the night away from the lodge, and Buck offered no explanation. Hamlet jumped out of Don's lap to greet Pard. The two soon disappeared into the kitchen together. Don grinned as he watched them go.

"That little cat has the energy I wish I had," he said. "I managed to dig up quite a bit of info while you were gone. Got time?"

"All the time in the world," Buck said. "Let me fill Pard's water bowl, and I'll be right back. Don pulled a comfortable chair in front of his makeshift desk. Buck sat in it when he returned from the kitchen. "Yellow Paint Woman was right. They're thick as thieves and sharing water out of the same bowl. Now, tell me what you found."

"Like you said, Haskel Doonkeen was a sniper in the army. What he didn't tell you is that he didn't receive an honorable discharge."

"That so?"

"Doonkeen's discharge was for medical reasons; in his case, mental."

"Doesn't surprise me," Buck said. "Any specifics?"

"One of my buds got me the report. Seems he's an extreme sociopath. A possible menace to other people."

Pard wandered back into the room and sat on the floor beside him. Buck rubbed his head.

"That doesn't surprise me either."

"His release has requirements. He meets with a psychiatrist at the VA hospital in Muskogee once a week. When I called the doctor, he tight-holed me."

"We know as much as he does about Doonkeen. What else?"

"He was involved in criminal activity during his last tour in Afghanistan."

"Such as?" Buck asked.

"Smuggling. He worked with an organized group running everything from opium to stolen antiquities. Army investigators didn't have enough evidence to convict him. They used his mental health to wash him out of the service. Stolen antiquities ties in with what he's doing now."

"Forbidden Treasures?" Buck said.

"You're a step ahead of me," Don said.

"Thorn Little Deer, the archaeologist I know, checked the tag with the Caddo Nation. The corporation owns his Corvette."

"And the truck that ran the old man off the road."

"Then maybe we can tie Pascal LeFlore's death with Blade and get him convicted of murder," Buck said.

"Don't think so. According to reports, someone stole the truck and wrecked it. The thief got away on foot."

"Does Doonkeen have an alibi?"

Don nodded. "He was here at the lodge with Mr. Big Shoe."

"Fits in with what I saw last night," Buck said. "Big Shoe and Blade drive identical Corvettes."

"Then he's likely connected to Forbidden Treasures."

"Looks like it," Buck said. "Big Shoe introduced him to Jake Huntington as a hunting and fishing guide. Know anything about that?"

"I found nothing that suggests he's a guide."

"They concocted the story?"

"Looks like it."

"But why?"

"So Cryptid Hunter will take him on the expedition."

Buck let that bit of information digest for a moment. "It's way past lunch. You hungry?"

"I brought an apple from home."

"Save it. Let's check out the lunch specials at the lodge. We'll talk more about Blade while we're eating."

"Twist my arm," Don said.

Pard wagged his tail and barked when Buck said, "Guard the cabin while we're gone, big boy."

The weather was mild, temperature in the eighties. A gentle breeze rustled the needles of the stately pines surrounding the lodge. Semis filled the auxiliary parking lot, some coming, others going.

Film crews from several networks had cameras running, reporters with microphones conducting interviews. Jake Huntington, dressed in starched camouflage fatigues was in the thick of things. Rimless glasses perched atop his snowy white hair like a tiara. He waved when he saw Buck.

"Missed you last night. They had a hell of a party at the swimming pool on the roof. Colley got drunk and threw a reporter into the water."

"Was there a fight?"

"Hardly. The reporter was female. She ended up in bed with him before the night was over."

Buck grinned. "Jake, this is Don Boone. He works for Clayton. He's helping me here at the lodge."

Using some secret fraternity grip, Jake shook his hand. "How do you like working for my best friend?"

"Just started yesterday. Haven't met Mr. O'Meara yet, though I already know he's a first-class individual."

"That he is," Jake said. "He's on his way here."

"You have quite an operation going," Buck said. "You sure we're gonna need all this equipment?"

"Better safe than sorry. Blade says we'll need every pound of it to complete our project. He could be right."

"Join us for lunch?" Buck asked.

"Still got work to do. Where are you eating?"

"Don't know. Someplace in the lodge."

"Sit on the deck at the Bistro. It's on the

second floor and faces north. The view is spectacular, and they have the best Reuben you ever sank your teeth into."

"We'll give it a try," Buck said.

"When Clayton arrives, I'll send him to join you."

They waved and headed to the Bistro. "Wow," Don said. "I had everything I could do to keep from asking for his autograph. The boys will never believe I met the Cryptid Hunter."

"Speaking of whom, what does your family think of your new job, and your new truck?"

"They're thrilled. I can't tell you how close the wolf was to our door."

"Don't have to," Buck said. "Been there myself more than once."

The outside deck at the Bistro Bar and Grill was everything Jake had said, and more. A fine mist of water coming from a rubber hose with tiny nozzles lowered the temperature on the muggy day.

Buck felt comfortable beneath the gaudy red umbrella blocking the sun from their table. And, like Jake had said, the view of the valley was spectacular. They could see the interstate many miles to the north. Cars, trucks, and semis looking no bigger than tiny insects traversed the highway.

"It's beautiful," Don said. "Wish I could bring Josie and show her."

"Why not? You're making plenty of money now, and I'm sure Clayton will give you the company discount."

"You think?" Don said.

"It would be a great chance for your boys to meet Cryptid Hunter in person."

"Booked solid is my guess."

"There were people checking out when we came through the lobby. Go see. I'll wait for you."

Don returned to the table with an ear-to-ear

smile. "They had a balcony suite on the third floor. I called Josie. She and the boys are packing for the weekend."

"What are your boys' names?"

"Don Jr. and Doug."

"They'll love this place. Soon as you meet Clayton, take the rest of the weekend off, and go get your family."

Though vehicles crowded Interstate-40 in the valley below, there was no such hustle and bustle at the restaurant. A lone hawk circled high above them as they finished eating.

"Something about Blade you haven't told me?" Don said.

"You're good," Buck said. "The Black Cup the old man in the pickup gave me. Someone stole it last night from the Spiro Museum."

"Blade?"

Buck nodded. "Bet it's in his room here at the lodge."

"Sitting on his coffee table."

"You're reading my mind."

"I'm pretty good at nosing around places where I'm not supposed to be," Don said. "Want me to retrieve it for you?"

"Enjoy your family this weekend. I'll get the Black Cup."

Clayton came strolling across the deck, his constant smile spread across his face. In starched jeans, snakeskin boots and a pink Hawaiian shirt, he had everyone's attention. Don stood to introduce himself.

"Glad to meet you," Clayton said. "Buck here has told me all about you. Welcome aboard. Anything I left out of your employment package?"

"No sir," he said.

"Don lives in the valley," Buck said. "I talked him into staying at the lodge for the weekend with his wife and two sons."

"Take your boys horseback riding. They'll love it, and I want to meet them and your little lady before the weekend is over," Clayton said.

With introductions complete, Don departed to get his family. Clayton settled into his chair, soon sipping whiskey provided by a pretty waitress.

"What's up?" he asked.

"Didn't you see all the commotion in the parking lot?"

"I did. There's enough gear and equipment down there for an attempt at Mount Everest. What else?"

"You remember me telling you the man that ran the old Indian off the road was staying here at the lodge?"

"Yeah."

"His name is Haskel Doonkeen. Turns out, he's close friends with Ezekiel Big Shoe."

Clayton sipped his whiskey and said, "I'm listening."

"Thanks to Big Shoe, Haskel Doonkeen has Jake's ear, and is helping him plan the expedition."

"What the hell's going on?"

"Don't know yet," Buck said.

Clayton's smile disappeared. He slugged his drink and motioned a passing waiter to bring him another.

"What's Big Shoe got to do with all this?"

"Wish I knew."

"Jake's chopper pilot is on his way to Guthrie to pick up KK, Lana, and Sara. They were shopping in Dallas when I left the ranch. What else?"

"Doonkeen's nickname is Blade. He earned it by being an army sniper that scalped his victims and carried the trophies on his waist."

"Sounds like a crazy man," Clayton said.

"According to a psychiatric report Don dug up, he's a sociopath and not a psychopath. I'm not sure there's much of a distinction. He threw his knife at Colley the first night we met him and missed his ear by about an inch."

"Good God!" Clayton said. "I better talk with Big Shoe."

Buck shook his head. "Don't do it."

"Because?"

"I'm working on their connection and don't want to tip them off."

"Whatever you say. You think it's safe here for the girls?"

"Big Shoe seems to have Blade's ear. I don't think he would hurt his associate's employer and family. I have to do something a little dirty later on tonight and I need you to have my back in case I get caught."

"Damn, Buck, I'm gonna have to get that pretty little waitress to bring me the whole bottle of whiskey. What now?"

"Someone broke into the Spiro Museum last night and stole the Black Cup. I'm pretty sure it was Blade, and that the relic is in his room. I need to know which room he's in."

Clayton checked an app on his cell phone. "Try 218," he said. "How do you plan to get in?"

"Haven't figured it out just yet," Buck said.

"Big Shoe has a master passkey to every room at the lodge. He keeps it with him."

"Then how am I supposed to get it?"

"We're having a party at our cabin later tonight. Big Shoe and his latest squeeze will be there. If I know KK and Lana, we'll soon be skinny dipping in the spa. Big Shoe will be drunk and his clothes in the outside dressing room."

"Clayton, you have larceny in your heart," Buck said. "Now, if I could just figure out how to keep Blade away from his room for awhile."

"He's Indian, ain't he? Get him a bottle of whiskey. Never seen an Indian yet that could hold his liquor."

"Clayton, that's politically incorrect in so many ways. I'm a third Cherokee. I can hold my liquor just fine."

"Maybe not politically correct, though still pretty much true. I'll find out where he hangs out and make sure his well doesn't go dry."

"How you gonna do that?" Buck asked.

"I know all the waiters and waitresses. Not only am I their boss, I'm also the best tipper on the planet. Just let me take care of this. When he passes out, I'll call you."

"And if he doesn't?"

"I'll make sure he does."

Buck could only shake his head. "Clayton, you missed your calling. You should have been a politician."

"Always glad to help," he said.

Chapter 16

Clayton was talking on his cell phone when Jake Huntington joined them. Though he'd been in the sun for several hours, he looked as fresh as if he'd just come from a nap and a shower.

"Clay lives with that phone plugged in his ear," he said.

"Got that right," Buck said. "Need a drink?"

"In the worst way," he said.

The shift in the bar had changed. Kristen, Big Shoes' squeeze had taken over as their waitress. Khaki shorts highlighted her long legs. The undone buttons of her gingham blouse revealed much of her black lacy bra. Jake and Buck didn't seem to mind.

"What are you having, handsome?" she asked.

"Bombay Gin and Fentimans Tonic Water, if you have it," he said.

"Sweet thing, like I told you the first time we met, we got most everything behind that big oak bar. I already know what you want, good looking," she said to Buck.

"Bet you do," he said. "Since I can't have it, I'll make do with another Coors."

The exchange went over Jake's head, though Kristen was smiling as she returned to the bar. Finished with his phone conversation,

Clayton joined them.

"What's wrong, Clay? You're not smiling." Jake said.

Clayton's grin returned. "Hell, Jake, I'm not rich and famous as you. Some of us got to work for a living."

"If I had your money, I'd burn mine."

"Then let's trade and see who comes out the best," Clayton said.

Jake glanced at Buck with a shake of his head. "I've known this man for twenty years, and I've never once got the better of him in a conversation."

"And you never will, little brother," Clayton said.

"How long have you known each other?" Buck asked.

"We met when I finished my master's degree from Duke. Dad knew Clayton and got me a job with his company to learn the ropes."

"His plan must have worked," Buck said.

"I learned more in five years about whores, smoky bars, and the dark side of the oil business than most people do in a lifetime."

"You bragging or complaining?" Clayton asked.

"I'm not complaining, although I'd like to have some of those brain cells back we sent up in smoke."

"Bitch, bitch, bitch!" Clayton said. "Remember those two little strippers we picked up in the Scorpio?"

"How could I forget it? It wasn't all I picked up that night. I thought my whanger was going to fall off."

"There you go again, thinking only of the negative."

"Clay saved my life on more than one occasion," Jake said. "Problem is, if he hadn't got us into one awful situation after another, he wouldn't have had to."

"I don't see any missing body parts," Clayton said.

"I had a hell of a time. What's happening, big brother?"

"Rent, taxes, and world-class women."

"You came all this way just to check on me?"

"And to have a hell of a good time," Clayton said. "Excitement and beautiful women seem to follow you around."

"I learned it from the master."

"When's that pilot of yours going to get here with my wife and girlfriends?"

Jake had to smirk. "Maybe never if they're as gorgeous as I suspect they are. Colley Hornbeck is the definition of womanizer."

"Hope he's a real man. Otherwise, he'll have trouble handling those three. Ain't I right, Buck?"

"Yessir, you sure are," he said.

"Buck and KK used to be a number," Clayton said.

"Your wife?" Jake asked.

"The woman I live with. Lana's my wife, and she lives with Sara over at the pagan compound."

When Jake looked at Buck for an explanation, he said, "Don't ask."

"I take it all three of these women are gorgeous beyond belief," Jake said.

"Lana's a red-headed Amazon with an ass-kicking body and a brain to match. Sara's dazzling and more than a tad jealous. KK is every man's wet dream."

Kristen caught the last of the conversation as she appeared with fresh drinks. Plopping in Clayton's lap, she grabbed his head, squeezing his face into her breasts.

"Is she sexier than me?" she asked.

"Baby," he said. "You're gonna be my wet dream if you wiggle that sweet ass of yours one more time."

Knowing they were watching her every move, she strutted back to the bar.

"Damn, Clayton, you still got it," Jake said.

"Yeah, and I may have to go change my boxer shorts."

An hour passed, Jake and Clayton exchanging stories as Buck listened. The windows behind them rattled as a chopper landed outside in the parking lot. Clayton glanced at his Rolex.

"That your chopper?" he asked.

"Sounds like it," Jake said.

"Then I better go rescue the girls before that whore dog pilot of yours convinces them otherwise."

"Bring them down. I'd love to meet them."

"Have to head over to the cabin and get them situated. Then I got to go talk to Big Shoe and get the straight skinny about what's going on at the lodge. We're having a party later on tonight at the cabin. It goes without saying that you're both invited."

"Where's your cabin?" Buck asked.

"A hundred yards south of the one you're in. Just follow the sound of country music."

Clayton stopped to exchange pleasantries with Kristen before leaving the bistro. Jake slowly shook his head.

"One of a kind," he said.

"He is that," Buck said.

"Now that we're alone, we need to talk about the expedition."

"I'm listening."

"I need to know if you're onboard."

"I'm not sure what you mean," Buck said.

"What I mean is lots of people think I only do the show for money and fame. That isn't true. Do you believe Bigfoot is real?"

"People I trust claim to have seen it," Buck said.

"I have no reason to doubt them."

"But do you believe it?" Jake asked.

"I don't know a fraction of what you do on the subject. Maybe you can enlighten me."

Jake nodded. "I've been on Bigfoot's trail for going on two decades. I got a fleeting glimpse of one in Idaho a few years back, but it's the closest I've come. I don't just believe they're real. I know they are."

"Tell me," Buck said.

"In the last fifty years, there have been more than five thousand quality sightings."

"I'm an ex-cop," Buck said. "Eyewitness accounts are usually unreliable."

"What's your point?" Jake asked.

"If there's a Bigfoot out there, then why hasn't someone credible photographed it?"

"Pandas weren't discovered until 1869. No one knew about them because they lived in a jungle away from humans."

"There isn't such a place in the United States," Buck said.

"Yes there is. Over twenty-five percent of this country has never been foot surveyed. Why? Because it's too wild," he said, answering his own question.

"You mean like the mountains in southeast Oklahoma?"

"Exactly," Jake said.

"Then where did these creatures come from?"

"My personal opinion is that they're hominids descended from Neanderthals."

"Aren't they extinct?"

"Perhaps not. Europeans and Asians have Neanderthal DNA. Neanderthals were sturdier and likely hairier than Homo sapiens. Maybe they crossed the Bering Strait to the New World first."

"But did they have feet like a Bigfoot?" Buck asked.

"There are caves in France with lots of Neanderthal bones. We know what they looked like. Their feet were bigger and flatter, and their heads much larger. Researchers have found many suspected Bigfoot prints."

"Most of the photos I've seen look like fakes," Buck said.

"I've studied many of the pictures with a magnifying glass. Some are faked, though others have dermal ridges."

"Pardon me?"

"Like fingerprints on articulating feet; something impossible to fake. The bottom line is, I'm convinced Bigfoot is real, and I'm determined to find one to prove I'm right. Let me show you something."

Jake retrieved a folded topographic map from one of the big pockets of his camo safari jacket. After unfolding it on the table in front of Buck, he pointed to an X marked in red.

"The place you're expecting to find Bigfoot?"

"Ezekiel Big Shoe tipped me off about this valley and his man Blade. Take a look," he said, pushing the map closer to Buck.

The contours pictured a mountain range. The place to where Jake pointed was in a valley deeply incised between two steep ridges, the color green indicating forestation. No roads or trails appeared on the map.

"This is a box canyon not far from here in the Ouachita National Forest. It's where Blade says we'll find Bigfoot. There's one strong reason why I believe he's not just blowing smoke."

"And that is?" Buck asked.

"Limestone comprises this valley, according to the state stratigraphy map."

"Which means?"

"Most large caverns form in limestone formations. My guess is there are many caves in this valley. Like where they found Neanderthal remains in France. This would be a perfect place for Bigfoot to live. Are you buying my hypothesis?"

"Sounds logical to me," Buck said. "Does Blade know about the caves, or does he have other reasons for choosing this canyon?"

"That, I don't know," Jake said.

"What about Yellow Paint Woman's assessment?"

"I'll keep an eye on Blade. He's not killing anyone or anything without my permission."

"Good," Buck said.

"Then tell me, are you in or out?"

"All in. I want to be there when you find Bigfoot, and I think you're going to."

Jake reached across the table and shook his hand.

"We'll surely find a footprint. I'm counting on you to verify if it's real or fake."

"Any footprint we find will be real because no one's ever been there to plant a fake."

"You don't like Blade, do you?"

"No sir, I don't," Buck said.

"Because of your fight in the locker room?"

"My dislike for Blade has nothing to do with this expedition. I'm confident he can lead us to a location favorable for finding Bigfoot."

"He seems like a dangerous man."

"Yes he is."

"I can only trust Ezekiel Big Shoe's judgment. I've known him for many years. His son is the quarterback for the New Orleans Saints."

"Met him last night," Buck said. "He's one big dude for a quarterback."

"And has an arm like a rifle," Jake said.

"You sound like a Saints fan."

Jake nodded. "I love New Orleans. When I finish this expedition, I'm going to check out the Manchac Swamp near there. Lots of reports of swamp monsters."

Buck grinned. "And those coonasses down there never lie."

"You're right about that. Doesn't matter because it gives me an excuse to spend time in my favorite city. Ever been there?"

"I spent a memorable Mardi Gras in New Orleans several years ago, and have meant to return ever since."

"Let's get this one under our belts, and I'll take you with me," Jake said.

"Sounds like a plan," Buck said. "Right now, I need to tab out. My new girlfriend's coming up tonight to spend the rest of the weekend with me."

Kristen walked up behind them and heard Buck's comment.

"You got a girlfriend?" she said. "I'm crushed. I thought I had you all to myself."

Buck gazed into her dark eyes. "Something tells me you're pulling my leg," he said.

"Who, me?" she said, touching her chest with both hands.

"Go ahead and pull," he said. "I like it."

Kristen grabbed the back of his head and rubbed her breasts in his face.

"I can't believe you're leaving me," she said.

"I won't be far away. You hot tubbing with Ezekiel tonight?"

"If his wife don't show up," she said. "She does her best to keep him on a short leash."

"I think she's failing. Ezekiel's a little old for you. Why aren't you going after his son? He's single, good looking and wealthy."

"And has more women chasing after him than you can shake a stick at. He's hot, and he knows it."

"Someone's gonna snag him. Why not you?"

"Maybe I like you better," she said.

"I'm calling bullshit on that one," he said.

"Gotta go. I better clear my tab."

She plopped in his lap, put her arms around his neck, and licked his eyelid.

"On the house," she said. "Clayton said to give you anything you want."

"I'm calling bullshit on that one, too," he said.

Chapter 17

Darkness cloaked the mountain, Hamlet asleep beside him and Pard licking his face when he awoke from his nap. As he dragged himself off the couch, he realized his visit with Esme had zapped him more than he'd realized.

Pard wagged his tail and barked when he said, "Hungry?"

There were two bowls in the kitchen and Buck filled both. Hamlet was a fussy eater. After sniffing the contents of his bowl, he jumped on the couch, curled up, and closed his eyes. Pard wasn't as particular.

When he finished eating, he and Buck walked one of the dim trails down the mountain from the lodge. Stopping on a scenic overlook, he tossed a rock over the ledge. He didn't hear it land.

Lady was asleep in her stall, and Pard waited as Buck retrieved a lariat from the tack room of his hauler. The night was warm, an owl hooting in the distance. Stars filled a clear sky saturated with the aroma of crushed pine straw.

They returned to the cabin, Buck's cell phone ringing when he stepped from the shower. It was Clayton, sounds of laughter and loud music echoing in the background.

"You ready?" he asked.

"Yes sir," Buck said.

"You're in luck. Blade hangs out in one of the second-floor bars. He drinks Stoli. We're mixing his vodka with 190-proof Everclear. His eyes are drooping."

"You are devious," Buck said. "Now, if I can just get my hands on that passkey."

"The party's just getting cranked up over here. Big Shoe is in the hot tub with that pretty, little waitress. His clothes are hanging in the dressing room."

"Then I'll drop by and borrow his keys," Buck said.

"You'll have no trouble. Big Shoe is drunk as a skunk."

"From the music and laughter, I'd say he isn't the only one."

"You'd be right about that. I got a half dozen women tossing lime and lemon slices at me."

"Damn!" Buck said. "Must be a giant spa."

"Plenty of room for ten acquaintances, or twenty close friends," Clayton said.

"Take your word for it. See you in a bit. Pard, guard the cabin," he said. "I've got work to do."

When he opened the front door, he found Thorn standing there, a red plastic cup in her hand and a silly smile on her face.

"I made it," she said.

He pulled her into the cabin, spinning her around to get a look at her outfit. A deerskin miniskirt highlighted her tanned legs and cowboy boots. She'd plaited her dark hair and had woven a hawk's feather into one of the braids. A turquoise necklace draped over the open top button of her silk blouse. When she kissed him, he could smell alcohol on her breath.

She beamed when he said, "You're the most beautiful woman in Oklahoma."

"You're a liar," she said. "But I like hearing it

anyway. Sorry I'm so late."

"It's after midnight," he said.

"Doesn't matter to me. I'm ready to party."

"I gotta take care of a little business first. Why don't you just rest on the couch till I get back?"

"Monkey business, maybe. There's nothing you need to do at midnight that can't wait until Monday."

"Yes, there is. Promise I won't be long."

"Whoa, buster! You're not going anyplace without me. My red cup needs a refill, and it's way too early to go to sleep."

Buck thought about the situation. He didn't want to take her to a wild party with a bunch of naked crazies. If he didn't, he'd have no chance of retrieving the Black Cup. He led her outside and locked the door behind them.

"I hear country music," she said. "Want to dance?"

Buck twirled her once and then tugged her hand. "My boss is hosting a party. It's gonna be wild, and I hate taking you there."

"I love wild parties," she said, pulling him toward the sound of music and laughter.

Buck clasped her hand. "I have to warn you first. Your boyfriend Zeke's daddy is at the party. He's naked and in a spa with a woman other than his wife."

Thorn cocked her head and gave Buck a look. "You're kidding?"

"Nope," he said. "And everyone there is likely naked."

"Good. That makes me want to go even more," she said.

Buck wasn't happy as he led her out the door. A six-foot fence surrounded Clayton's cabin that was bigger than the one Buck occupied. Clayton's was an A-frame that reminded him of ski chalets he'd seen in the Rockies. They entered the yard through an open gate.

A wooden deck began at the stairs leading into the chalet, tiki torches lighting the deck. Clayton was sitting at a patio table, smoking a big cigar as he sipped his whiskey. Everyone else was in a circular spa inset in the deck.

Fingers of steam wafted up from the spa along with loud laughter and conversation. Someone had turned down the country music to a mild roar. Thorn's expression began to beam as Buck led her to Clayton's table.

"Clay, this is Thorn Little Tree. I need to do what we talked about earlier. Can you watch her for me?"

"Hi, Clay," she said, shaking his hand. "Despite what Buck thinks, I'm a big girl and can take care of myself."

"Bet you can," Clayton said.

"Come on, Buck. Let's get in," she said. "I love hot tubs."

"There's something I have to do and it can't wait until tomorrow."

"Clayton? Can it wait?"

Clayton shook his head. "Just checked with my contact. It's now or never."

"Gotta go, baby. I'll be right back."

"Fine," Thorn said, shedding her clothes as she walked toward the steamy spa.

Clayton pointed toward the changing room. "Quite a looker you got there. I'll try and keep an eye on her."

"Thanks," Buck said.

Wolf whistles and rude comments sounded behind him as he entered the changing room. Everyone's clothes were hanging on a rack, and it took him a minute to locate Big Shoe's. He had no trouble lifting the wallet and borrowing the master passkey to the lodge. Stopping at his cabin, he patted Pard and grabbed his lariat.

In the hallway outside Blade's room, he waited as a drunken reporter fumbled with his drink and electronic passkey. When he stumbled inside, Buck opened Blade's door and entered.

The room was dark except for the ambient light shining through the open curtain leading to a tiny deck. Using the flashlight on his keychain, he surveilled the room. The door to the bedroom was ajar. He peeked inside, wondering if Blade was already there and passed out on the bed. He wasn't.

When he was sure he was alone, he began searching the room for the Black Cup. He found a small package addressed to an office in McAlester. Since it was about the size and weight of the Black Cup, he decided to open it.

Cutting the tape with care, he removed an object wrapped in tissue and bubble wrap. It was the Black Cup. Searching the coffee table, he found a dirty ashtray about the same size and weight. Without bothering to dump the butts, he stuffed it in the box. Something across the room caught his eye.

It was a copier, a sheet of paper protruding from the cover. Buck opened it, his find something he hadn't anticipated. Two more sheets of paper lay by the printer. Putting all three into the feeder, he pressed the start button.

The cheap printer was noisy and seemed to take forever to copy the sheets. It was still humming when he heard footsteps outside in the hallway. He switched off his flashlight as someone stuck a passkey into the entry slot.

Grabbing his copies, he fumbled to return the originals to where he'd found them. He managed to slip out to the deck as Blade stumbled through the door. He was stuffing the sheets into his shirt when he realized he'd left the Black Cup by the copier.

Blade staggered to a little refrigerator, groping inside for a bottle of pink bismuth. After fumbling to open the bottle's childproof top, he chugged most of the contents.

Pink liquid dribbled down his chin and shirt as he belched. Squatting behind a large potted plant, Buck saw him stumble to the couch. For a long moment, he just sat there, Buck wondering if he was going to have to hit him on the head and knock him out. It was something he didn't want to do.

The patio door was ajar, and he soon heard the sound of a loud snort. Blade, it seemed, had fallen asleep sitting up. As quietly as he could manage in his boots, he opened the door a crack and slipped inside. When he did, Blade opened his eyes and wheeled around.

Buck hugged the wall and froze, bending at the knees to become less visible. Blade either didn't see him or else was too drunk and sleepy to realize someone was in his room. His head drooped, and he again began to snore.

While the patio door was less than six feet from the copier, it took him several minutes to reach it. When he did, he bumped the Black Cup with the back of his hand. Grabbing it before it hit the floor, he hurriedly returned to the patio.

Blade's room was on the second floor, too high to jump. Tying his lariat around the post of the cast iron railing, he vaulted over it, climbing to the ground. He released the noose from the post in time to step into the shadows as Blade stuck his head out the door. Seeing nothing, he went back inside, shutting the sliding door with a thud.

Buck's heart continued to race as he stood in the darkness. The adrenaline rush that had helped him survive had begun to dissipate, leaving him with a headache. Grasping the Black Cup, he gazed at it, making sure it wasn't a dream.

With any luck, Blade would mail the dirty ashtray without checking it first. McAlester wasn't far away. The package could reach its destination as early as tomorrow. When it did, he would become Blade's number one suspect.

He bypassed his cabin on the way to Clayton's, not daring to leave the cup there. Someone was at the party that would know how to safeguard it. That person wasn't Clayton.

Chapter 18

The party was going strong when Buck reached Clayton's cabin. A noisy commotion began as he returned the passkey to Big Shoe's wallet. Curious about the uproar, he peeked out the door.

Steam wisped up from the empty spa, everyone standing in a semicircle as Thorn and her former boyfriend Zeke Big Shoe shouted insults at each other. Dressed in jeans and Saints' jersey, Zeke wagged an angry finger at naked and defiant Thorn. White terrycloth robes draped Clayton and the others.

Damp hair clung to Thorn's bare shoulders. Beads of water dripped between her bare breasts as she glared at Zeke. Colley Hornbeck had his arms around an attractive woman whose blond hair was as wet as Thorn's. Buck recognized her as Candice Jacobs, a popular reporter for one of the cable stations. Ezekiel Big Shoe stood behind his son. Kristen, her arms crossed, had taken over Clayton's place at the patio table.

"I'm sorry I ever gave you the time of day," Zeke said.

Thorn was quick to respond. "And I'm sorry I wasted two years of my life waiting for an alley cat like you."

"If I'm an alley cat, then you're a slut," he said.

"Take that back," she said.

"Fuck you!" he said.

His words were more than Thorn could take. Lunging at him, she scratched red marks into his face with her fingernails. Zeke pushed her away, and into the spa. She landed with a splash as Jake Huntington came strolling through the gate. Rushing to help, he threw a punch.

Zeke grabbed his wrist and backhanded him, sending his glasses careening across the patio. Not finished, he wheeled him around, shoving him into the hot water with Thorn. Kristen grabbed Ezekiel's arm.

"Let's get the hell out of here," she said.

Big Shoe wheeled his son around. "You idiot," he said. "Go with Kristen. Now!"

The big pro quarterback gave his dad a condescending look and then followed Kristen out the gate. Big Shoe turned to Clayton and Lana.

"Sorry, folks," he said. "The boy's always been a little headstrong, just like his mother. I can't control him anymore."

"It's okay," Clayton said. "He put on quite a show."

Buck was the first person Big Shoe saw when he stormed into the little changing room. Grabbing his clothes, he hurried out the door.

As Buck walked out to the patio, Clayton, Lana and KK were helping Thorn and Jake out of the spa. Sara wrapped a robe around Thorn's shoulders and led her to the patio table.

"You okay, boss?" Colley asked.

"I'll live," Jake said.

"Good because I got to get this little lady to bed. She's interviewing you tomorrow at seven."

"I may be a little late," Jake said.

Sara grabbed his elbow. "Let's get you out of these wet clothes," she said.

Country music continued to blare as Buck

grabbed Lana and Clayton's shoulders.

"I need to talk to both of you. Now's as good a time as any," he said.

"You sound serious," Lana said.

"As a heart attack."

They turned off the music and outside lights, and went inside. Cabin was a misnomer for a structure constructed of massive logs and native stone. Animal skins and woven rugs covered the wooden floors. A chandelier made of antlers hung from the vaulted ceiling. Though unneeded, a crackling fire burned in the massive stone fireplace.

Lana got Buck a beer, and then directed him to a room with a large conference table. She shut the door behind Clayton as he followed them inside. Her makeup had washed off in the spa, long red hair damp and mussed. Didn't matter because her piercing eyes left Buck weak in the knees.

"What's up?" she said.

"This," he said, handing her the Black Cup. "Haskel Doonkeen stole it from the Spiro Archaeological Museum last night. I found it in his room."

"Who is Haskel Doonkeen, and what the hell were you doing in his room?"

"A thief and a murderer. I was retrieving stolen goods before he had a chance to dispose of it," he said.

"What stolen goods?"

"The Black Cup of Oklahoma, for one. The object you have in your hand."

"Maybe you better start from the beginning."

"Someone is stealing priceless antiquities from all over the state. So far, this is the most valuable relic stolen."

"Are the police involved?"

"State police and O.S.B.I. Thorn says they've made little progress."

Lana turned the cup in her hand. "What is it?"

"A thousand-year-old Native American artifact, likely the most valuable Mississippian relic in existence."

"It doesn't look like much. What makes it so valuable?"

"It was the Holy Grail of the Mississippians."

"How do you know?"

"Esme told me. I saw her last night."

Lana backed up a step. "You saw Esme? I thought she was dead."

"She isn't."

"Then where is she?"

"In another place and time," Buck said.

"You'd better explain."

"Esme is a time traveler. She lives in a world that precedes us by a thousand years."

"I find all this hard to believe," Lana said.

"Then suspend your disbelief. Esme visited Clayton a few nights ago, didn't she Clay?"

Lana moved her gaze to Clayton, waiting for his explanation.

"Is that true?" she asked.

"Yes, dear. I thought I was dreaming. Now I realize I wasn't."

"What did she want?"

"Buck's help. I sensed she needed me to send him to Spiro," he said.

"As I said, I'm finding all this hard to believe."

"I traveled back in time. Esme implored me to stop Doonkeen."

"Tell me about this Haskel Doonkeen," she said.

"An associate of Ezekiel Big Shoe. He's staying at the lodge and is leading Huntington's Bigfoot expedition. The Army suspected him of dealing in smuggled antiquities. He's part of a company called Forbidden Treasures. I feel there's a good possibility Big Shoe is somehow involved."

”Clayton, are you keeping something from me?” she said.

Clayton poured more whiskey into his tumbler from a bottle at the wet bar in the office.

“Buck wanted to hire a security man for the lodge. Big Shoe refused, threatening to quit and take the entire staff with him. It’s possible Big Shoe is complicit in the thefts of these antiquities.”

“Why didn’t you share this with me?”

“I’m telling you now,” he said.

“What’s the problem?” Buck asked.

“Big Shoe is a minority owner of the lodge,” Lana said.

“Twenty percent,” Clayton said. “Not that minor.”

“Don’t fight,” Buck said. “I need your help.”

“Such as?” Lana asked.

“The Black Cup isn’t safe here at the lodge, or in the museum at Spiro. Do you have a place to keep it for awhile?”

“You already knew the answer, or you wouldn’t have asked,” she said.

Removing an Indian rug from the wooden floor, she lifted up a slat to reveal a hidden safe. Opening its heavy door, she placed the Black Cup inside it.

“It’ll be safe for the moment. I’ll have someone from Lycaia security pick it up tomorrow and transport it back to our bank vault. What else?”

“Don’t tell anyone that I retrieved the Black Cup. Not even Thorn or Jake.”

“You suspect them?”

“I’m not sure what I suspect,” he said. “But I have a hunch. I found something else in Doonkeen’s room.”

Pulling the folded sheets of paper from his shirt, he handed them to Clayton.

“What the hell is it?” he asked.

“A map that was in Doonkeen’s copier and an old article I found beside it. I was wondering what interest he had in going along on Jake's expedition. The map and this article explain why."

"Give us a hint?" Lana said.

"Jake showed me a topo map of the area in the mountains Doonkeen intends to take us. The article is from an old science magazine. It discussed a map found in the Prado Museum in Madrid. Some Spanish explorer had learned the location of La Ciudad Perdida del Oro and had drawn a map."

"Translation?" Clayton said.

"The Lost City of Gold."

"In eastern Oklahoma?"

"The map in the article looked a lot like what I saw on Jake's topo. The place we are going is part of the Ouachita National Forest. Jake had to get permission from the feds. Because of Doonkeen's military record, I'd say he had no chance of ever obtaining permission on his own."

"This all seems so coincidental," Lana said.

"Maybe not. Big Shoe contacted Jake about conducting an expedition into the valley. He also touted Blade as the person to lead them."

"Even if the City of Gold is in the valley, what can anyone do about it?" Lana asked.

"Don't know," Buck said.

"What else do you need from us?" she asked.

"Your help in stopping Blade."

"There are some things you'll need to get me," she said.

"Name them," he said.

"We'll have to start with what we've got. You say the state police and O.S.B.I. are already working on these antiquity thefts?"

"Yes."

"Then I'll need copies of their reports and photos of the stolen property. Any information you can provide me with."

"Thank you," Buck said. "I promised Esme I

would do my best to shut down this theft ring. I can't do it on my own."

"Esme was like my sister," Lana said. "You can count on me."

"What about Jake?" Clayton asked.

"Don't know yet," Buck said. "I'm not ready to tell him about Blade, though I need to check this article against his map."

Lana tapped her long red nails on the desk. "Something else is bothering you. I sense it concerns Clayton and me. It's about Adam, isn't it?"

Buck lowered his head. "You tricked me into conceiving him with you. You and Clayton promised I would have visitation and that he could spend time with Jim and Carol. None of this has happened."

Lana clutched his hand. "You're hurt."

"Of course I am. Adam is two, and it's starting to look like I'll never have the chance to take him fishing, or teach him how to sit a horse."

"Clayton?" she said. "Did you make promises to Buck?"

He nodded. "Afraid I did. Now, I feel like a number one heel."

Lana still had Buck's hand in hers, and she squeezed it. "Adam is my prince. I've had a hard time trusting him out of my sight."

"Lana," Clayton said, trying to speak.

Lana's stern glance silenced him. "I'm not finished," she said. "When I return to Lycaia, Clayton and I will have a talk with Adam. I don't feel that it's time yet to tell him you're his real father, but you will get your visitation. I promise."

"And Jim and Carol?"

"I see no reason why he can't spend a week or two with them," she said. "Will this make things better?"

Buck nodded. "You can't imagine. Mind if I call

Carol and tell her?"

"Knock yourself out," she said. "It's late. Let's convene this meeting and check on the others."

Aroma of bacon and eggs wafted from the kitchen as they exited the conference room. KK and Sara, dressed in matching pink baby doll nighties, had cooked.

"Comfort food, buffet style with paper plates and plastic forks," KK said.

"Where's Thorn and Jake?" Buck asked.

"Jake went to his own room. Thorn was beat. We put her to bed upstairs. Anyone for breakfast?"

"Clayton and I will take ours to go," Lana said. "We still have lots of work to do."

"It's two in the morning," Sara said. "Can't it wait?"

"Yeah," Clayton said.

"We haven't seen each other in more than a week, and we have important business that can't wait," Lana said.

Clayton grumbled as he freshened his whiskey. He seemed happier after piling his paper plate with scrambled eggs and bacon. Lana made do with grapefruit juice and French toast.

"Poor Clayton," KK said when the door to the office shut behind them. "That woman can be a real bitch."

"Try living with her sometimes," Sara said.

Buck filled his own plate, trying to ignore KK's skimpy nightie. Her honey-blond hair was still damp from the spa. Sara was shorter than KK and not as curvy. It didn't mean she was hard to look at. They both knew what effect they had on men. KK laughed when Sara rested her elbows on the table, giving Buck a gaping view of her tiny breasts.

"If you two have nothing better to do than torture me, I'm taking my plate and heading back to my own cabin."

"Don't be such a party pooper," KK said.

"Thorn's passed out upstairs. There's no one waiting for you at your cabin."

"Story of my life," he said.

"Then spend a little time with KK and me," Sara said. "We could do more skinny dipping in the spa."

"And have Lana and Clayton on my case?" he said. "I think not."

"They aren't jealous types," Sara said.

"I'm not taking the chance. Besides, it's two in the morning."

"Spoilsport," KK said.

Buck finished eating, slugged his coffee, gave them both a hug, and then started for the door. He returned, grabbing a biscuit and a couple of slices of bacon for Pard and Hamlet.

Chapter 19

Buck awoke from a strange dream the next morning with the feeling someone was staring at him. When he opened his eyes, he saw they were.

Thorn stood at the foot of his bed, her arms crossed, and a frown on her pretty face as she stared at him.

"I'm not too happy with you right now. I was anticipating a fun weekend. Instead, you abandoned me with strangers, and I had to depend on another stranger to take up for me."

"I'm guessing you're not here to jump in bed with me and have a go at wild sex?"

"In your dreams," she said. "I started to go home without saying anything. I couldn't because I was too pissed. Now, you're just laughing at me."

Buck wrapped the sheet around him and got out of bed.

"I'm sorry. No one was as excited as me about your visit. I didn't want to leave you alone. I had no other choice. There was something I needed to do and only one chance to do it."

Thorn's arms were still crossed. "Like what?" she said.

"Rescue the Black Cup."

Her arms dropped to her sides. "You have the Black Cup?"

"It's in the safe at Clayton's cabin. Lana's having someone from Lycaia security pick it up later today. They'll keep it in the bank safe until we're able to end this rash of artifact theft."

"I'm still mad at you," she said.

"Please don't be," he said, venturing a touch to her arm.

When she didn't move away, he embraced her. "Guess you see why Zeke's not my boyfriend anymore."

"He's a jerk and doesn't deserve an angel like you."

"An angel with a horrible hangover," she said with a giggle.

"Thought you didn't get hangovers."

"First time for everything."

Thorn was warm and soft, heat beginning to rise in his loins.

"Sure you won't change your mind about joining me in bed?"

"Having sex is the last thing I want to do. If you just hold me, I'll lie with you awhile."

They lay there, Thorn's thoughts a million miles away. Buck was thinking about other things he'd already realized weren't going to happen. Pard and Hamlet joined them on the bed.

"Hey, baby," Thorn said, hugging the dog with the wagging tail. "Whose cat?"

"Long story. They're both hungry, and I'm sure Pard needs someone to take him for a walk."

Hamlet rubbed against her legs when she stroked his back. "Beautiful animal," she said. "I never took you for a cat person."

"Yellow Paint Woman gave him to me. If I mistreat him, she might cause one of my body parts to fall off."

"Might do you some good, Buck McDivit. Tell me where your leash is. I'll take Pard for his walk," she said.

"You're a princess," he said.

Pard licked her face as Buck pulled on his jeans and buttoned his shirt. "No need for a leash with Pard. Start down the trail just outside the door. I'll catch up soon as I get my boots on."

He could see them just ahead as he rushed down the steep trail behind his cabin. A cold front had set in overnight, leaving behind a haze of damp, morning fog. Thorn was sitting on a boulder overlooking the valley when he caught up with them.

"I just love Pard, and so does Maggie. Give him to me?" she said.

"No way," he said. "Unless I'm included in the package."

"Don't know about that," she said. "Think I'm still mad at you."

"Don't be that way," he said. "You know you were having fun until Zeke showed up."

"Your friends are crazy. KK's a blast, and so is Sara, though Lana's kind of a snob."

"And Clayton?"

"Love him. He's so handsome. Reminds me of an old movie star."

"Don't call him old, at least to his face," Buck said.

"Colley was a trip, and so full of himself," she said. "The woman with him is a Fox anchor. They were having more fun than anyone else."

"And Ezekiel Big Shoe?"

"I can't believe he has a girlfriend. His wife Madelyn is a classy woman. She'd die if she knew how much he'd disgraced her."

"Will you tell her?" Buck asked.

A shake of her head answered his question before she spoke.

"Someone else other than me will have to break the news to her. It's so sad."

"What?"

"Even her son is in on the sham. What a prick. I can't believe I loved him."

They continued down the trail, a cool summer breeze blowing up the mountain. Buck felt a drop of rain on his shoulders.

"We better head back before the bottom drops out," he said.

They almost made it to the cabin before the skies turned dark and opened up in a torrent of summer rain. Buck was pulling his shirt off before he got through the front door.

"There's an extra robe on the hanger behind the bathroom door," he said. "We can throw our wet clothes in the dryer."

He was in his own terrycloth robe and feeding Pard when Thorn emerged from the bathroom.

"Don't get any ideas," she said. "Just because I'm naked under this robe doesn't mean we're going to do anything."

"Just as well," he said. "I need to show you and Jake something, and I don't need sex on my mind."

"Good luck with that," she said.

Jake answered on the second ring.

"Jake Huntington," he said.

"It's Buck. How's your schedule look?"

"Tight," he said. "Just finished my interview with Colley's girlfriend. She gave me hell about my black eye. What's up?"

"Thorn's here with me. She's cooking breakfast."

"Oh?"

"There's something I need to ask you. Can you come to my cabin?"

"You say Thorn's cooking?"

"Yes, and it smells wonderful."

"Where's your cabin?"

After giving him directions, Buck checked to see if he could make good on his promise of breakfast.

"Jake's on his way over, and I told him you were cooking. Are you gonna make a liar out of me?"

"You can help," she said. "I can't believe how hungry I am."

"Yes I can," he said.

She kissed him. "Think maybe we can get our weekend back on track after the meeting with Mr. Huntington?"

"A horseback ride followed by watching the sunset over a bottle of chilled champagne? How's that sound?"

"And then early to bed after an excellent dinner?"

"You're reading my mind," he said.

She kissed him again and then shooed him out of the kitchen. "I'll take care of breakfast," she said. "You take over from there.

When Jake arrived, the aroma of bacon and eggs wafted through the door.

"I don't know who's doing the cooking, but I think I'm in love," Jake said as he took a seat at the table.

Thorn poked her head through the door, laughing when she saw Jake's shiner. Wiping her hands on her apron, she rushed out and gave him a hug.

"You saved my life last night," she said. "Thank you."

"I did the best I could. That big jerk almost broke my jaw."

"You were wonderful," she said, finally pulling away to return to the kitchen. "Don't want the biscuits to burn."

"You okay, Jake?" Buck asked.

"Nothing that a little trip to my dentist won't fix. What you got?"

"Do you have your topo map with you?"

"I don't go anyplace without it," he said.

"What's up?"

"Let's eat, and then I'd like to take another look at it," Buck said.

They helped Thorn put the meal on the table, and then Jake held out his hand. "We've never met. I'm Jake Huntington."

"Thorn Little Deer," she said.

"Thorn's a state archaeologist and runs the Spiro Archaeological Park. You can call her Dr. Little Deer."

"Ph.D.? I'm impressed," Jake said. "Where did you go to school?"

"OU," she said.

"Wish I'd been so lucky. My parents wanted me to go to the University of Texas. Now, every football season, all my friends either hate me or can't stop gloating."

"I thought you went to Duke," Buck said.

"My master's degree. Most of my Oklahoma friends disregard it."

"Sounds like a personal problem," Buck said.

Jake sprinkled pepper on his scrambled eggs. "That it is," he said. "I try to be out of town during OU versus Texas weekends. What about you, Thorn? Are you a big football fan?"

"I love going to the games. It's always crazy and exciting."

With breakfast eaten and the table cleared, Jake spread his topo map on the table.

"This quadrangle encompasses part of the Ouachita National Forest. The reserve extends into Arkansas and is much larger than just this quad. It's where our target lies," he said, pointing.

"Looks rough," Buck said.

"No roads or even trails. Nothing in the quad has ever been foot-mapped."

"How large is the area on the map?" Thorn asked.

"About sixty square miles. Shampe Canyon

encompasses most of the map."

Thorn glanced at Buck. "Shampe is Choctaw for mythical monster," she said.

Jake nodded. "Bigfoot. Almost every tribe has a name for it."

"What better place to search for Bigfoot in Oklahoma than Shampe Canyon?" Buck said.

"Genius, as a matter of fact," Jake said. "A box canyon fifteen miles in length. Steep mountains on either side and trees so tall and lush that little light penetrates."

"Mind if I take a closer look?" Buck asked.

"Go ahead," Jake said.

Buck studied it, intent on every feature of the canyon. Someone had blacked out the descriptive information in the title block. Likewise, they'd used a marker on the longitude–latitude descriptors.

"Where is this located?" he asked.

"I deleted the location information for a reason," Jake said. "No one knows where it is except Blade and me."

"Not even Colley?"

"That's right. I can't take the chance of being claim-jumped. There's too much interest here."

"I won't tell anyone," Buck said.

"Sorry. I trust only myself."

Buck returned his attention to the map. "No one has ever foot-mapped the canyon. Have you thought about the possibility of what else you might find there?" he asked.

"Such as?" Jake said.

"Indian artifacts."

Thorn was all ears. "You think it's possible?" she said.

"You tell me. There was activity all over this area long before the Spaniards arrived."

"You're right," she said. "Shampe Canyon could be a treasure trove. If there's any validity to what you say, and I think there is, then no one is visiting Shampe Canyon without me."

"I can't allow that," Jake said.

"As Buck said, I'm an archaeologist for Oklahoma. I'm also affiliated with the Federal Government. If I don't go, no one goes."

"Too dangerous. No place for a woman."

"Keep your sexism to yourself. I'll bet I'm fitter than you are."

Her words brought a smile to Huntington's face. "I've always considered myself liberal. You're right. I can't believe those words just spewed out of my mouth. I'm sorry."

"Thank you," she said. "If we find artifacts that need protecting, I'll be there to make sure it happens."

"I don't like that arrangement," he said. "I'm only looking for Bigfoot and could care less about artifacts. We're going to have to talk about this."

"More reason why I should be along for the ride," Thorn said.

Buck ignored their banter as he studied Jake's topo map. "There's another problem. If the canyon has never been foot-mapped, the trees are likely hundreds of years old."

"And your point is?"

"Cutting an LZ may well be impossible. How are we going to establish a base camp if Colley has no place to land?"

"LZ?" Thorn said.

Jake was scratching his chin when he said, "Landing zone. What do you suggest?"

"Flyover," Buck said. "See if we can locate a natural landing spot not shown on your topo."

"And if we don't find such a spot?"

"Then go to Plan B," Buck said.

"I think we should spend some time together going over Plan A," Thorn said.

"Me too," Jake said. "Can you spare this lovely young woman for a few hours?"

Buck glanced at Thorn with disappointed eyes.

"We had other plans, though I guess it's okay."

Thorn and Jake were laughing and acting like old friends when they left the cabin. An hour had passed before she called.

"This is taking longer than I thought."

"No horseback ride?" he asked.

"There'll be time for many horseback rides. Okay?"

"Then call me when you finish with Jake," he said.

Chapter 20

Buck found a website that sold topo maps for download. Locating the quadrangle with Jake's box canyon was the problem. An hour passed with no luck in finding the duplicate of Jake's map. Demoralized but not discouraged, he did an internet search for Shampe Canyon. An obscure reference in an old Bureau of Indian Affairs publication gave him the answer he needed.

Pard barked when he finally said, "Got it!"

He was still beaming after purchasing, downloading, and printing the map. When he compared it to the article he'd found in Blade's room, he knew they were one and the same. He had little time to start missing Thorn as he had a call from Don Boone.

"I'm glad I took your advice and booked a room. Josie and the boys love this place. We went horseback riding down the mountain and had a blast exploring the trails."

"Great," Buck said. "I'd love to meet your family."

"We're going swimming at the main pool after lunch. Want to join us?"

Don had signed off when Buck's cell phone rang again. This time, it was Clayton.

"Just checking on you," he said.

"I'm meeting Don, your new employee, and his family at the main pool at one."

"Lana and Sara returned to Lycaia. It's just me and KK. Mind if we join you?"

"Lucky you," Buck said. "A little of Lana goes a long way. I'm sure Don wants to introduce his family to you."

"We'll see you there," Clayton said.

Only a few swimmers remained at the main pool as many of the guests had checked out and gone home. Don was already in the pool with his wife and two boys. He waved when he saw Buck taking a seat at a table with a colorful umbrella.

There was no doubt that Don was the father of the boys, the family resemblance unmistakable. Josie had a pretty face, a pixie smile, and carried a few extra pounds for her height. The boys shook Buck's hand, and Josie hugged him.

"We can't thank you enough," she said.

"Don't thank me. Clayton O'Meara is the man responsible. He's on his way over," Buck said.

After a bit of small talk, Josie and the boys returned to the pool. Don stayed, pulling up a chair.

"Did you rescue the cup?" he asked.

"Yes and there'll be hell to pay when Blade finds out. It was in a box addressed to an address in McAlester. I replaced it with a dirty ashtray."

"McAlester isn't far away. I'd like to be a fly on the wall when someone opens that package."

"Me too," Buck said. "They won't be happy, and I'll be Blade's number one suspect. I also found out why Blade wants to be part of Huntington's expedition."

"I'm all ears," Don said.

Though Buck was in his bathing suit, he'd brought along the article and the topo map he'd downloaded.

"This is the map of the box canyon where

Blade says we'll find Bigfoot. I found this old article when I rescued the cup. A Spanish soldier drew the map in the inset. Though the two maps aren't the same scale, I think you'll get the picture."

Don glanced at the maps. "Blade's got gold on his mind and not Bigfoot," he said.

"And he can't get to it without Jake's help. Something else bothers me," Buck said.

"What?"

"Jake didn't make it easy for me to find this topo. He had the location blacked out on his copy and told me only he and Blade know the canyon's location."

"Your point?"

"Blade may have murder on his mind. If he killed us, no one would ever find our bodies in that million-acre wilderness."

"The chopper pilot will know the exact location," Don said.

"Not yet he doesn't, and Jake doesn't intend to tell him until the day of the flyover. Wouldn't be hard to booby trap a chopper. If it goes down out there, it could take months, maybe years to locate."

"Roger that," Don said. "Wonder how Blade intends to exploit the situation even if he finds his City of Gold."

"He'll figure a way. I didn't show this article to Jake and Thorn Little Deer. I did bring up the possibility of there being Indian artifacts in the canyon."

"And?"

"Thorn's hell bent on joining the expedition."

"Blade will already know you're on to him by then. Hope you got a great plan working."

"Lana wants the police reports of all the thefts."

"Get them for her tomorrow, and find out what else they have. They may already have the

Oklahoma thefts linked with similar jobs around the country."

"Great," Buck said. "I was hoping to implicate Blade in the old Indian's death and get him sent away for a good long time. Don't know if that'll work out now, or not."

"Maybe we should just kill him and throw his body into a deep ravine."

Buck folded the article and put it away. "You sound serious."

"The best way to get rid of a mad dog is a bullet between his eyes."

"Hope it doesn't come to that," Buck said. "If it does, I'll take care of it myself. I don't have a wife and two strapping kids."

Clayton and KK arrived before they had a further chance to talk about popping Blade. Clayton's bathing suit showed off the toned body of an older man. KK's black bikini caught the eye of everyone in the pool area. Don jumped up and stood at attention, doing everything except saluting. Clayton grabbed his hand and pumped it.

"This is Don Boone, our newest employee."

Don motioned for Josie and his two sons to join them. Following introductions, they returned to the pool, leaving Buck, KK, and Clayton alone.

"Awful nice folks," Clayton said. "How's he working out?"

"He's a keeper. A true professional who knows how to get things done."

Don and his boys were practicing diving at the deep end of the pool, splashing and having a wonderful time. Stretched out on a lounge chair, Josie sipped a drink through a long red straw as she caught some rays.

"Water looks great," Clayton said. "Think I'll join them."

To the delight of Doug and Don Jr., he was

soon demonstrating how to do a cannonball.

"He's the biggest baby out there," KK said.

"That's a fact."

"You okay, Buck McDivit?"

"Couldn't be better."

"You seem a bit off-kilter. How's your sex life?"

"Lately, it's been non-existent," he said.

"I just love Thorn. She's beautiful and has the most gorgeous blue eyes. Sort of Debra Wingerish-looking in that old movie, *Urban Cowboy*."

"She's a looker. No doubt about that."

"You've had sex with her already, or you wouldn't be spending the weekend together."

"Nope."

"She playing hard to get?"

"It just hasn't worked out for us. I wasn't planning for her to get wasted last night and pass out at your cabin."

"You like her?"

"A lot."

"Then what's the problem?" she asked.

"I think she's still hung up on her ex-boyfriend."

"If you're talking about that hunk of eye candy at the pool last night, I can see why. He's a dreamboat."

"And a jerk," Buck said.

"Do I detect a hint of jealousy?"

"Maybe a little. I'm not sure exactly why, but I'm starting to feel used and abused."

"You think she's using you to make her ex jealous?"

"Kind of seems that way. You're starting to depress me. Let's talk about you for awhile. How are you and Clayton doing?"

KK sipped her glass of chardonnay before answering. "It's been interesting. Growing up, I always dreamed of romancing King Arthur and living in Camelot. As it is, I'm lady-in-waiting in a four-way with Arthur, Queen Guinevere and her female lover."

"I don't even try to explain your relationships to people anymore," he said. "What about kids? You and Clayton ever going to have any?"

"You kidding? My biological clock is ticking so loud, it's starting to give me a headache."

"Talked to Clayton about it?"

"Our age difference again. Guess when he grew up, men and women didn't discuss sex. It embarrasses him."

"You think he wants a child of his own?"

"We've tried. Clayton can't have kids."

"How do you know?"

"Don't ask. Just believe me; he's sterile."

"And you?"

"A baby factory waiting for some active sperm."

"What's the plan?" he asked.

"Find the perfect man and lure him into my bed. You game?"

Buck almost choked on his Coors. "If you'd gotten me drunk and whispered in my ear, I might have obliged you. Now that I know your plan, I wouldn't touch you with a ten-foot pole."

KK reached under the table and ran her palm up his leg. "Sure about that?"

"Someone already tricked me into fathering a son I rarely see. Unless I'm married, no more kids for me."

"Spoilsport," she said.

"You're gonna get us both in trouble," he said.

"Clayton's having the time of his life clowning in the pool with those boys. You could strip me butt naked, lay me out on the table, and have your way with me. He'd never notice."

"I wish you'd shut the hell up. I don't have a towel and this bathing suit is about to embarrass me."

"Braggart," she said, tossing him a towel.

Just in time, as Thorn and Jake came through the gate and joined them. A waiter almost spilled his drinks as he turned to get a glimpse.

Thorn's cutoffs and ruffled blouse revealed a bit too much of her shapely body. Cowboy boots served only to highlight her legs. If she'd had spurs on the boots, she could have subbed as the star of an x-rated movie. KK glanced at the towel thrown across Buck's bathing suit and flashed him a wicked grin.

Jake was wearing cutoffs as well, though his came almost to his knees. His tee shirt said University of Texas. They were both laughing as they joined Buck and KK.

"Thorn took me horseback riding," Jake said, motioning a passing waiter.

"Didn't know you liked horses," Buck said.

"I don't, and they don't like me. I've never been so terrified in my entire life."

"You're such a liar. You know you loved it," Thorn said.

"We saw some beautiful scenery. Clayton, Lana, and Ezekiel have done a marvelous job. The Sunset Lodge is world-class."

Buck grimaced when the waiter brought Thorn a frozen daiquiri. Here we go again, he thought.

"Where's Clayton?" Jake asked.

"In the pool with the rest of the kids," KK said.

"Those boys with him are two of your biggest fans," Buck said.

"Then maybe I need to meet them," Jake said, sipping his Bombay Gin before heading toward the pool.

"Jake seems like a wonderful person," KK said.

"Oh, he is," Thorn said.

Realizing she may have hurt Buck's feelings, she glanced in his direction. When KK nudged him with her knee, he looked the other way.

"You two have plans for tonight?" KK asked.

Thorn realized almost too late that KK was inquiring about her and Buck, and not she and Jake.

"My plans are up in the air," she said.

Jake returned to the table before the conversation could get any stickier.

"Business in Fort Smith. I have to leave this party early. Colley's warming up the helicopter." He grabbed Thorn's hand and kissed it. "Thanks for the lovely afternoon," he said.

Don's boys were waving and shouting as Jake exited the pool area. Thorn looked distraught and didn't try to hide it.

"I'm going to the cabin and change," she said, following on Jake's heels.

"I see what you mean," KK said when they were gone.

"I'm starting to feel like an old whore," Buck said.

He smiled when KK said, "Or Rodney Dangerfield. What now?"

"Looks like another lonely night," he said. "Maybe I better start in on the hard stuff."

Chapter 21

Buck had that stiff drink before returning to his cabin for a much-needed nap. Hamlet, his new black cat, was lying on his chest when he awoke. It was dark, and he had the same strange feeling someone was watching him. When he flicked on the lamp beside the bed, he realized it was Thorn.

"Still sleeping with the cat?" she said.

"Long story," he said. "Thought you'd left."

She sat on the side of the bed. "I feel like such a fool."

"How so?"

"I chased after Jake; told him I'd go to Fort Smith with him. He invited me along. When we landed, his wife was waiting on the tarmac."

Buck sat up and wiped the sleep out of his eyes. "He's married?"

"I'm such an idiot. Just because he's a celebrity, I was ready to jump in his bed."

"What are you doing back here?"

"Guess he wasn't expecting his wife to be waiting for him. He introduced me as Colley's girlfriend. I came back with Colley, and he was all over me."

"You okay?" he asked.

"Except for my self-esteem. It's registering zero on the ego meter."

"Like I said, why are you here?"

"We had a date. Remember? I had meant to spend the weekend with you. I know it sounds crazy. I simply thought we might salvage some of it."

Buck gave the cat a stroke. "You have to be at work in a few hours, and my ego meter's the same as yours."

"I'm so sorry," she said. "When Jake and I went riding, I had stars in my eyes. You have every right to be mad at me."

"I'm not mad. I don't know what you're looking for. I'm pretty sure it isn't me."

"You could be wrong about that. I got to thinking about our steak and champagne, and moonlight horseback ride," she said.

"Don left some bologna in the refrigerator."

She leaned close to him and ran her hand through his hair. "I'm sorry," she said. "Forgive me?"

"Maybe."

"What kind of answer is that?"

"I can't be too upset because all we've ever done is kiss and hold hands. Since we're both in the bedroom, we could change things."

Thorn startled Hamlet when she jumped up. Springing to the floor, the cat ran to the kitchen.

"Is sex the only thing you have on your mind?" she asked.

"I thought you said you were sorry."

"Forget it. I have so many things on my plate, there's no room to even think about sex."

"We could walk up to the lodge and get something to eat."

"I'm confused, not hungry."

"About what?" he asked.

"I'm almost full-blood Caddo, yet I think like a white man. I went to white man's school. I studied white man's books. I scoffed whenever anyone in my family said anything about my Native American heritage.”

“Sounds like you've had too many daiquiris.”

She giggled and put her hand to her mouth. “Like I said, Colley was trying to get in my pants all the way from Fort Smith. He had a flask of whiskey.”

Buck grabbed his shirt draped over a chair, and went into the kitchen.

“Amazing,” he said.

“Don't you care about my feelings?”

“I bought a mule for Yellow Paint Woman,” he said. “I'm going to take it to her. Come with me?”

“You bought a mule?”

“Yes ma'am, I did.”

“For an old Indian woman? Why?”

“There's a general store at the lodge. People who live around here, as well as the tourists, buy all sorts of souvenirs and goods there. Yellow Paint Woman's mule is too old to help her. She's been walking from her cabin to get her groceries and then carrying them home. A mule was for sale at the stables. I bought it.”

“How much did you pay?”

“What difference does it make?

“A good mule can cost a thousand dollars or more.”

“Sixty bucks,” he said.

“You can't buy a mule for sixty dollars. Something must be wrong with it.”

“He looked fine to me.”

“Did you interact with him?”

“You kidding?”

“What if the animal has a mental disorder?”

“I'm going to get him. Coming?”

Damp clouds hung low above the grounds of Sunset Lodge as Thorn and Pard followed him out the cabin door. Gentle drops of rain began dampening their shoulders. The night attendant of the stables met them at the entrance to the barn.

The little man had no shirt beneath his overalls, his mussed hair the color of dry straw. Pard stood back on his heels, barking at the man.

"Kinda late for a ride, folks," he said.

"I bought your mule. I'm here to pick him up."

"Ain't gonna be easy," the man said.

"Something wrong?"

"That mule's crazy as a coot. He don't let nobody come near him."

"Then how do you feed him?"

The man snickered. "Throw a bale of hay over the fence, and then run like hell."

"Is he in his stall?"

"Why hell no! We don't waste no stalls on crazy-ass mules. He lives out there in the pasture."

"Which pasture?" Buck asked.

The man pointed and then started to walk away. "I'd help you," he said, "I ain't gettin' my teeth kicked out. You're on your own, bud."

"Maybe you should just leave him here and get your money back tomorrow," Thorn said.

Buck tossed the Jeep keys to her. "Can you back it up to the gate? I'm going to find out what we're dealing with here."

Pard raced under the barbed wire as Buck climbed over and gazed into the darkness. When lightning flashed, illuminating the sky, he saw the red eyes of the mule. Putting his fingers to his lips, he whistled, the sound echoing down the mountain.

"Stay behind me, Pard," he said.

The mule issued a sound halfway between the neigh of a horse and the bray of a mule. When Buck approached it, he grew animated, pawing at the damp earth beneath its feet.

"Come here, boy," he called.

The mule's bray became a snort as he moved toward him. Rain had begun falling, and the mule flinched when thunder struck nearby. Buck was within twenty feet of the beast when it lowered its head and rose up on its hind legs. Finally, it charged toward him.

Pard began barking as Buck raised his hands straight in the air and stood his ground. The mule slid to a stop before hitting him. Buck stepped forward and put his arms around the big animal's wet neck.

"Whoa, big fella," he said, letting go with one hand as he caressed the mule's face.

Buck grew angry when he felt the crease in the mule's head and saw its chipped teeth. The deluge had begun, rain falling in sheets.

"It's okay, Thunder. Let's get out of this downpour."

Buck grabbed the mule's mane and led him to the hauler where Thorn was waiting, gate open and ramp down. The mule went into the hauler and didn't protest when Buck shut the door behind him.

"I may be tipsy, but I can see you got a set of balls on you. Where did you learn to handle a crazy mule like that?"

"Hell, he's scared to death of the lightning, and somebody has beaten him. When I come back tomorrow, I'm going to find out who, and then kick his sorry ass. Get in the truck before we drown."

"I'll drive," she said. "You've done enough work for one night."

Buck climbed into the passenger seat as Pard piled into his lap.

"You are one good man, Pard," he said. "I knew you wouldn't let that big mule pound me into the mud."

Pard licked his face and wagged his tail as Thorn headed for the road to Spiro.

"You'll have to tell me where to go," she said.

"If I can remember. I wasn't thinking too well

the other day."

"And I bet she has no cell phone to call and ask directions."

"She doesn't even have electricity. Hope she has some candles burning."

The storm intensified, wipers keeping up with the rain as they started down the steep road.

"Slow down," he said. "The turn is just around the next corner."

The Jeep was creeping when she pulled off the main road to follow the narrow trail through the woods. Wind was blowing, trees swaying like planted dancers. Darkness and motion began playing with their perceptions of reality. A glowing lantern on a rickety wooden porch beckoned when they reached a clearing.

"This is it," he said. "Pull up to the porch."

Yellow Paint Woman was sitting in a rocking chair, a black cat, and a lop-eared hound at her feet. The dog began barking when they got out of the Jeep.

"I've been waiting," she said.

"This is Thorn," he said.

Yellow Paint Woman embraced her. "Though you don't know me, I've known you my whole life."

Thorn began to cry.

"Brought you something," Buck said.

"A mule," she said.

"You knew?"

"Prescience is both a curse and a blessing. I know the beast is a tortured soul. You brought him to the right person because I will heal his wounds."

She and Thorn followed him to the back of the hauler. When he opened it, she climbed inside with the mule.

"Don't let her go in there," Thorn said. "That crazy mule will kill her."

Yellow Paint Woman heard her. "It's okay, child. I'm not afraid of death. What's his name?"

she asked.

"I'm calling him Thunder," Buck said.

"A strong name for a beautiful animal," she said as she led him down the ramp. "There's a harness on the porch. Will you get it for me?"

When Thorn brought her the harness, she placed it on the mule's head. Lightning flashed across the sky, Thunder braying. Yellow Paint Woman put her arms around his neck and hugged him.

"It's okay," she said. The old Indian woman led Thunder to a barn that backed up to a rock escarpment. "You'll never have to worry about the storms again," she said.

They followed her as she led Thunder to a spacious stall. Fresh hay covered the ground. The great beast found a container of oats waiting for him.

"This is your forever home," she said, shutting the door to the stall.

"I can't believe you two," Thorn said as they returned to the porch. "That mule is dangerous."

Yellow Paint Woman shook her head. "From now on, he'll be gentle as a lamb."

Chapter 22

Rain continued falling as lightning streaked the sky above the clearing. The hound remained on the front porch as Pard and the black cat followed them into the log cabin. A wonderful aroma emanated from the black pot hanging over an open flame in the stone fireplace. The young woman stirring the pot turned and smiled.

"This is my granddaughter, Inger," the old woman said.

Inger looked nothing like her grandmother. Instead of straight and black, her hair was blond and curly. Khaki shorts highlighted her toned legs. Her white tee shirt said University of Arkansas. Thorn cast Buck a glance, wondering what the woman was doing there.

"I often spend summer weekends with Grandmother," she said as if sensing Thorn's question.

"How's your cat?" the old Indian woman asked.

"Good, I guess. Left him at the cabin with a man I work with. They are like new best friends."

"You hungry?"

"Not until I got a whiff of whatever it is you're cooking in that pot," he said.

"What is it?" Thorn asked.

"Eat a bite, and then I'll tell you," she said.

They sat at her little table as Inger served them each a bowl of stew.

"Tasty," Thorn said. "Please tell me you'll give me the recipe."

The old Indian woman put her hand on Thorn's shoulder. "There is no recipe, child. I make my porridge from many things gathered in the forest and fields near my house. Wild mushrooms, hazelnuts, asparagus, chicory, and sheep sorrel, to name just a few. The ingredients of the porridge are never the same."

"Grandmother is a gatherer," Inger said. "She has herbs that cure almost anything. She knows more about wild plants than anyone in the mountains."

"Love it," Thorn said.

"Yes," Buck agreed. "And this is the best water I've ever tasted."

"From the well my grandfather dug many moons ago," Yellow Paint Woman said. "He lived more than a hundred years drinking water from that well."

"I believe it," Buck said.

When Yellow Paint Woman gave Inger an almost imperceptible nod, she began lighting candles. When she finished, she extinguished the lamp.

"Coal oil gives off lots of light, though the fumes and soot will choke you to death. I prefer candlelight," the old woman said.

Rain continued outside the open window, the tattered old curtains whipping in the breeze. Lightning flashed, lighting up the darkness. Inside, there was only the gentle glow of scented candles.

Sensing that Buck intended to stay awhile, Pard curled up at his feet and went to sleep. The old woman had a look of concern on her face as she glanced at Thorn.

"Child, you seem so forlorn. You have

questions for me?"

"I'm confused," Thorn said. "I'm starting to feel I've lost my identity."

Thorn stole a peek at Buck when Yellow Paint Woman asked, "This is about a man, isn't it?"

"Is it?" Thorn said.

"Maybe we need to smoke the pipe."

"Excuse me?"

"The cloud blower," Yellow Paint Woman said. "It clears the head. Inger, will you fetch it for me?"

An ornamental pipe lay on the shelf behind Thorn. Inger's gaze settled on Buck as she placed it on the table in front of the old woman. Thorn didn't miss her smile.

"Have you ever smoked native tobacco?" she asked. Both Thorn and Buck shook their heads. "It's potent and produces euphoria far stronger than tobacco sold in stores."

"What euphoria?" Thorn asked.

"You aren't a smoker, are you?"

"I never started."

"And you, Buck?"

"When I was younger. I remember getting a rush while smoking a cigarette."

"Nicotine gave you that rush."

"What's your point?" he said.

"Grandmother's tobacco produces euphoria much greater than cigarette-smokers experience. You may even have a vision. If so, it will likely foretell your future."

"How do you know so much?" Thorn asked.

There was pride in Yellow Paint Woman's voice when she said, "Inger knows many things."

"Is Yellow Paint Woman your real grandmother?" Thorn asked.

"We both are kin of the storm, the sky, and the ground we walk on," Inger replied.

"You don't look like an Indian."

"What's an Indian supposed to look like?" she

said.

"I'm sorry. I didn't mean to be malicious. It's just that you have fair skin, blue eyes, and blond hair."

"Your eyes are also blue, and you are Indian," Inger said.

"I can't believe that you are. Nordic, maybe."

Tears appeared in Inger's eyes. Turning so no one could see, she ran out the door, letting it slam behind her. Thorn followed her.

"That can't be good," Buck said.

Yellow Paint Woman grabbed his arm. "They are sisters. Sisters fight. Let them settle this among themselves. I'm glad we're alone because I have something to ask you."

"Name it," he said.

"You have tasted tea from the Black Cup."

"How do you know that?"

"Haven't you?"

"Twice," he said. "Though I don't remember the first time."

"You are a sensitive. I can tell by the way you handled the mule. You are also a walker."

"I'm not sure what you mean," he said.

"Yes, you do. You have traveled through time."

"I think I have, though I can't be sure because it felt so much like a dream."

"Did you visit the pyramids?"

"Yes," he said.

"Not the flat-topped pyramids of the Mississippians. The ones in the valley where you intend to look for the People of the Night."

"You better explain."

She shook her head. "They are Mayan."

"Is it the City of Gold?"

The front door slammed in the wind as Thorn and Inger entered before the old woman could answer. Thorn's arm was around Inger's waist, smiles on their faces. Yellow Paint Woman also smiled.

"Everything okay?" she asked.

"Yes," they both answered.

"Then let's smoke the pipe."

Thorn and Inger sat at the little table as the candle flickered.

"First, explain why you and I have blue eyes," Thorn said.

"You already know the answer," Inger said.

"I think I do. I'd like to hear it from you."

"Vikings visited these mountains long before the Spanish. Some even settled here. Many Native Americans from here to Arkansas have blue eyes."

Heavener was a town less than fifty miles from where they sat. As a state archaeologist, Thorn knew all about the runestones carved in the rock near there. There was a question about who had carved them. The possibility remained that it could have been Vikings.

"Enough," Yellow Paint Woman said.

Inger handed her the pipe. Grabbing a tom-tom sitting by the fireplace, she began drumming an addictive beat. The old woman lit the pipe with the candle, took a puff, and then gave it to Buck.

Following his experience with the tea from the Black Cup, he was apprehensive about smoking the pipe. After taking a small puff, he passed it to Thorn.

Thorn was more adventurous, inhaling so much smoke that she started to gag. Inger stopped drumming and patted her on the back. When her eyes uncrossed, she took another puff before passing it to the old woman.

They passed the ceremonial pipe around the table several times. Even though Buck tried not to inhale, his head began to swim. Yellow Paint Woman's head began rotating on her neck. Her disjointed eyes opened and closed. Finally, her head slammed against the table. When he moved to help, Inger raised her hand.

"She is okay," she said. "Like most Indian witches, she suffers from epilepsy. The People call it Witch Frenzy."

Though her eyes remained closed, a whistle began issuing from the old woman's lips. It changed into another sound—a voice straight from the dead.

"Demon of darkness, unanswered desire, mistaken judgment, Sister of Fire, Arrow of Justice, or death in the mire."

The voice grew silent as Inger set her tom-tom aside. She helped the old woman from her chair and walked her to bed in a dark corner.

"Grandmother is asleep. She won't awaken until tomorrow when the sun appears over the rise. The animals are also asleep. You have tasted of the Holy smoke. Now, you must come with me."

Impaired by the powerful smoke, Buck's head buzzed. Purple light rippling in harmonic waves began replacing the candles' glow. Inger stripped away her clothes as she walked toward the door, her perfect body emanating an aura of gold.

Buck and Thorn followed her into the storm still raging outside the log cabin. Her golden body glowing, Inger started down the hill. Locked in a state of altered reality, Buck unbuttoned his shirt and tossed it to the ground. His jeans followed. Thorn shucked her clothes, gentle rain beading off their naked bodies.

The golden aura radiating from Inger lighted a path down the hill. She awaited them where a mountain stream intersected a rock-bottomed pond. When they embraced, her electric touch sent waves of pleasure surging through their bodies. They followed her into the warm water.

"We've returned to the womb," she said. "There

is nothing here to fear; nothing from which to hide. When you're in the water of the belly of the earth, you feel only love. Come to me."

They sat on a rock ledge, half submerged, Inger in the middle, Buck and Thorn on either side of her. Inger felt soft, warm, and real. Buck's body had come alive with sensations not experienced since his first wet dream. Thorn was also affected, her arms around Inger as her fingers and lips explored both hers and Buck's.

There was no time, only the instant that lasted an hour, eternity, or perhaps only a fleeting moment. A loud clap of thunder caused Inger's body to grow rigid. Grabbing their hands, she spread her arms and began to levitate. Buck's heart went into his throat as they rose into the air.

"We're flying," Thorn said.

"Floating," Inger said. "Don't let go of my hands or you will fall."

The storm continued, lightning illuminating the sky and their thoughts. They floated upwards through damp clouds. Buck thought he was dreaming. It didn't feel like a dream as they glided above the ancient mountain range. They were soon floating high above a canyon.

Below them, people moved about a primordial city rife with golden pyramids. Seeing them, they dropped to their knees and began to pray. He got only a glimpse of the city, though it was all he needed to see.

Chapter 23

Lying in the grass ten feet from a muddy farm pond, Buck awoke to morning light shining on his face. Thorn was beside him.

"What the hell!" she said when she opened her eyes.

"Don't have a clue. My head's pounding and I could use a handful of aspirins."

"Where are our clothes?" she said.

"I don't even know where I'm at and I've never felt so screwed up."

"Did I have sex with you?" she asked.

"You tell me," he said.

"I feel like I've made love," she said. "My body's all warm and aglow. I feel great, except for my headache."

Their arms were touching. It was the first time he'd gotten a good look at her naked body. His sexual reaction was almost instantaneous. When she saw his erection, she sprang to her feet.

"Watch it, buster. It's Monday morning, and I'm already late for work."

She started up the hill, gathering her clothes as she went. Buck pulled on his socks, jeans, and boots as he followed her. They both were clothed when they reached the top of the hill.

An old pickup sat parked in front of the

doorway. Yellow Paint Woman was in the pasture, hugging her new mule. An older man dressed in boots, jeans, and cowboy hat, walked toward them.

"Who are you?" he asked.

"Buck and Thorn. We brought Yellow Paint Woman a new mule. We were down the hill looking at the pond. And you?"

"Her grandson, Charlie," he said.

The man looked every bit of seventy, and it made Buck wonder how old Yellow Paint Woman was.

"Are you related to Inger?" Thorn asked.

"Don't know anyone named Inger," he said.

Buck glanced down the hill. "Yellow Paint Woman's granddaughter."

"Ain't no Inger in our family. Thanks for giving grandmother the mule. Gotta go now."

Yellow Paint Woman waved as Charlie's old pickup rattled away down the narrow dirt road.

"Where's Inger?" Thorn asked.

The old woman clutched Thorn's hand. "Sometimes visions are empty and have no meaning." She kissed Thorn's forehead and then grasped Buck's hand. "Thank you for Thunder. You are a good man."

With that, she walked away. When Thorn glanced at her watch, Buck handed her the keys to his Jeep and unhitched the hauler.

"Take it," he said. "You don't have time to ride back up the mountain. Pard and I will walk to the lodge. You can return the yellow beast to me when you come for yours."

She gave him a peck on the lips. "When I do, we need to have a long talk. I'm not exactly sure what happened last night. It's almost like a dream."

"You remember Inger, don't you?" he asked.

"Jeez," she said, rubbing her head. "I'm not

sure what we smoked last night. I can hardly remember my own name."

As the yellow Jeep disappeared in the trees, Pard ran down the hill, jumping into Buck's arms.

"You miss me, boy?"

From his wagging tail and doggie kisses he gave him, it was obvious he had. A crowd of reporters had gathered in the parking lot in front of the Sunset Lodge when they made it up the mountain. The chopper sat on the blacktop, Jake doing an interview as cameras rolled. When Jake saw them coming up the road, he excused himself.

"Where have you been? We're doing the flyover today."

"Sorry about that. I did a little flyover myself last night, and got wasted."

Jake chuckled. "No problem. Jimi, my camera operator, didn't arrive until an hour ago. We've got unexpected baggage."

"Oh?"

"Colley twisted my arm. Talked me into bringing his new squeeze, Candice Jacobs."

"I thought that's who she was when I saw her at Clayton's party," Buck said. "You don't sound overjoyed."

"Though it may not appear that way, our show is scripted. I've known Candy forever. She's not shy about sleeping with anyone that can help advance her career. She's also full of herself and about as nosy as they come. It's a given she'll try to take over the show."

"Sounds like you know her pretty well."

"A little too well. She almost got me divorced a few years back."

Buck glanced at the crowd of people waiting near the chopper.

"This is just the flyover. You know lots of powerful people. Call in a few chits. Have her sent to someplace far away before the real expedition begins," he said.

"You mean someone like Clayton?" he said.

"Or Lana. Either of them can help you with the problem."

Jake nodded and tapped his shoulder. "Good idea. You ready now? Everyone's waiting."

"I have to take care of Pard, and I'd like to shower first, and change clothes."

"No time. Gotta go."

"Cowboy boots weren't made for hiking," Buck said.

"Everything you'll need is in the chopper. You can change when we get there, and I'll find someone to care for your dog. We must get airborne."

Don was on the edge of the crowd, a duffel bag in his hand. He waved when Buck spotted him.

"They want to do the flyover right now. Can you watch Pard and the cat while I'm gone?"

"You bet," he said, handing him the duffel. "I packed a few things I thought you might need."

"Thanks," Buck said.

Don scratched Pard behind the ears. "No problem. Got some news for you."

"Tell me," Buck said.

"Someone tore up your cabin again this morning. My guess is it was Blade looking for the Black Cup."

"The package made it to McAlester quicker than I thought."

"And, like you said, someone was pissed."

"Blade must think I still have the cup."

"Looks like it to me. Watch your back on the flyover."

Buck bumped his fist. "Pard hasn't eaten," he said as he followed Jake to the helicopter.

Don waved as the chopper lifted off in a rush of noise and rotor-generated turbulence. "He won't go hungry," he shouted. "Stay safe."

Blade, Candice Jacobs, and Jake's camera operator were in the passenger compartment with him. Dressed in camouflaged jungle fatigues and combat boots, they looked ready to explore. Blade stared out one of the windows, doing his best to ignore him.

Candice Jacobs narrated as the man with the camera shot film through an open porthole. She looked at least forty years younger than Colley. After Jake's wry comment, he wondered if she'd slept with him just to secure a spot on the expedition. In any event, Colley was happy and didn't mind. When she noticed him looking at her, she moved into the seat beside him.

"We haven't met. I'm Candy Jacobs."

"Glad to meet you, Candy. Buck McDivit."

"And what's your purpose on this expedition?"

"Blade and I are guides."

Blade didn't look when he heard his name. Buck sensed he wasn't smiling. Candy had tied her long hair in a ponytail, and she wore no jewelry or makeup. All business, he thought. The man with the camera stopped filming and waved when she introduced him.

"Jimi Olsen hails from Sweden. He's Jake's camera operator. Don't mind him. He never smiles."

Olsen's baby face belied his big and beefy, NFL fullback frame.

"Hello," he said, giving Buck a fake salute.

"Tell me a little about yourself," she said.

"I handle security for Clayton O'Meara, an owner of Sunset Lodge, and friend of Jake's."

"Blade won't let me interview him. What about you?" she asked.

"Why not? I'm not shy."

"Believe me, no one's ever going to mistake you for a shrinking violet," she said. "Jimi, I got an interview."

Candy waited while Jimi situated the camera for the best angle to film both her and Buck. When he gave her the nod, she began.

"This is expedition guide and security expert Buck McDivit. What exactly is your function on this expedition, Mr. McDivit?"

"I'm here as an assistant to Mr. Huntington."

From her expression, Candy didn't like his clipped answer.

"Is that all?"

"My grandfather was Cherokee. He taught me how to track."

"You intend to track down Bigfoot?"

"That and other things."

"What other things?" she asked.

"Seeing to the safety of everyone on the expedition."

"You think there's danger afoot?"

"We're visiting a part of the world never touched by man. No telling what we might encounter."

"Are you carrying a weapon?"

Buck shook his head. "Mr. Huntington doesn't believe in violence. There are no weapons on his expeditions."

"How do you propose to deal with wild animals, and the unforeseen?"

"Take things as they come," he said.

Candy turned to the camera, microphone in hand. "That was Buck McDivit, one of the guides for Cryptid Hunter's Bigfoot Extravaganza," she said. "He anticipates danger but carries no weapon. Candice Jacobs reporting from the wilds of the Ouachita Mountains in Oklahoma."

No reporter as savvy as Candy had ever interviewed Buck. When Candy failed to get the responses she sought, she reacted by making him seem the bumbling idiot. He somehow felt violated.

Candy and Jimi returned to filming the forest

below as Blade flashed Buck a wry smile, its meaning unmistakable. The chopper vibrated as mountain turbulence moved it around in the air. Colley and Jake were in the cockpit as they banked toward the Ouachita National Forest. When they reached the valley, Colley descended, searching for a clearing in the trees.

"What are we doing?" Candy asked.

"Looking for a place to land."

"There's not enough room to do that, even for our fabled pilot. What's your next plan?"

"There is no next plan," he said. "The trees are too large to clear a landing zone, at least without a bulldozer. If we can't find a place to land, Blade and I will have to rappel in."

Jake left the co-pilot's seat and signaled Blade and Buck to huddle with him.

"Can either of you spot a possible LZ from this topo?" he asked.

Buck glanced over Blade's shoulder as he took a turn at scanning the map. Shaking his head, he handed it to Buck.

It took him a moment before he saw something. "Maybe here," he said, pointing to the northeast edge of the map. "Looks like a clearing on this rock ledge."

Jake climbed back into the cockpit. Colley turned the chopper around and headed toward the northeast edge of the canyon. They were soon hovering over a rocky ledge that didn't seem large enough on which to land the chopper. Colley tried it anyway. When Jake gave the signal, he shut off the engine. Blade opened the door and stepped out.

"What's it look like?" Jake called.

"A steep descent into the forest. I can get down. Don't know about the rest of you."

"If you can make it, then so can we," Jake said, following him out the door."

Blade had already started down the slope before anyone else vacated the chopper. The forest was thick and he disappeared from sight. Jake was about to send Buck down after him when his words rang from below.

"I'm at the base of the bluff," he said.

"How far down?" Jake asked.

"A good two-hundred feet."

"Impossible," Jake said. "We're at treetop level here on the ledge."

Blade's voice echoed up the bluff when he answered. "These trees are the biggest I've ever seen. They're at least that tall."

"Can the rest of us make it down?" Jake said.

"If you're careful. Lower the equipment on a rope first, then use it to help those that need it."

After lowering the equipment, Candy was the first to follow. Buck tied the rope around her waist.

"Pick your way down. If you slip, don't worry. We won't let you fall," he said.

Candy disappeared through the top of the trees as Buck fed the rope through his gloved hands. Colley, Jake, and Jimi also had hold of the rope. Missing a foothold, she screamed, dropping ten feet before they halted her fall. They could hear her crying as she dangled below them.

Chapter 24

They'd reached the end of the rope when Blade's voice echoed from in the canyon.

"I got her," he said. "Send the next one down."

Jimi went next, and then Jake. Neither lost their footing, and both made it to the base of the ledge with no trouble.

Colley saluted when Buck said, "Keep a good hold on the rope, old buddy. I love my cowboy boots, but they weren't meant for rock climbing."

When he reached bottom, Jake called up to Colley.

"We're staying overnight. I'll let you know when to pick us up," he said.

Colley's voice echoed from above them. "Will do, boss."

They couldn't see the chopper as it lifted off the ledge, though they could hear its turbine-powered engine. When the sound faded in the distance, Buck took his first long look at their surroundings. It was like something out of a fairytale.

The only trees he'd ever seen as big were redwoods and sequoias of northern California. These trees were every bit as large, their first branches towering high above them. The leafy canopy covered the valley, only muted light filtering through the foliage. Even stranger, no undergrowth, thickets, or vines grew beneath the towering giants; only toadstools, fairy rings, and grass. The rippling sound of moving water focused his attention.

A creek flowed through the valley. Though dry in places, many deep pools marked its course. An egret, fishing in one of the pools, lifted skyward through a gap in the trees. Jimi's camera was working, Candy voicing a running commentary into her microphone.

"This is like no place I've ever seen," she said. "I didn't realize that such a Garden of Eden even existed in the world, much less in Oklahoma.

"The trunks of the trees are eight to ten feet wide, the trees towering two hundred feet into the air. There's lots of distance between each behemoth, the ground covered with putting green grass."

Buck agreed with her assessment, and so did Jake.

"What now?" he asked.

Blade pointed to a spot in the distance. "Find a place to set up camp." When Jimi turned his camera on him and began filming, Blade was quick to react. "If you don't want your equipment smashed, erase what you just filmed and don't ever point it at me again."

Jimi was reluctant to comply until Candy gave him the nod. When she did, he lowered the camera, the button he pressed producing a whirring sound. Returning the camera to his shoulder, he turned away without saying a word. Neither did Jake, although Buck sensed his concern.

Their backpacks contained bedrolls, tents, canteens, and three days of meals ready to eat. Buck's had his hiking boots and camouflage fatigues he'd yet to make use of.

Thick forest didn't cover the entire valley. Like the open patch of sky the egret had flown from, they began noticing many small clearings, swaths of sunlight in a forest of shade. Wildflowers, herbs, squash, and grapes grew in these patches. Jimi began digging in the dirt, pulling out a potato-like tuber.

"What is it?" Jake asked.

"Cassava," Jimi said.

"I'm not familiar with it."

"Main source of protein in many Caribbean countries, Central and South America," he said.

Candy was interested. "What's it doing here?"

"These patches of vegetation aren't random," Jimi said. "Someone cut the trees around them on purpose to provide light so they could grow gardens. I saw the same thing in the Amazon Basin."

"Total bullshit!" Blade said. "I've seen cassava all over the world. That's not cassava. Even if it is, it's no garden. No one cleared these patches. You couldn't cut one of those trees with an industrial chainsaw, much less a stone axe."

Jake glanced at Jimi, and then at Buck as Blade kicked dirt on the bushy plants.

"What do you think?" he asked.

Buck earned a dirty look from Blade when he said, "Looks like someone's garden to me."

"Let's move on," Jake said.

Buck's brain was buzzing. He wondered how cassava had found its way from South America to a box canyon deep in the Ouachita Mountains.

They began getting glimpses of deer, wild hogs, squirrels, rabbits, turtles, and snakes.

"Wonder what else is out there?" Jake asked.

"Maybe your Bigfoot," Buck said.

"Hey you guys," Candy called. "Take a look at this. Looks like a big saddle."

A huge knob of solid limestone near the escarpment had become the focus of Jimi's camera. The formation formed an elongated circle thirty feet in diameter and rose forty feet into the air. As Candy had said, the beveled top of the formation made it look like a saddle.

"Guess we'll call it Saddle Rock," Jake said.

Candy ran to the top of the formation. "Look at me," she said.

"How did you get up there?" Jake asked.

"There's a path. You can see all the way to the cliffs from up here. And something else."

Jake held up his hands. "Don't keep us in suspense."

"A waterfall plunging from the top of the cliff into a gorgeous pool."

Buck followed her along the worn pathway winding to the top of the huge limestone remnant.

"What a vantage," he said. "This must have been an observation post."

Jimi and Jake joined them, marveling at the panorama. In the distance, water plummeted from the sheer rock cliff. The waterfall had hollowed out several limestone pools, each diverting the water. They had formed five separate tiers. Crystal water rippled at the base of the cliff. Behind it lay the mouth of a large cavern.

"Feeds into the creek," Buck said. "It's primary source must be somewhere west of here."

"It's beautiful," Candy said.

Jimi was busy filming the enormous natural water park. Ferns and lichens clung to the limestone. Water hyacinths floated in the largest tranquil pool.

Jake had already descended from the vantage point at the top of the big rock. When he reached the fall, he cupped his hands beneath the water spraying from the cliff.

"Best I've ever tasted," he said.

From their vantage, they could see just how high the escarpment was. Birds soaring above them looked like moving spots of color. Blade wasn't smiling when he arrived.

"Let's camp on the other side of those boulders for the night. We can powwow later about what we need to do," he said.

If Jake was unhappy about Blade taking charge, he didn't show it. They set up camp beside the limestone pool. Blade drew a map in the sand with the point of his knife.

"The end of the canyon is at least ten miles west of here. We can't all make it there and back before Colley returns. I'll recon it for us."

"What do you think, Buck?" Jake asked.

"Why not? We'd just slow him down. This is a reconnaissance. We can all have a look when the real expedition starts."

"When do you plan to leave?" Jake asked.

"Now," Blade said, hoisting his large backpack.

"What are we supposed to do while he's away?" Candy asked.

"Rest, and then explore the area. Me, I'm gonna get out of these boots," Buck said.

Grabbing his backpack, he headed to a part of the pool cloaked by tall bushes. His jeans and shirt were still muddy from lying on the ground in the rain the previous night. After stripping them off, he waded into the cool water to wash sand and grime out of his hair.

Feeling better, he stood dripping in the shallow part of the pool when a broken twig snapped behind him. Wheeling around, he saw Candy, hand on her hips and a wicked grin on her face.

"Nice ass, cowboy, among other things," she said. "Didn't mean to scare you."

"You're scaring me now," he said.

"Don't think so. Mind if I join you?"

"Why the hell not?" he said, watching as she tossed off her camouflaged fatigues and waded into the water.

He was up to his knees when she reached him.

Standing on her tiptoes, she kissed him.

"You know you want it as bad as I do," she said.

"You had me at hello," he answered.

"You're going to have to wait."

She dove in and swam toward a small waterfall. When she touched the rock ledge, she climbed up to a beveled tier about ten feet above the pool.

"This is great," she said. "Like a water park for adults. Join me? The water's warmer up here."

"It's pretty hot down here, too," he said.

Before he could follow her up the path, Jake appeared through the tall bushes, Jimi right behind him.

"Hate to interrupt you. We've found something you need to see," he said.

Buck got out of the water and put on his camouflage fatigues. Candy joined them. "No one's leaving me out of this," she said.

"What is it?" Buck asked as he and Candy followed them to the mouth of the large cavern.

"You'll see," he said. "Jimi and I found something interesting while we were checking out the cave."

The big Swede led the way, climbing what looked like handholds carved in the limestone. Thirty feet above the valley floor, they encountered a path that led them to the open mouth of a cavern. Corncobs lay everywhere, covering the floor of the mountain opening. Jimi had the heavy camera on his shoulder and Candy pushed past him.

"What is it?" she asked.

"Cave dwelling," he said.

"Whoever lived here consumed lots of corn," Jake said.

"They also ate meat and knew how to start fires," Jimi said, nudging a pile of charred bones with the toe of his boot.

"You think this could be the home of Yellow

Paint Woman's People of the Night?" Jake asked.

Buck picked up a cob and tossed it over the ledge, listening until it hit the ground and bounced.

"No one has lived here for hundreds of years. I visited a cave like this in northern Arkansas. It's prehistoric all right. Ancient Indians lived all over this area."

"Want some film?" Jimi asked.

"A few minutes of footage won't hurt. If we decide to use it, we can dub some sound in later. What we're after is a picture of Bigfoot."

"Amen to that," Candy said. "I could use something to eat. Anyone else hungry?"

"Starved," Jake said.

Buck agreed. "I haven't eaten since last night," he said. "Sounds good to me."

"No need asking Jimi," Jake said. "He's always hungry."

They'd gotten a late start. Darkness had descended on the valley as they finished their meals ready to eat. Though the night was warm, it didn't stop them from building a small fire. They sat around it, chatting, as sounds of the night began encompassing them. They heard the flutter of wings as an owl captured some small animal foraging after dark. Far in the distance, animals howled at the moon.

"What's making that noise?" Candy asked.

"Wolves," Buck said.

"There are no wolves in this part of the country."

"Guess they didn't get the memo," he said.

"What'll we do if they attack?"

"Build up the fire before we go to sleep," he said. "We'll be fine."

"Sure about that?" she asked.

"You can stand guard from the top of Saddle Rock if you like. Me, I'm gonna get some shuteye."

"Fine," she said.

They stayed awake listening to crickets, frogs, and wildlife on the prowl. Something else was bothering Jake.

"Despite what Blade said, I'm curious about those patches of vegetation. You think someone planted them?" he asked.

"Don't know how else to explain them," Buck said.

"Jimi?" Jake said.

"You already know how I feel about it," he said.

"I think so too. Why is Blade so adamant that they aren't?"

"I'm sure he has his reasons," Buck said.

"Screw your gardens," Candy said. "What about the wolves?"

"Our tents are high tech, constructed of rip-proof fabric. Not even a bear can get into them. I'm turning in," Jake said.

The others soon followed. Buck had closed his eyes and rolled over when something scratched on the flap of his tent. It was Candy.

"Let me in. I'm not sleeping alone."

When he unzipped the door, she scurried inside and threw herself on top of him. She was insistent as he felt the warmth and passion of her bare body.

Chapter 25

Later that night, Buck awoke to someone shaking his shoulder. It was an agitated Candy.

"Something's out there," she said.

She wasn't dreaming. There was movement outside the tent. As they listened, it emitted a guttural yelp and crashed into the forest surrounding the campsite. Buck crawled out of the tent, pulling on his pants as he did.

"You can't go out there," she said.

"Yes I can," he said.

Still dark, the time on his cell phone said six-thirty. With her flashlight casting a beam through the night, Candy followed him out of the tent.

"What was it?" she asked.

"Don't know. Hand me the flashlight."

Their voices woke Jake and Jimi.

"What the hell's going on?" Jake asked, flashing his light in Buck's face.

"An animal of some sort wandered through camp," Buck said. "Something disturbed it and caused it to run away."

"Must have been a skunk from that god-awful smell," Jake said, holding his nose.

"Don't think so," Buck said. "It sounded much bigger than a skunk."

"You forget something, Candy?" Jake asked.

"Who cares? It's not like you've never seen me naked before now," she said.

Buck's light illuminated something on the ground.

"What the hell is it?" Jake asked.

"One huge footprint. If this big boy were human, he'd have a hard time finding shoes to fit him."

"A bear?" Candy asked.

"Not a bear track," Buck said, focusing his light on the moist earth near the sparkling pool.

Jake moved closer for a better look. So did Candy and Jimi.

"Then what is it?" he asked.

"Your Bigfoot," Buck said.

"Oh my God! Are you sure?"

"What else could it be? There are no hoaxers anywhere near here."

Jimi had already gone for his camera as the hazy morning sky began to lighten, and then turn red. Buck grabbed instant coffee and a heating device from his pack. Candy returned to her tent, fully clothed when she emerged. He handed her a cup of coffee when she joined him under the canopy they'd erected.

"Jake's got his Bigfoot," Buck said.

Candy sipped the coffee from the metal cup. "I'm not sure I believe it."

"Believe it," Buck said. "That print's not quite human, but it's definitely not a bear's."

Jake had a smug grin on his face when he joined them, reaching for the hot metal cup of coffee Buck handed him.

"What do you think now?" he asked.

"That Blade had this valley pegged."

"Wish we'd had some infra-red cameras set up around the perimeter last night."

"This trip is only preliminary. When we return,

you can bring enough equipment and supplies to last all summer if need be."

"Unless the creature gets spooked and moves elsewhere before we return," Jake said.

"It wasn't us that scared Bigfoot," Buck said. "There are other predators in this valley."

"Maybe I should rethink my stance on bringing weapons."

"Maybe you should," Buck said.

"Just kidding. Never gonna happen."

"At least bring propane stoves and pots of real coffee. This instant stuff tastes like swill," Candy said. "Let me order the supplies for you."

"She's right," Buck said, dumping the last of his coffee on the ground. "You could peel paint with it."

"Pretty crappy, I'll admit," Jake said. "Makes me wish I wasn't such a caffeine head."

"Any coffee's better than no coffee," Candy said. "Pour me another, please."

Jimi had taken his camera to the waterfall. They were still carping about Jake's instant coffee when he called to get their attention.

"Hey, something over here I think you want to see."

They found him staring at something in the sand.

"What is it?" Jake asked.

"Another footprint. This one has a little extra."

Buck knelt to get a better look. Something red stained the print, and he stuck his finger in it.

"Blood," he said. "Must be the reason he yelped and ran away."

He began sweeping the area, finding something on the bark of a tree. Jake joined him.

"What is it?"

"Blood stain. Something cut Bigfoot, and he must have brushed the wound against the tree."

"See any other prints of whatever it was that

spooked him?"

"Just our boot prints. Lots of them around," Buck said.

"Then what drew the blood?" Jake asked.

"Maybe he stepped on something sharp," Candy said.

"That wouldn't explain the blood on the tree," Buck said.

"Could have been an owl," Jake said.

They all looked at Jimi when he said, "Or a bat."

"Neither owls nor bats would attack a Bigfoot."

"What, then?" Candy asked.

One of the boot prints was bigger than the others. Blade's boot. Buck kept the thought to himself until he had time to think about it.

"Don't know," he said.

Candy had other things on her mind. "My stomach's growling. I'm hungry enough to eat a horse."

"No horse on this trip," Jake said. "All we have are some Army surplus MRE's."

"Bet they're no better than your World War II surplus coffee. Probably tasted like shit the day they packaged it," she said.

"Quit bitching, Candy. GI's all over the world drink it every morning."

"If we gave them real coffee, we might win some of those wars we've been fighting for fifty years."

"If you don't like it," Jake said, "There's plenty of water around here to drink instead."

Candy shot him the finger and beat everyone back to the provision table. Producing a silver flask from her back pocket, she laced her coffee with the vodka in it.

"Anyone else?" she asked.

"What is it?" Jake said.

"It ain't Bombay Gin, though I guarantee it'll

make your horrible Java a bit more tolerable.”

Jake frowned as he took the flask, using it to dose his coffee. Jimi and Buck followed suit.

“How was it?” he asked when Candy pushed the rest of her MRE aside.

“Mexican chicken stew isn’t what I dream about when I’m hungry for bacon and eggs.”

Having already finished his meal, Jimi grabbed the rest of Candy’s and ate it in silence.

“Jimi likes it,” Jake said.

“He’d eat the rear end of a cow,” Candy said.

“Knock it off,” Buck said. “We have more important things to talk about.”

“Such as?” Jake asked.

Buck finished the last of his coffee and sat the cup on the little utility table before answering.

“I think someone attacked our Bigfoot this morning with a knife,” he said.

“Where did you come up with that idea?” Candy asked.

“The bloodstain on the tree. It wasn’t blood spatter. Someone used the bark to wipe off the blade of their knife.”

“Who?” Jake asked.

“There’s only one person in this valley with a knife that I know of.”

“You think Blade did it?” Jake asked. “For what reason?”

“I’m not a mind reader,” Buck said. “The nearest boot print to Bigfoot’s print was Blade’s. He’s the only one of us that wears boots that big.”

“Our prints are all over the place,” Jake said. “You said it yourself. The proximity of his print was just coincidence.”

“I don’t believe in coincidences,” Buck said. “I think Blade was here, standing outside our tents early this morning. Either he disturbed Bigfoot or vice versa.”

“And what the hell do you think he was doing?”

Jake asked.

"Guess that's the sixty-four dollar question."

"Don't be defensive," Jake said. "I'm only trying to get to the bottom of this."

"Jake's right," Candy said. "Blade's fifteen miles from here. It couldn't have been him."

"Blade was a soldier with special training. A trained soldier can force-walk fifteen miles in less than six hours. That's while carrying all his equipment on his back. Assuming he ever left sight of us."

"Nothing you're saying makes any sense," Jake said.

"Forget it," Buck said. "Maybe you're right."

Still barefoot and shirtless, he returned to his tent. Once inside, he realized why Blade had returned to camp. Someone had cut a small slit in the back of the tent. That someone had also rummaged around in his pack, looking for something. Buck knew what that something was.

They spent the rest of the morning exploring the area around the pool. After lunch, they doffed their clothes and went swimming. Candy and Jimi were roughhousing at one end. Buck sat on a rock beneath falling water when Jake joined him.

"I took your advice about Candy and called Clayton. He said he'd take care of things. After finding the footprint, I think it's best to get rid of her."

"Your expedition; your call," Buck said.

"Though she has a good heart, when it comes to business, she takes no prisoners."

"It's okay," Buck said. "Why are you still trying to convince me?"

"I just thought . . ."

"That since we'd slept together I'd take her side of the argument?"

"Something like that," Jake said.

They had no chance to finish the discussion

as Blade came striding through the trees. He wasn't smiling when he saw them romping in the mountain pool.

"Am I the only one on this expedition doing my job?" he asked.

"We worked all morning," Jake said. "We're taking a break. Join us?"

"Not interested in what I found?"

"Of course we are," Jake said. "Grab a seat at the table, and I'll be right there."

Blade could only frown and shake his head as he gulped water from his canteen. Jake grabbed a towel and dried off behind a tree. After pulling on his pants and shirt, he joined him at the table. Seeing the party was over, Buck, Jimi, and Candy got dressed. Likely expecting tales of a dozen Bigfoot sightings, Jake awaited the report. When Blade seemed reluctant to began, he prompted him.

"Well?"

"Nothing. Not one damn thing. I'm now convinced we won't find Bigfoot in this valley."

Jake glanced at Buck, and then at Candy and Jimi. "Impossible. There was one here last night."

"You saw it?" Blade asked.

"We heard it and smelled it. It fled when we climbed out of our tents. It left two footprints. Want to see?"

"Why not?"

He followed them to the first print they'd found. After seeing it, he looked less than amazed.

"What?" Jake said.

"An obvious fake."

"What the hell are you talking about? That's no fake," Jake said.

"Yes, it is," Blade said.

Jake glanced around again. "I hope you're not suggesting that one of us faked the print. For what reason?"

"We all know the answer to that question," Blade said. "Ratings, of course."

Jake's eyes narrowed, and he came close to taking a swing at the big Indian sniper. Buck grabbed his elbow to make sure he didn't.

"Preposterous," he said.

"Is it? Your pussy cameraman, slut reporter or your dance hall cowboy. I have no doubt they'd do anything you ask them to do."

Blade's words were more that Jimi could take. When he took a swing, Blade wheeled him around, tightened his arm around his neck, and put his knife to his jugular.

"You kill him, and you're a dead man," Buck said.

"You all saw it. He attacked me. I'm within my rights to cut his throat, here and now."

"Don't do it," Buck said.

"You talk mighty big for someone that's got no weapon," Blade said. "I could kill you, too."

Blade was right, and Buck knew it. Without a weapon, he had little chance against the knife.

"Maybe," he said. "And it could be your day to die, not mine. Let him go. Now."

Blade still had a bruise under his right eye from his last scuffle with the big cowboy. Lowering his knife, he pushed Jimi aside and sheathed it.

"Call your pilot," he said. "I've had about enough of this happy horseshit I can stomach."

Chapter 26

Blade left them standing as Jake fumbled with his cell phone to call Colley.

"I'm already in the air," the pilot said. "I'll be waiting when you get here."

Jake wasn't smiling when he addressed the crew. "Colley's on the way. Fun's over. Let's break camp."

Blade had climbed the rope ladder to the ledge, waiting in the chopper when the others reached the cliff. Buck followed Candy to make sure she didn't fall. When they reached the escarpment, he realized what little space on which Colley had to land.

The group exchanged few words on the trip to Sunset Lodge. Candy's phone rang about halfway back. Unlike her normal outgoing self, she lowered her voice so no one could hear.

A crowd had gathered to welcome the returning group, Thorn among them. Her eyes opened wide when Candy kissed Buck after exiting the chopper. Blade didn't wait around, brushing past reporters and cameras without a word. Don emerged from the crowd, Pard at his heels, the little dog jumping into Buck's arms.

"Lots to report," Don said. "Lana and I have Blade on the run. She's good."

"So are you," Buck said, shaking his hand.

Jake joined them, doubt in his voice when he said, "What now?"

Jake's altered disposition disturbed Buck. "Nothing's changed," he said. "None of us planted that footprint. It was real, no matter what Blade thinks."

"You saw Bigfoot?" Don asked.

"I wish," Buck said. "It ran away before we got out of our tents. It left behind two footprints."

"I have something to report," Candy said. "My network called while we were in the chopper. They have a plum assignment for me in London."

"Congratulations," Jake said.

"I'm not taking it. I wouldn't miss the rest of this expedition for any assignment."

Thorn joined them, frowning when she caught Buck's eye. Candy didn't seem to notice as she put her arms around his waist and snuggled closer. Jake glanced at his Rolex.

"I have business to attend to. Can we all meet at dinner later tonight? I'll call with details."

Candy accompanied him as he returned to the chopper to brief Colley.

"Looks like you had a fine old time on the flyover," Thorn said.

"We had some excitement. "Even evidence of human habitation."

"Oh?"

"A cave littered with corn cobs," he said.

"Then that clinches it. I'm coming along on the expedition. I won't take no for an answer."

"Then you better mend your fences with Jake."

The chopper's rotor had finally stopped turning. Jake and Colley stood beneath it, chatting with a reporter. Thorn glanced at them, and then back at Buck.

"You and I can talk later," she said as she started away to the chopper.

"Trouble in paradise?" Don asked.

"Something like that. What you got?"

"I'm trying to match our stolen objects with antiquities for sale on the Internet. I think I'm on the right track."

"I'd be happy if we could just pin the old Indian's murder on Blade."

"That one's not so easy," Don said.

"I gotta call Clayton. Any chance we can get together later?"

Don nodded. "You bet. I left something in your cabin you need to see. Can you wait a minute?"

Buck was scratching Pard's ear when an explosion rocked the area. Everyone watched in stunned amazement as a black cloud of smoke billowed into the air. As a group, they hurried to see what was on fire.

Buck and Pard ran with them. Squealing tires caused him to turn in time to see Blade's black Corvette racing out of the parking lot. He watched it disappear before sprinting toward his cabin.

Little remained except for dying flames and smoldering ashes. The odor of natural gas pervaded the area. No one seemed to notice as the crowd had gathered around a person lying on the ground. Buck's heart skipped a beat when he realized it was Don. He pushed his way through the onlookers for a better look.

"Is he . . . ?"

An EMT administered to him, her uniform indicating she worked for the lodge. She glanced at Buck and shook her head, meaty arms working Don's chest as smoke billowed out of his mouth.

Someone must have turned off the natural gas to the cabin because the flame died in an instant. When the big nurse put an oxygen mask on Don, he opened his eyes for an instant. It was all Buck needed to see. Backing out of the crowd, he stepped into the rubble of the cabin, hoping to find some answers. The roof had collapsed though it didn't cover what he wanted to see.

He'd finished looking and was back in the crowd when members of Big Shoe's new security staff arrived. They began cordoning it off with yellow crime tape. Satisfied there would be a detailed investigation, he returned to check on Don.

Two more EMT's had arrived, loading Don on a stretcher. Pushing through the crowd, they took him to the chopper. Colley had its motor cranking, awaiting their arrival. Buck spotted Thorn and Jake.

"Where are you taking him?"

"Hospital in Poteau," Jake said.

"Have you heard anything about his condition?"

"Touch and go right now. He inhaled some flame. He may have damaged his lungs."

"Can I go with you?" Buck asked.

"Not enough room. I'll call with a report when we get there."

There was enough room for Thorn as he watched her climb into the chopper. They lifted off and flew away, disappearing over the tall pines surrounding the lodge. The crowd had dispersed, yellow tape surrounding the smoldering remains of the cabin. When Buck glanced down, he realized Pard was at his heels.

"Good boy," he said, giving the dog a head rub.

Pard grew alert, his ears pointing toward the sky. He was staring at something in the nearby shrubbery. Buck hurried after him to see what it was.

When Pard barked, a frightened cat poked its head out of the greenery. It was Hamlet, its black fur singed. Pard licked its face and wagged his tail as Buck lifted the forlorn creature. Cradled in the big cowboy's arms, the little cat seemed to relax.

When his cell phone rang, he returned him to the ground. It was Clayton.

"Just had a call from Big Shoe. He said your cabin exploded. You okay?"

"I was nowhere near it when it blew. Colley's flying Don to a hospital in Poteau."

"What happened?" Clayton asked.

"Someone booby-trapped the cabin hoping to kill me. You know who my main suspect is."

"Stay away from him," Clayton said.

"He tore out of here already and thinks I'm dead."

"Jimmy is warming up the jet. We'll head to Poteau and check on Don."

"Then you'll get there before I do," Buck said.

"Stay safe," Clayton said. "Lana's already talking with the police. Maybe we'll have some answers by the time we get to the hospital."

His cabin destroyed, Buck had no place to go. Picking up Lady from the stable, he loaded her into the hauler. With Pard and Hamlet in the front seat, he started down the mountain to Poteau.

Hazy sunlight, reflecting through puffy clouds cast a soft filter on the valley. A buzzard, checking out last night's road kill scurried out of the way when it heard the Jeep approach. Spreading its wings, it lifted off the road like a large kite in a gentle wind. Hamlet crawled into Buck's lap and went to sleep.

Pard was having none of it, tapping his paw on the window until Buck lowered it. He then assumed his favorite riding position. After stroking the little cat's head, Buck relaxed for the first time that morning.

It was noon when they reached the hospital at Poteau. The day mild, he left the windows down in the Jeep and told Pard to keep an eye on the cat. Giving him a head rub, he had little doubt both Pard and Hamlet would be there when he returned.

The room occupied the only floor of the little hospital. An I.V. dripped fluid into Don's vein, the plastic nozzle in his nose supplying oxygen. His wife and two boys stood at his side, holding his hands.

Sunlight shined through the open window. Flowers filled the room, their fragrant scent almost overpowering. Buck gave Lana, Thorn, and Clayton a nod. Clayton looked solemn as he clutched his big Stetson in front of him. Lana's frown told him all he needed to know about her disposition. Josie began to cry when he embraced her.

"I'm so sorry," he said.

"Not your fault," she said.

"I feel like it is. I wish there were something I could do."

"He's going to make it," she said. "The nurse gave me her guarantee."

"Then that's good as gold," Buck said. "Has he spoken to anyone?"

"Just some gibberish. He keeps talking about a cat named Hamlet."

"Is he on drugs?"

"Morphine," she said.

When Buck bent down for a closer look, Don opened his eyes and tried to speak. Josie and the two boys were on top of him, hugging, and kissing him.

"Hamlet saved my life," he said, his voice a soft rasp.

"Who is Hamlet?" Josie asked, looking at Buck.

"My cat. Found him in the bushes near the explosion site. He had scorched hair and was coughing up smoke."

"He saved my life," Don repeated, his voice stronger. "If I had gone into the cabin I'd be dead now. When I opened the door, he jumped straight into my arms. I tripped and fell backwards off the porch. It's the only thing that saved me. Was the place booby-trapped?"

Buck nodded. "Someone set a trap for me. I'm so sorry, Don."

"Not your fault." Josie began crying when he ventured a smile. "It wasn't my day to die."

"I just hope your lungs are okay," Buck said.

"I'll make it. I'm a tough old bird. You say Hamlet's okay?"

"Outside in the Jeep," Buck said.

"You're kidding!"

"We want to see the cat," the boys said. "Is it okay, Mom?"

"The nurses won't allow a cat in here," she said.

"Then don't tell them," Don said. "Buck?"

"I'll get him." Hamlet was still asleep in the front seat when Buck picked him up. "You may as well come with us," he said to Pard.

When he placed the cat on the bed, the little animal went straight to Don's face and began rubbing against it.

"How you doing, little buddy?" he said.

The black cat circled his chest, kneading dough on it. It finally closed his eyes and went to sleep.

Chapter 27

Don's sons were all over the cat, stroking and petting it. Don smiled as Josie looked on.

"That cat has no place in a hospital," she said.

"Mom, it saved Dad's life," son Doug said.

"He's a hero," Don said.

"I'll take him back to the car," Buck said.

"Please," Don said. "Can he stay here with us?"

"Of course he can," Buck said. "If it's okay with Josie, and the hospital staff."

Josie saw something in her husband's eyes that resonated with her. Grabbing Buck's hand, she led him into the hallway.

"Thank you," she said. "That's the first response we've had from him since we got here. I believe he's going to make it."

"Me too," Buck said. "Sorry about the cat."

"What's his name?" she asked.

"Hamlet. I just got it. Don has taken care of it while I was away. I think he's grown attached."

"You know he has a heart of gold. It hasn't been easy for us these past few months," she said.

Buck took her hand. "Sorry about the explosion. His job isn't supposed to be dangerous. It'll get better, I promise."

She smiled and hugged him. "I saw the look in the boys' eyes when they heard their dad speak.

Would it be asking too much for you to give us the cat?"

"Though I love all animals, I've never had a cat in my life. He's Don's cat now."

They were both beaming when they returned to the hospital room.

"Buck just gave us Hamlet. Are you responsible enough to care for him?"

"Yes," they chimed as one.

Don squeezed Buck's hand, tears in his eyes.

"I'm gonna get out of here and let you get some rest. I'll check on you later today," Buck said.

Lana, Thorn, and Clayton also said their goodbyes, and then followed him into the hallway.

"I missed breakfast this morning," Clayton said. "Any chance of getting some good grub around here?"

Thorn nodded. "There's a café around the corner. Their green chile omelet is to die for."

"You can ride with me," Buck said.

Pard jumped into Thorn's lap, wagging his tail and licking her face. Clayton and Lana sat in back.

"Nice wheels," Clayton said.

"You should know," Buck said. "You bought them."

"Where you gonna park this buggy? Maybe we should just get out and walk."

"Stop worrying," Buck said. "Poteau's not that big."

Buck found a parking spot in a vacant lot on Main Street next to the café. After pouring a bowl of water for Pard, he lowered the windows.

"Not worried about theft?" Clayton asked. "Pard ain't big."

"He knows where I'll be. He'll come get us if someone starts messing with the vehicle."

"Smart dog," Lana said. "Does he have a sister?"

"He's not fixed, so there's a chance he'll father

puppies someday."

"Then put me first in line," she said. "I like the offspring of smart males of all species."

Understanding Lana's cryptic meaning, Buck and Clayton smiled. Thorn cast them a questioning glance. Clayton's eyes grew larger the moment they opened the door of the little café.

"Think I'm gonna like this place," he said.

"A Mexican couple owns it," Thorn said. "Everything they cook is spicy."

"The hotter, the better," Clayton said.

"You may be singing a different tune when we leave," she said.

He just chuckled, and said, "Bring it on."

They were soon feasting on green chile omelets, jalapeno hash browns, and homemade biscuits. The smiling waiter, also the owner, was happy to oblige Clayton with his hottest peppers. Clayton had to finally call uncle and ask for a pitcher of ice water. Lana never missed a beat, shaking her head as she ate.

"Talk about the Peter Pan Syndrome," she said. "Clayton hasn't aged a day since he was thirteen."

"And you love it," he said.

"Yes I do," she said.

Lana seemed out of place in her expensive dress and designer boots. Her good looks captured the attention of the café's patrons. Her appetite as ravenous as Clayton's, she cleaned her plate before pushing it aside.

"What do you know about the explosion?" she asked.

"That I was the intended target. I hope the investigators are able to link it to Blade." Buck watched as Lana and Clayton exchanged somber glances. "What?" he said.

"The investigators have already ruled the explosion an accident. The result of a broken gas line inside the cabin."

"That's crazy. I had a look at the bombsite before Big Shoe's security men taped it. I found part of a flip-phone along with broken Christmas lights. The gas line wasn't broken. Someone had opened it."

"I feel like such an outsider," Thorn said. "What does any of that mean?"

"Someone planted a bomb made from Christmas lights and an old flip-phone. The explosive material Tannerite is a mixture of ammonium nitrate and aluminum powder."

Lana finished the explanation for him. "The two common substances are benign by themselves, though explosive when combined."

"Blade set the trap to explode thirty seconds after someone opened the front door. The timer made sure the person had entered the cabin before it exploded. The cat prevented Don from doing so. It saved his life."

"So the two compounds resulted in the explosion?" Thorn said.

"Along with a cabin filled with natural gas. Blade opened a line after setting the devices."

"The bomb squad found no explosive devices," Clayton said.

"Because Big Shoe's men cleaned up the site before they arrived," Buck said.

"And Blade isn't implicated in any way," Lana said.

"Figures," Buck said.

Lana tapped her fork on the plate. "His day is coming. Someone will pay for this. I promise."

"Where do we go from here?" Buck asked.

"Don's meticulous. He's checked every site on the web for artifacts matching those stolen from Oklahoma. He even wrote a computer program that employs artificial intelligence to help him. He'll get better. When he does, we'll break this case."

"What about Blade?" Buck asked.

"He pissed me off when he hurt Don," Lana said. "I promise you, I'll see him burn in hell."

"Excuse my ignorance," Thorn said. "You think a single person stole our antiquities and tried to kill Don?"

"Blade has help," Buck said.

"Ezekiel Big Shoe?" Thorn asked.

"We think so," Lana said.

"Thorn glanced at Buck, her gaze asking a silent question he didn't want to answer. Lana motioned the waiter for more coffee, and Clayton took a silver flask from his sports coat. When the coffee arrived, he laced it with whiskey from the flask.

"Thirteen-year-olds don't drink whiskey," he said, still smarting from Lana's Peter Pan remark.

"I'll bet you did," she said.

When Clayton stopped grinning, he asked, "What about the expedition?"

"There is a Bigfoot out there. We didn't see it, though it did leave a couple of footprints."

"So the expedition continues?" Lana asked.

"Yes, and Thorn is coming with us to check for archaeological significance. From what we already saw, I'd say she'll have her hands full."

"Your City of Gold?" Clayton said.

Someone dropped a plate in the kitchen. Patrons of the café listened as it bounced across the cement floor, applauding when it shattered.

"What did you say?" Thorn said, staring at Clayton.

Realizing he'd spoken out of turn, he didn't answer. Instead, he poured more whiskey into his coffee.

"Private joke," Buck said when Thorn looked at him for answers.

"I like jokes," she said.

"Tell you later. Where are you two headed from

here?"

"Back to the ranch for me, and Lykaia for Lana," Clayton said. "Can you drop us off at the airstrip?"

"And I need a ride," Thorn said.

They weren't far from the little airport, Clayton and Lana's plane waiting on the runway. Someone in a golf cart headed their way to pick them up. Clayton reached over Buck's seat and handed him a set of keys.

"You'll need a place to stay. Plenty of room in our cabin."

Buck, Thorn, and Pard watched as Clayton and Lana's jet lifted off from the runway. After it had disappeared into the clouds, Buck took the liberty to put his arm around Thorn's waist.

"You look great," he said. "I've missed you."

Her frown was telling. "Always trying, aren't you?"

"Never know. Someday I may get lucky."

"Sounds like you got lucky with that Candy woman."

"Who told you that?"

"Jake filled me in."

"It's not what you think," he said.

"It's okay. We aren't exactly in the middle of a big love affair."

"Thorn, I . . ."

She stopped him. "Mom drove me to the lodge. She'd never seen it. I was going to spend the night with you. It angered me when I saw you with the reporter woman. Jake was nice enough to give me a ride in his helicopter."

"Like I said, it's not what you think."

"Jake told me about her. He said it wasn't your fault."

"Good old Jake. Always looking out for me."

"Don't worry about it. Like I said, we weren't exactly going steady."

"Can't we start over again?" he asked.

Thorn ignored his question. "Jake told me about Bigfoot visiting your camp. He's upset that Doonkeen thinks one of you planted the footprints you found."

"We saw things that need explanation. I'm glad you're coming with us on the expedition," he said.

"Who's keeping Pard?"

"Haven't thought about it."

"Mom's watching my little ranch, feeding my animals while I'm off looking for Bigfoot. Let's take Lady and Pard to my place. Maggie would love having Pard around for a few days, and you can meet my mom."

"Does this mean you're not mad at me anymore?"

"I'm not quite ready to say that."

"Is your mom as beautiful as you are?"

"To me, she's the most beautiful woman on earth. Dad was a lineman for County Electric. He died a few years back when he fell from a telephone pole."

Buck reached across the console and touched her hand. "I'm so sorry."

"I'm still not over it, though more so than Mom. They were inseparable."

"Losing a spouse can't be easy."

"Do you still have your parents?" she asked.

"I'm an orphan, though a wonderful couple helped get me through my teen years."

Thorn stared as if she were seeing him for the first time. "I can't imagine what it's like having no parents," she said.

"Like a great open void in your heart."

"Lana made a strange comment about children. She was staring a hole through you when she said it. Want to tell me about it?"

"You're good," he said. "Lana is the mother of my son, Adam."

"Aren't Lana and Clayton married?"

"In a manner of speaking. He lives with KK, and Lana lives with Sara."

"Who has Adam?"

"Lana, at least most of the time."

"You had an affair with her?"

Buck shook his head. "More like a dream. She and Sara drugged and tricked me into fathering Adam. They promised I would have privileges as a father. That's never been the case."

"Despicable," she said.

"I didn't realize how upset I am until lately. I confronted her and Clayton at the party the other night. She's agreed to give me regular visitations."

"Will she?"

"Don't know," he said.

"How old is Adam?"

"Two going on ten."

Thorn glanced out the window as a rabbit ran across the road in front of them.

"It'll work out," she said. "Let's go to my place."

Chapter 28

Sunlight filtered through dark clouds drifting overhead, a hawk disappearing into the vapor. Buck remembered the rutted turnoff to Thorn's house and slowed to avoid jarring the horse trailer. The roof of her barn appeared when they crested the last rise.

"I love your ranch," he said. "It's beautiful, and I could get used to the seclusion."

"Don't get too attached. I still don't like you much, though I'll take Lady and Pard."

"Package deals only. Take them, you take me too. That your mother?"

A woman on the front porch was feeding Thorn's bird dog. Her hair as dark as Thorn's, she was a couple inches shorter.

"My mom, Rosie Little Deer."

"She doesn't look old enough to be your mom."

"I'm twenty-six, and she had me when she was eighteen. You do the math."

"I see where you get your looks."

"Whatever you do, Buck McDivit, don't flirt with her, or I'll kill you."

"Don't know if I can help myself. Older women turn me on," he said.

"You're pressing it," she said.

Rosie Little Deer met them as they opened the Jeep's door. Pard bounded out and went running, looking for Maggie.

"I'm Rosie," the woman said.

"Buck. Thorn hasn't quit talking about you."

"And she's told me lots about you."

"All good, I hope."

"For the most part," she said.

Rosie's appearance left little doubt of her relationship with Thorn. Dressed the same, in worn jeans and western shirts, they could have passed as sisters. Thorn had already opened the door to the trailer and was leading Lady toward the corral.

"My horse, Lady," Buck said.

Rosie gave her a pat on the rump as she passed. "What a beautiful animal," she said.

Except for Lady, the corral was empty. Chester was in another nearby pen. When he saw Lady, he whinnied and ran to the fence.

"Have to keep an eye on that one," Thorn said. "Unless you want a pregnant horse."

"Don't know if I'm ready for that," he said.

Lady snorted and trotted over to the fence, rubbing noses with Chester.

"Looks like those two are," Rosie said. "I have coffee brewing. Like a cup?"

"Love one," he said.

Buck followed her to the front porch where Pard and Maggie were rubbing noses and wagging tails.

"No doubt these two remember each other," Thorn said as she joined them. "Best as I can see, he likes the ladies as much as you do."

Buck let the remark pass as he followed her to the table in the little kitchen. Rosie rested her hand on Buck's shoulder as she poured his coffee.

"I'm so glad Thorn's finally taken an interest in a strong man. Her boyfriend in high school was the class nerd."

"Knock it off, Mom," Thorn said. "Zeke isn't a nerd. I went with him for three years."

Rosie's eyes flashed when she said, "Now that boy has muscles."

"Mom liked him more than I did," Thorn said.

"His mother's a sweetheart. I don't even want to tell you what I think about his dad. He tried to hit on my little sister while his wife was in the same room."

"Mom, Buck doesn't want to hear about Zeke and his family."

"Well, it's the truth. What do you do for a living, Buck?"

"Security advisor for a rich oilman."

"Sounds exciting," she said.

"Usually pretty boring, though it has its moments."

"I'm so happy you met my beautiful daughter. I am so proud of her. She has a doctorate degree, you know?"

"Mom, please," Thorn said.

"Did she tell you she was a Junior Olympian?"

Buck could see by the way Thorn was rolling her eyes, that her mom told the same story to everyone she met.

"She didn't tell me," he said.

"Thorn's dad taught her how to shoot a bow and arrow. We spent years taking her to archery tournaments around the country. Would you like to see her medals?"

"Mom," Thorn said. "Buck doesn't want to see my medals."

Thorn's exasperated tone caused Rosie to change the subject. "My baby says you saw Bigfoot."

Thorn gave her mother another dirty look when Buck glanced at her for confirmation.

"It was uneventful, at least for the most part," he said. "What else did you tell your mom?"

Rosie grinned when Thorn said, "Just that I'm sure you had no time to become bored," she said.

Buck let the remark pass as her cat came through the pet door. Rosie petted the gorgeous calico rubbing against her leg.

"All the time she was growing up, Thorn would bring strays home for me to take care of," she said.

Grabbing the cat, she took her to an empty food bowl and opened a can for her.

"I still do," Thorn said.

He'd turned to get a look at the shiny rear of Rosie's jeans as she bent over to feed the cat. Thorn caught him looking, and motioned him to follow her out to the porch.

"What did I do now?" he asked.

"Pard and Lady can stay. You have to go."

"Bye, Rosie," he called through the screen door. "Nice meeting you."

"Leaving so soon?" she said.

"Have to get back to the lodge. We're returning to Shampe Canyon soon."

"Be careful. Thorn said it could be dangerous. And Buck," she said. "Please take care of my beautiful baby on the trip."

He had many things on his mind as he slammed the door on his Jeep. A chaparral with a lizard in its mouth blocked the dusty road as he drove away from Thorn's little ranch. The sky had darkened, and drops of rain sprinkled his windshield. Feeling alone, he drove around the stubborn bird without disturbing it.

Still worried about Don, he returned to the hospital instead of taking the road to Sunset Lodge. Josie and the boys had gone home, Don asleep on the bed. He opened his eyes and smiled when he sensed he was no longer alone.

"Just checking on you," Buck said.

Don's voice was hoarse when he spoke. "They took me off oxygen. I finally had to get angry with Josie to get her and the boys to go home and get some rest."

"You got a keeper there," Buck said.

"You're telling me. I've meant to tell you about this computer program I wrote."

"Lana mentioned it. Didn't know you could code."

"Took an online course. Never came in handy until now."

"You don't sound so good," Buck said. "Maybe you better tell me about your program in a few days when you're feeling better."

"Just this," Don said. "Lana's a dream to work for. Every idea I come up with, she makes it better. We got a handle on the case now, putting facts and evidence together. One thing still worries me."

"What?"

"Blade's bent on killing you. Better watch your back."

Buck tapped his shoulder. "Anything I can get you?"

"I'm good," he said, coughing. "The doctor said there's no permanent damage to my lungs."

"Wonderful news. How long are they keeping you?"

"Until tomorrow, maybe."

A nurse with a clipboard brushed past Buck to take Don's temperature.

"Mr. Boone is doing just fine. Now, it's late, and he needs his rest," she said.

"Just leaving," he said, clasping Don's hand. "I want to say again how sorry I am. I should be the one in the hospital and not you."

"Fate doesn't work that way," Don said.

***

Steady rain continued as Buck reached Sunset Lodge. The parking lot was empty, most of the network support vehicles gone. When he drove past the remains of his cabin, he remembered the chaos that had occurred earlier in the day.

Clayton's party cabin was dark as he

pulled into the driveway. Drizzling rain dampened his shoulders. Thunder rattled the windows as he opened the front door.

Feeling lonely, he wished Pard were there. A hidden light from the vaulted ceiling illuminated the room when he flipped the switch. A printed note from Lana, attached to the front of the refrigerator with a magnet, caught his attention.

"Take the bedroom at the top of the stairs," the note said. "It's sort of like the honeymoon suite. Hope you and Thorn enjoy the bottle of chilled Dom. And Buck, don't do anything I wouldn't do."

Lana, he thought, must have emailed the note to someone on staff, having them supply the Dom and place the note on the refrigerator so that he would find it.

"So much for that idea," he said.

Having missed lunch, he rummaged through the refrigerator. Lana had stocked it with German beer, Dutch cheese, and French pastries. What he wanted was a chopped beef sandwich slathered with Oklahoma barbecue sauce. He settled for smoked salmon and brie on a sliced croissant.

A winding wooden stairway leading to the balcony made the great room spectacular. What it missed was another human, or canine, with whom to talk. Feeling glum, he grabbed the chilled bottle of champagne and started upstairs with it.

The bedroom was everything Buck expected. Someone had turned down the covers and sprinkled fragrant rose petals on the sheets. As lonely as he felt, he had to chuckle.

A warm breeze wafted Lana's silk curtains through the open balcony door. Shucking his boots and clothes, he went outside and let an overstuffed chair swallow him.

Rain fell in waves, the overhang shielding him from all except a gentle mist. He removed the cork with a loud pop. Foaming champagne dribbled on his feet, the cork bouncing as it hit the ground. Not bothering to wipe his foot, he drank cold Dom Perignon straight from the bottle. Lana would have had a cat, he thought.

The champagne was almost empty when the downpour finally abated. Thunder persisted, and dense fog cloaked the valley as humid air saturated the surroundings. Only the hazy glow of a cloud-cloaked moon penetrated the growing soup. The bottle dropped from his hand, bouncing but not breaking when it struck the deck.

Champagne blurred his vision as he tried to focus on something over a distant mountaintop. It was a splinter of flickering light moving toward him. He blinked, thinking it was his imagination.

The light continued moving toward him. He watched until it stopped before reaching the balcony. The muted light glowed brighter as it grew larger. Something wrapped in sheer white cloth appeared. His eyes popped as the vision of Inger moved in and out of focus.

"Hope I didn't frighten you," she said.

Buck couldn't believe what he was seeing. "You're floating," he said.

"You and Thorn floated with me the other night."

"I was dreaming. Now I'm drunk. You're not real."

"I am real, a spirit of the forest, my home since the advent of time."

"I don't believe you."

"You don't believe your eyes?"

"I can see you better when I close one of them. Why are you here?"

"Grandmother's prophecy. I think you may have forgotten."

"Remind me," he said.

"Demon of darkness, unanswered desire, mistaken judgment, Sister of Fire, Arrow of Justice, or death in the mire."

"What does it mean?"

"Five questions only you can answer," she said.

"And if I don't?"

Blue eyes flashed when she said, "Your salvation lies in the riddle's solution. Solve it you must."

"Or?"

"You die."

Her image grew dimmer. "Wait," he said. "Give me a clue,"

Warmth radiated through his hand when she grasped it. "Your clue is in the riddle. You must solve it alone."

Her grasp left only fingerprints that glowed red as her image burst into an explosion of dissolving light.

Chapter 29

Buck awoke in the chair on the balcony as warm sunlight shined in his eyes. Someone had covered him with a gold and black Afghan. It felt as if he'd just awoken from a dream. It didn't explain the fingerprints indenting his hand.

When he reached the bedroom, he lay on the rose petals and closed his eyes. The ringing of his cell phone woke him, his dream forgotten, and the fingerprints gone. It was Jake calling.

"What's up?" he asked.

"Disaster."

"Like what?"

"I'm having an early dinner by the pool with the crew. I'd prefer telling everyone once rather than repeating the story several times. Can you join us?"

"What time is it?"

"After seven. Did I wake you?"

Buck couldn't believe he'd slept so long, and he didn't bother answering the question.

"Give me twenty minutes to shower and change clothes," he said.

Warm water alleviated some of his wooziness, though his head continued to pound. As he toweled off and padded into the bedroom, he longed for a glass of Thorn's hangover remedy.

Lana had saved him from having to wear the same jeans and shirt. Inside the closet, he found clothing, boots, and a note from her.

"Since you lost everything in the explosion, I took the liberty to have the staff supply you with new clothes and everything else you might need," it said.

He was dressed and halfway down the stairs when the vague memory of seeing Inger crossed his mind. It seemed so real to him, he couldn't reject the possibility that it was something other than his imagination.

Jake had arranged a big table, complete with white tablecloth and silver place settings, near the pool. Thorn, Jimi, Candy, and Colley had joined him. Pouring coffee from an urn, Buck swallowed a slug before speaking.

"Hi, gang. Sorry to keep you waiting."

"Glad you could make it," Jake said. "I have something important to tell everyone."

Candy arose from the table. "Jimi and I already know. Maybe we should just excuse ourselves."

"Does this mean . . . ?"

"Yes it does," she said, interrupting him. "I'm taking the assignment in London. Just wanted to give you a heads up."

"Jimi?"

"Sorry, boss. The network has reassigned me to another show. Guess this is goodbye."

After shaking Jake's hand, he departed without saying a word to anyone else. Candy waved goodbye over her shoulder as she followed him out the door.

Jake motioned a passing waiter. "I'm going to need something stronger than coffee. Can you send someone to take our cocktail order?"

"Amen to that," Colley said. "That little bitch Candy wouldn't even give me a kiss on the cheek.

Far as I'm concerned, she can kiss my ass."

"Shut up, Colley. We have more important things to talk about than a little rejection."

Knowing when to close his mouth, Colley rolled his eyes, making a face after sipping his coffee.

"What the hell's going on?" Buck said.

"You were right about Blade. I should have listened. He held a press conference yesterday and called me a charlatan."

"And the reporter's believed him?"

"Yes they did," Jake said. "Candy and Jimi were the only two that didn't check out of the hotel and go home last night. The network canned the episode. Ordered me to take a leave of absence while they try to repair my reputation. The expedition ain't gonna happen."

"That's total horseshit," Buck said. "We saw the footprints."

"Blade accused me of planting them. He incited the media; told them I was perpetrating a fraud. The network is livid. I thought they were going to fire me."

Kristen was working the bar and appeared with drinks for everyone except Thorn.

"Didn't know what you were having, honey, and I didn't want to bring you a Shirley Temple."

Thorn tried hard not to take offense. "It's okay. Coffee's all I need."

Kristen cupped her hand to Colley's ear and glanced at Thorn. "Lightweight," she said, loud enough so everyone could hear.

"Sorry about that," Jake said when she was gone.

"Don't worry about it," Thorn said. "I've known Kristen since we were ten. She knows who I am."

Colley tapped his knuckle on the table. "Women!" he said.

Jake let his comment pass. "I'm so sorry this

whole affair is ending like this," he said.

"Then don't let yourself get railroaded," Buck said. "We have all the supplies we need, and you own the helicopter. Let's go anyway."

"What would it prove?"

"If you let this lie, everyone will believe Blade. You'll never live it down."

"He's right," Colley said. "Your oil company could buy the network if you wanted it to. Why are you letting them push you around?"

"Maybe so. The problem is we're missing a few important cogs."

"Such as?" Buck said.

"A camera, for one. Someone to operate it, for two."

"Can't you find someone?" Thorn asked.

"I've never worked with anyone except Jimi. I confess, I know little about what he did. We always counted on him to do his magic."

Delivering more drinks, Kristen caught the drift of the conversation.

"I could be your cameraman," she said.

"Excuse me?" Jake said. "It's not that easy, young lady."

"I have a two-year degree in filmmaking from Oklahoma Community College."

"Never heard of it," Jake said.

"It's accredited. I learned every aspect of making motion pictures. That includes cameras and how to operate them."

"You're mighty pretty," Colley said. "But you ain't big enough to tote around a motion picture camera."

"A movie shot with an iPhone recently won an award at Sundance. There are some nice motion picture cameras built from magnesium, lots lighter than aluminum. And with digital refinements only dreamed of a few years ago."

"You sound knowledgeable," Jake said. "Do

you own a camera such as you describe?"

"I wish. I don't have an extra twenty grand lying around."

Jake raised his hands. "Then there you have it."

"Bullshit," Buck said. "Lana could have you the lightest most sophisticated digital camera available here tomorrow. If Kristen can operate it, then give her a chance. What have you got to lose?"

All eyes turned to Kristen. "I'll nail it for you, I promise."

"Are you in the union?"

"Come on, Jake," Buck said. "Lana can handle that as well. Give Kristen a hand up. She's trying to help. The way I see it, this is your ass if you don't do something."

"Buck's right," Colley said. "What have you got to lose?"

"My reputation."

"If you don't counter Blade's lies, it's already gone," Colley said.

Jake still wasn't convinced. "What if we find nothing in the valley?" he asked.

"We already found footprints. You have pictures of them on film. What better reason do you need?" Buck asked.

"Blade said they were fakes."

"They weren't faked."

"I don't know," Jake said.

Buck pushed his chair aside and started for the door.

"Clayton didn't tell me you're a coward," he said. "I'm out of here."

"I'm coming with you," Thorn said.

The table shook when Colley slammed his whiskey glass against it.

"Damn it, Jake, we've been together for fifteen years. Don't matter none cause I quit. I won't work for a loser."

Buck, Thorn, and Colley were halfway to the exit when Jake, in a loud voice, said, "I give up. The expedition is back on. Kristen, you're our new cameraman. Starting tomorrow, that is. Tonight, you're still the cocktail waitress. Can't speak for everyone. Just keep bringing me drinks till I pass out."

Kristen hugged his neck, and then kissed him full on the mouth. "Yes sir, boss," she said. "When are we leaving? I have to talk mom into taking care of my baby while I'm away."

"Heaven help us," Jake said, grabbing his forehead.

As Buck, Colley and Thorn returned to the table, Jake seemed more than convinced. He called Lana. Within an hour, she'd located all the camera equipment they'd need. She also vouched for Kristen's degree.

"Let's drink a toast," Jake said.

Kristen brought a round of shots, and one for herself. Buck was starting to get sick after slugging his Tequila.

"I need something to eat," he said.

Colley tossed a menu across the table. "Pretty good grub here. Try the Sundown Burger with well-done fries."

"Wish I had a shot of Thorn's hangover medicine," Buck said.

Thorn was already a step ahead. Kristen was grinning when she brought him the concoction she'd ordered for him.

"Rough night, cowboy?"

"You could say that," he said, between bites of his Sundown Burger.

He felt better after eating and taking Thorn's hangover remedy. Colley and Jake were already into their cups, meaningful conversation futile. Pushing aside his plate, he slapped Jake's shoulder.

"Leaving?" he asked.

"Put a fork in me. I'm done."

Thorn gave Jake a kiss, begged off from another drink, and followed Buck out the door.

"You were wonderful," she said, clasping his arm.

"Like me one minute, hate me the next," he said. "My head's spinning."

"There's a scenic trail leading down the mountain. Let's take a walk, and then . . ."

She smiled when he said, "Then what?"

"I'm still not sure about you. Let's walk first and then I'll decide."

The eastern sky had darkened as he shadowed Thorn down the steep trail, wondering where the day had gone. At least his pounding head had finally departed with it.

They sat on a boulder, looking down at the lights flickering in the valley below. She clutched his hand and pulled him closer. In the distance, a coyote howled. Lost in a moment of passion, neither of them heard it.

"I hope Lana has some champagne," she said.

"She thought we'd be together last night and left us a bottle of Dom Perignon. After drinking it all myself, I'll be happy if I never see another bottle of champagne as long as I live."

"Pussy," she said.

They held hands all the way up the trail, often stopping to embrace and kiss. She hurried inside the massive log cabin after he opened the door for her.

"This is gorgeous," she said, glancing up at the rafters. "I could get used to it."

"You and me both."

Thorn wasn't listening as she rummaged through the cabinets, looking for champagne. She soon found a wine refrigerator behind a folding door.

"Oh my God!" she said. "I've died and gone to heaven. I waitressed during college, and I've never seen a wine and champagne cache like this. Some of these bottles are priceless."

"Clayton isn't into wine, and I doubt Lana's lips have ever tasted Ripple."

Thorn grinned. "Then she doesn't know what she missed. Cheap wine makes for the best sex."

"Hope not," he said. "There's no Boone's Farm in that stash."

"Then we'll make do with what we have," she said.

Despite his better judgment, he was soon swilling expensive wine straight from the bottle. They'd gravitated back to the chair on the balcony where he'd slept the previous night. Thorn was on his lap and acting like anything but a puritan.

"You're built better than Zeke. Ever play professional sports?"

"Wasn't good enough," he said.

Thorn pulled him to his feet. "Even if the rose petals are a bit crushed, I love that bed. Let's find out how good you are."

Chapter 30

Thorn was standing by the open door to the balcony when Buck opened his eyes next morning. A warm breeze whipped the sheer curtains, molding against her naked body. When she saw he was finally awake, she rushed to the bed and climbed on top of him.

"You're the best lover I've ever had," she said.

"How many is that?"

"Just you and Zeke," she said.

Buck's cell phone rang before he could comment. It was Clayton. "You ain't gonna believe this," he said.

"What?"

"Someone murdered Ezekiel Big Shoe last night. Cut his throat."

"You kidding me?"

"Nope, and I guess we both know who did it."

"I'm sure you're right," Buck said. "But I'm too good a P.I. to jump to that conclusion without checking it out first."

"Whatever," he said. "Don't make no difference cause Big Shoe's deader than a doornail. Lana and me are flying down in an hour or so. She's taking charge of the lodge until we get a handle on things."

"What?" Thorn said when Buck signed off.

"Ezekiel Big Shoe. Someone murdered him last night."

Thorn's hand went to her mouth. "Oh no! I have to call Mom."

Without bothering to dress, she hurried down the stairs. When Buck followed, he found her sitting in an overstuffed leather chair, crying her eyes out as she talked on the phone.

"You okay?" he asked when she finally stopped talking.

"I just can't believe this. The news is all over the valley. Short of the Chief, Ezekiel was the most important person in our tribe."

"I'm so sorry. I didn't realize you were so close."

After burying her face in her hands, she ran toward the stairs.

"I have to get to town. There'll be people coming from all over to attend the funeral. I'm sure I'll have relatives staying at the house."

Buck didn't follow her back to the bedroom, brewing coffee in the kitchen instead. He'd already finished his first cup when she blasted down the stairs.

"Gotta go," she said, after giving him a quick peck on the lips.

"What about Pard and Lady?" he said, calling after her. "Should I come get them?"

"They'll be fine," she said, slamming the door behind her.

Disjointed by the events of the previous two nights, he was in no hurry to encounter the rest of the day. Hours later, he stood in front of the range, smoke billowing up from a skillet, as he tried to fry eggs. A familiar voice caused him to turn and look. It was Clayton.

"Who taught you to cook?" he said.

"No one. Guess that's my problem."

"Sit down," Clayton said, pointing to the kitchen table. "I'm a little hungry myself. Relax and watch a master at work."

Clayton found a frilly apron in a cabinet. Though he looked more than a little silly, Buck kept his mouth shut. Six-four Clayton was anything but feminine. Didn't matter. He was enjoying himself, his big teeth flashing beneath his silver mustache.

He was soon chopping jalapenos, onions, and tomatoes. When he folded the ingredients into his omelet, Buck's mouth began to water. He watched in awe as the older man peeled, diced, seasoned, and then fried a batch of hash browns. They feasted on omelets and potatoes, Clayton's laced with Louisiana hot sauce.

"Glad you showed up," Buck said. "I was getting ready to open a can of beans."

"Son, you need a woman."

"You're not a woman, and you can cook."

"Born in my left nut," Clayton said. "If I weren't a multi-millionaire oilman, I could have given Emeril a run for his money."

"Who taught you?"

"My third wife. We had nothing else in common except our love of food. She could cook like nobody's business. If she'd loved me, I'd still be with her to this very day."

Clayton grinned when Buck said, "Her fault, then?"

"Met this young filly in a bar one night. Next thing I knew, I was alone and sleeping in my office. Imogene remarried. Last I heard, she had three kids. Took me ten years to regroup and get back in the business after she took every penny I had."

Buck poured syrup on his hash browns. "Why is it I don't feel sorry for you? While you're at it, tell me about Big Shoe's murder."

"Don't know much more than you. He was working late last night. No one saw who entered his office and cut his throat."

"Any sign of a scuffle?"

"Don't know. Lana's over there now, along with a passel of police searching for clues."

"What's the plan?" Buck asked.

"Big Shoe was just about the most important man in eastern Oklahoma. There'll be senators, governors, and powerful business leaders at his funeral. And that's not to mention everyone in the county."

"And you?"

"Lana and I flew up today. KK and Sara will be along tomorrow. We'll be at the funeral with bells on."

"I'd like to take a look at the murder scene."

"Head over there," Clayton said. "Lana will see that you get a look."

"Think I will. Thanks for breakfast."

"No problem. If your life ever slows down, I'll give you a few lessons."

Buck didn't bother replying as the door shut behind him. Except for puddles in the blacktop, puffy clouds were all that remained of last night's rain. The main parking lot was empty except for some police vehicles. A truck came roaring up the hill, the driver honking when he saw Buck. He pulled to a stop next to him.

"Don," Buck said. "They let you out of the hospital already?"

"Yesterday."

"You look good. How do you feel?"

"My ears are still ringing, and I have a persistent cough and a few burns. Other than that, I'm good to go."

Buck shook his hand. "Guess you heard about Big Shoe?"

Don nodded. "Thought I'd get a look at the murder scene. I think we know who did it. I want to make sure."

"Me too," Buck said. "I'm on my way over.

Lana's already there, and Clayton says she can get us in for a look."

"Can we stop by the bombsite first?"

"You bet," Buck said.

The distance was short from the parking lot to the remains of the cabin. Didn't matter because Don was moving slow.

"Sorry," he said. "Can't get oxygen to my lungs fast enough."

"I'm in no hurry," Buck said. "Take your time."

When they reached the bombsite, he realized he hadn't taken a good look the last time he was there. Portions of three walls remained. The wall where the front door had been was gone. Yellow crime tape had blown loose in the thunderstorm. The roof was gone, having collapsed. Don put a hand to his head.

"A directional charge," he said. "Meant to kill the first person coming through the door."

"The bomber used a flip-phone as a timer. Like you said, the cat saved you."

"Right about that," Don said. "If I'd made it through the door, there wouldn't have been enough body parts left of me to put in a mayonnaise jar."

Buck tapped his shoulder. "It was a sophisticated bomb. The person that built it and set it up had special training."

"Army training," Don said.

When he finally turned away from the demolished structure, Buck tugged his arm.

"I don't know how an investigator could have mistaken this as a natural gas explosion."

"Maybe something to do with Big Shoe's murder."

"I think it has everything to do with the murder. Let's head over and see if we can get a handle on things."

When Lana arrived at the lodge, she'd

refunded the money of all the remaining guests, and checked them out. They found her standing alone in the deserted lobby. Seeing Don, she embraced him.

"You shouldn't be here," she said.

"I spent years in the army as a homicide investigator. Thought I might be able to help."

Lana frowned, shaking her head in disgust. "The people investigating don't seem to have a clue. The detective looks about fifteen, and is in over his head."

"You think he'll let me and Buck take a look?"

"I'll call his chief and get him fired if he doesn't."

"You can do that?" Don asked.

"You may get a chance to see."

"Where was Big Shoe killed?" Buck asked.

She pointed to a door. "In his office."

Buck glanced at the big, oak door as they entered. "No sign of forcible entry," he said.

"My money's betting on an inside job," Don said.

"What are you inferring?" Lana asked.

"Whoever killed Big Shoe knew him," Buck said.

"And likely very well," Don added.

The office was as regal as Buck had remembered it. A chalk outline of Big Shoe's body marred the polished pine floor. A detective from the county sheriff's department stood propped against the wall, watching a technician collect forensic samples. As Lana had said, he was young, trying his best to look older. His cookie duster mustache and cheap suit did little to advance his cause.

"Lieutenant Taylor, this is Don Boone and Buck McDivit, two members of my security team. If you don't mind, I'd like for them to have a look at the murder scene."

Detective Taylor was in awe of the tall woman in high heels and expensive dress.

"I have no problem with that," he said. "The sheriff said to consider you part of the department."

"Sheriff Davis and I've been friends for many years," she said. "Thank you."

The chalk outline was in front of the wet bar. Blood had pooled on the floor, staining a nearby rug. Shards of glass lay congealed in the sticky mess and some of the fragments were scattered across the floor. Don removed a pen from his pocket and began moving pieces of glass. Detective Taylor watched with an amused expression on his face.

"Got it figured out yet?" he said.

Don gave Buck a wink. "As a matter of fact, I do."

The Detective's expression changed. "You've only been here five minutes. You pulling my leg?"

"It's plain what happened here," Don said.

"Then maybe you better tell me."

Don skirted around the bloody rug, back to the wet bar. "What time was Big Shoe killed?" he asked.

"Two in the morning," the detective said.

"There's no sign of forcible entry. It's reasonable to assume Big Shoe knew the person that killed him. He died standing in front of the wet bar, a bottle of Stoli in his hand. When the murderer cut his throat, he dropped the bottle."

"What does Stoli have to do with anything?" Taylor asked.

"There's a half empty bottle of Dewar's on the bar, another empty bottle in the trash. My guess is that Big Shoe was a Dewar's drinker."

"He's right," Buck said. "I had a drink with him the first night we met."

"He dropped the bottle of Stoli, began to bleed

out, and then slumped to the floor. There's only one footprint in the blood. Size twelve or bigger, I'd guess. The print of the person that killed him."

Taylor began thumbing through his notes. "Big Shoe wore size nine," he said. "Go on with your story."

"There was a glass on the bar. The glass into which Big Shoe poured the Stoli. I presume no one has wiped the bar since the murder. Look close. You'll see the ring left behind when someone moved the glass."

"Who moved it?" Taylor asked.

"The murderer. After cutting Big Shoe's throat, he picked up the glass from the bar and drank the Stoli."

"Then where is it?" Taylor asked. "It wasn't on the floor."

Don pointed to the glasses sitting in rows on a shelf above the bar. "I'd say it's that one right there. All the rows are in perfect alignment. All the glasses except for that one."

Detective Taylor drew closer, craning his neck to get a better look. By now, even the technician had stopped taking samples and was staring at the rack of bar glasses. Don pointed again.

"There's a smidgen of vodka still in the glass. My guess is the murderer's prints are all over it. And the DNA you'll need to identify him and the evidence to make the charge stick in court."

"Sam . . ." Detective Taylor said.

He didn't have to finish his sentence. The technician was already moving toward the wet bar, evidence bag in hand.

"Why was the killer so reckless in returning the dirty glass to the rack?"

"Because he was drunk, and didn't think we'd be smart enough to figure it out."

"If what you say proves true, I'm gonna buy you the biggest T-bone you ever ate," the

detective said
     Don shook his hand. "I'm looking forward to it, Detective Taylor."

Chapter 31

Lana was smiling when they left Big Shoe's office, exiting into the deserted lobby.

"You're amazing," she said. "How did you interpret so much with so little information?"

"Years of practice," he said. "I can't begin to tell you how many homicides I've covered. Used to give me the creeps."

"I can imagine," she said. "I can't believe how stupid Blade was to leave his prints and DNA at the murder scene."

"Not stupid at all," he said. "Repeat killers often leave clues on purpose. I'm not a shrink and have no idea why they do it, but they do."

"What now?" Buck asked.

"Tie this case up with a pretty bow and put it to bed."

"Are we that close?" Lana asked.

"I think so," Don said. "We've known the connection between Big Shoe and Forbidden Treasures for a while now. Ever since Buck saw him driving an identical Corvette as Blade's. Let's find out who else is in on this."

"How?" Lana asked.

"The address in McAlester where the Black Cup package went. I'm going there to check it out."

"Not without me, you're not," Buck said.

"May I go?" Lana asked. "I want to be in on whatever you find."

"Of course you can," Don said.

"Then let me change out of this skirt and put on some work clothes."

They waited outside Clayton's cabin for her to return. Buck sat in the backseat of the crew cab, the big diesel in Don's truck humming.

"Why do you think Blade killed Big Shoe?" he asked.

"Maybe the explosion. Big Shoe owned a large chunk of the lodge. I'm sure he wasn't happy with his business partner blowing up one of his luxury cabins."

"My bet is there's more to it than that," Buck said.

"Like what?"

"Don't know. Maybe we'll find out in McAlester."

"Let's hope," Don said.

"What do you think of Lana?"

"Quite the woman; both beautiful and smart."

"She is that," Buck said.

Lana appeared from the cabin dressed in a yellow tee shirt and stylish blue shorts. She climbed into the front seat.

"What's the plan?" she asked.

"Just checking a lead," Don said as he powered down the mountain in the big truck. "Couldn't find anything on the web about the address."

The day had grown warm, so Don cranked the air conditioning.

"Nice truck," Lana said.

"You own it."

"Clayton has good taste."

"At least in trucks and women," Buck piped in from the backseat.

She took Buck's comment as a compliment,

smiling when she said, "Don't get me started."

The broad valley, surrounded by mountain vistas, flattened as they neared McAlester. They were soon on Main Street of the old town best known as the home of the state penitentiary; a facility the locals referred to as Big Mac. There were no skyscrapers. Most of the buildings were one or two-story structures constructed of red brick and native stone. They found the address they were looking for on E. Choctaw.

"Must be in the building on the right," Buck said.

No other vehicles were on the street, so Don did a uey and parked in front of a red brick building.

"Hope Clayton and I aren't paying your traffic tickets," Lana said.

"Used to be a small town cop," he said. "Believe me when I tell you nobody cares."

"If you say so," she said, as they climbed out of the truck.

Business was slow in downtown McAlester. Except for an old man coming out of a furniture store across the street, the sidewalks lay deserted. A boy pedaled past on a bicycle, his dog's ears flopping as he trotted behind him. The man's truck backfired as Buck held the door open for Lana and Don.

The building reeked of must and age. Its antiquated lights cast dim shadows on the black and white tile floor. Some of the offices had names on the doors, and numbers in worn gold lettering. Don pointed to a cracked door at the end of the hall. The name said Martino's Watch and Jewelry Repair.

"Help you?" the little man behind the counter asked.

"You Mr. Martino?"

"That's me. What you got?"

"We're looking for Forbidden Treasures," Don said. "Is it in this building?"

Mr. Martino rubbed his hand through his gray flattop. "Around the corner," he said.

"Know if anyone's there to help us?"

"Justin and his cat. You know Justin?"

"Can't say as I do," Don said.

"He's a little slow."

Lana was busy looking at the used watches and jewelry in the display cabinet on the wall.

"Slow?" she said.

"Autistic, I think is the word for it."

"Anybody else work there?" Don asked.

"Two Indian fellas drop by every now and then. The big ugly one with the bushy ponytail had me clean his Rolex once. Got mad when I charged him twenty bucks. Had to give him ten back cause I was afraid he might kill me."

"Sounds like a mean one," Don said.

"When I see him coming, I shut my door. He got into it with Justin yesterday."

"What happened?"

"I kept my nose out of it. The big Indian was yelling so loud his voice echoed down the hall."

"Did you call the cops?"

"Like I said, I kept my nose out of it. After he rushed out of here, I went down and checked on Justin. He was on the floor, against the wall, his nose bleeding, and his eye starting to swell. I gave him a bag of ice to put on it."

"Thanks for the info, Mr. Martino," Don said, starting for the door.

"Just a minute," Lana said. "How much is this watch?"

"Ma'am, you got quite the eye. That's the most expensive watch I got. I can't let it go for less than seventy-five bucks."

Lana handed him a hundred dollar bill. "Keep the change." When he started to put it in a box, she said, "Clean it for me, and I'll give you another twenty. I'll pick it up later."

"What was that all about?" Buck asked as they walked out the door.

"My mom had a watch like that. It reminded me of her. I couldn't resist."

"He would have sold it to you for ten bucks."

"Chalk it up as ten dollars for the watch, and the rest for the information and memories."

The door where Martino had pointed was unlocked and they entered without knocking. A young man of obvious American Indian heritage sat at a computer. As they approached him, a black and white cat ran from across the room and jumped into his lap. Lana motioned to Don to let her do the talking.

"Are you Justin?"

When the young man raised his head, they could see the swelling around his eye.

"That's me," he said.

"I'm Lana and these two men with me are Don and Buck." Justin returned his gaze to the computer screen without saying hello. "That's a nasty looking black eye you have. Are you okay?"

Justin continued to stare at the computer, but said, "Mr. Martino gave me some ice to put on it. It don't hurt so bad today."

"Mind if I take a look?" she asked. When Justin nodded, she knelt in front of him. He winced as she probed the purple splotch with her fingers. "We may have to get this looked at. What's your cat's name?"

"Whiskers," he said.

The cat stood on Justin's lap, her tail moving as she turned in slow circles. Lana gave the cat a stroke.

"I think she's trying to protect you. It's okay, Whiskers. We wouldn't hurt Justin for any amount of money."

Justin raised his head and said, "You have a nice voice. You remind me of my mom."

"Thank you," Lana said. "How is your mom?"

Justin lowered his head again. "She's dead."

"I'm so sorry," Lana said, touching his hand. "Who do you live with?"

"Whiskers and me live alone in a house down the block. My dad bought it for Mom and me."

"Oh? Who's your dad?"

"Mr. Big Shoe."

Lana glanced up at Don and Buck to catch their reaction. "Ezekiel Big Shoe?"

"Yes."

"Do you have other relatives; a grandmother or aunt, maybe?"

Justin shook his head again. "No one but Whiskers and me."

"Not ever? Who raised you?"

"My mom."

"When did she die?"

"Maybe a year ago," he said.

"How do you take care of yourself?"

"My dad gives me a hundred dollars a week."

"You buy your own food and cook it?"

"No."

"Then how do you eat?"

"I give the money to Lola."

"Who's Lola?"

"A nice woman that lives next door. She makes my lunch, and I eat breakfast with her kids."

"Do you know her last name?"

"Redbones."

"Is she married?"

Justin's head lowered again. "Got killed."

"How?"

"Accident where he worked."

"Justin, I'm so sorry," she said, patting his hand again.

"Lola buys cat food and feeds Whiskers.

Whiskers likes her and the kids."

"How old are her children?"

Justin raised his hand to his chest. "Hector is this tall. He's the biggest."

"Do you work for your dad?" Lana asked.

"Yes."

"Can you tell us what it is you do?"

"Keep the books and fill orders. When Mr. Doonkeen brings things, I take pictures and put them on the website. When someone buys something, I ship it to them."

"Is he the one that gave you the black eye?"

"Yes."

"Why was he so angry?"

"He pushed me away from the computer to look at the numbers. He didn't know how to use the program and made me show him. He got so angry that I thought he was going to kill me."

"He saw something in the numbers he didn't like?"

Justin blinked and touched his black eye. "He called Dad bad names. He was shouting and threw a chair against the wall, and then he slapped me. Lola was angry and wanted to call the police. I wouldn't let her because Mr. Doonkeen told me he would kill us all if I did."

It took a moment for Lana to compose herself. When she did, she said, "So you keep the books on this computer?"

"Yes."

"Mind if I take a look?"

Justin hugged the cat to his chest, letting Lana occupy the chair. With practiced fingers, she began moving from screen to screen. Finally, she glanced up at Buck and Don.

"There's information for everything we need on this computer. Invoices, addresses; you name it. Another program open is a database of antiquities. Pictures and information about where the artifacts originated."

"Bingo," Don said.

Buck glanced around the small room. "Where do you store the relics?" he asked.

"Warehouse on the edge of town," Justin said.

Lana let the young man return to his computer.

"Justin, you are amazing. Who taught you how to keep books?"

"Mom did."

"She taught you how to use the computer?"

"I am good with numbers. She only had to show me once."

"I've never seen a more beautiful set of books. They are perfect."

"Mom couldn't believe it either. She used to say I never make mistakes. She kept getting sicker, and I had to start doing all the work for her."

"Cancer?" Justin lowered his head. "Do you have a picture of her?"

A smile crossed his face for the first time. He disappeared into the back room, returning with an 8 x 10 photo in a gold frame. A young woman with black hair and even darker eyes was sitting on the front porch of an old wood-framed house. Ezekiel Big Shoe sat next to her, holding her hand. He was also smiling.

"She is so beautiful. What was her name?"

"Beth," he said.

"You must miss her a lot, don't you?"

"Yes."

"She would be so proud of you. Was yesterday the first time Mr. Doonkeen ever hurt you?"

"He hurt my mom once. I couldn't stop him. After I told Dad, he never hurt Mom again, but he always gave me dirty looks. When he's here, I have to put Whiskers in another room to keep him from hurting her."

"A despicable man," Lana said.

"Yes."

"I can't believe how good you are with numbers."

"Yes."

Lana reached into her wallet and removed a hundred dollar bill. "Your dad can't make it today. He asked me to give this to you."

Chapter 32

They were ten miles out of McAlester, heading back to Sunset Lodge before anyone spoke. The frown on Lana's face expressed her dark thoughts.

"You okay?" Buck asked.

"That sorry prick needs to have his balls cut off with a rusty knife, and I'm just the girl to do it," she said.

She cracked a smile when Don said, "Don't sugarcoat it, Lana. Tell us how you really feel."

"There's enough data on Justin's computer to put Blade in Big Mac where he belongs," she said.

"On death row," Buck said. "Why did he get so mad at Big Shoe?"

"They ran all their ill-gotten money through an offshore account in Nicaragua. It was easy to see from the books that Big Shoe was taking more than his fair share."

"How do you get money from an offshore account?" Buck asked.

"The easy answer is by credit card. If Big Shoe or Blade needed money, the bank in Nicaragua would credit their card with cash."

"I'm confused," Buck said. "He didn't use a credit card to pay for his share of the lodge, did he?"

"There are other ways of laundering money."

"Such as?"

"Casinos, horse tracks, and any number of betting venues. Winning or losing a bundle of money at a crooked casino, for example. It works both ways, and the Treasury Department is none the wiser. That's why the feds track the gaming industry. They aren't always successful at keeping out organized crime."

"There are so many Indian casinos in this state. Good chance Big Shoe was first cousins with some of the managers," Buck said.

Don tapped the brakes when a jackrabbit scurried across the road in front of the racing truck.

"So Blade found out his partner was cheating him and then killed him," he said.

"Looks that way to me," Lana said.

"I'm just thinking out loud here. The information on that computer is the only evidence we have to link Blade and Big Shoe," Buck said. "Maybe we should have brought it with us."

"Shit!" Lana said. "You're right. Turn around."

No vehicles were within a hundred yards of the truck as Don hit the brakes. Lana and Buck grabbed doorposts as they raced away in the opposite direction. After cresting a small rise, they saw a gray cloud of smoke billowing up in the distance. Something was on fire in McAlester.

They found the main street crowded with cars, cops, gawkers, and firefighters. The old building that housed Forbidden Treasures was ablaze. Smoke and flames billowed high above the roof. Don didn't stop, weaving through traffic and people before sliding to a halt.

Buck jumped from the truck and sprinted for the door of the burning building. Don tackled him before he'd gone five feet.

"No one in that building is alive," he said, holding Buck to the ground until he stopped struggling.

"I see Justin," Lana shouted, pushing through the crowd.

"He made it out," Don said. "And so did the cat and the old man."

A buzz-cut McAlester cop dressed in a khaki uniform was questioning Justin. A young woman, baby in hand and two toddlers hugging her legs clutched Justin's arm. Tears welled in her dark eyes, her face red.

"What happened?" Don asked.

"Some crazy Indian doused the building with gasoline and then lit it," the officer said.

"Everybody okay?" Buck asked.

"No one in the building except these two."

"What happened?" Buck asked after the cop had moved away through the crowd.

"Mr. Doonkeen took the computer, and then set fire to the building," Justin said.

"The crazy man could have killed him," the young woman said.

"Are you Lola Redbones?" Lana asked.

The woman nodded and started crying again. She was short, plump, and her dark hair mussed.

"I was so afraid," she said. "He burned Justin's house. There's nothing left but ashes."

"It's okay," Lana said, embracing her. "Everyone's safe. You shouldn't return to your house just yet. Do you have relatives you can stay with?"

Lola shook her head. "My husband Charlie was from Louisiana and moved to McAlester after Katrina."

"You have an Indian name. Can't your tribe help you?"

"Grandpa was full blood and grew up on a reservation. Charlie thought it was demeaning and never claimed his head rights."

"And you?"

"I'm Mexican," she said.

"You're coming with us until we can find you a place to stay."

Lana's words calmed the young woman, and she knelt to comfort her two barefoot boys.

"All our things are at the house," she said.

"We'll stop by and get what you need," Don said.

"Are you okay, Mr. Martino?" Lana asked.

He opened his palm, handing her the watch she'd purchased. "Lost everything except for this," he said.

He blushed when she kissed him on the forehead and said, "Mr. Martino, you are a doll. I'm so sorry about your shop."

"Maybe the best thing that ever happened to me," he said. "Been paying big premiums on my insurance for years. Now, they're gonna pay me. Maybe even enough to buy a little fishing camp down by the river."

"Good for you. If we only hadn't lost that computer. Justin, why are you grinning?"

Justin handed her a jump drive. "Mom taught me to back-up every day."

"All the data from your accounting program is on this?" She rested her hand on his shoulder when he nodded. "I wasn't going to tell you. Now, I think it's best. Justin, your dad is dead.

Justin was non-responsive as they gathered clothes and a few possessions for the Redbones. Buck sat up front with Don. Lana climbed into the backseat with Lola and her toddlers. Hector sat in her lap. Her free arm draped around Justin's shoulder.

"Everything okay back there?" Don asked.

"Good as it's going to get for awhile," she said.

"Justin, can you show me the warehouse where you store the relics?"

"Up ahead," he said.

The warehouse on the edge of town was little more than a large storage shed. It didn't matter because the door was open. Buck got out and looked.

"Empty. Blade cleaned it out already."

"Figures," Don said. "Where to now?"

"Back to the lodge," Lana said. "And please slow down."

Don slowed to the speed limit. They found Clayton waiting at the entrance to Sunset Lodge.

"I was starting to worry," he said.

Don and Buck helped Lola carry her meager belongings into the lobby.

"Go home and get some rest," Lana told Don. "You shouldn't have been working today, anyway."

"I'm not going anywhere," he said. "Blade is lurking around, and you need protection."

"Already taken care of," Clayton said. "Big Shoe's security people are working for me now. They're patrolling the grounds as we speak. The police finished their investigation. I got enough employees back to clean the place up and run the front desk. If I had a cook and some waiters, we'd be set.

"Good," Lana said. "We need rooms for Lola and Justin."

"Pleased to meet you," Clayton said, slapping Justin's shoulder and pumping Lola's hand. "You may have to eat my cooking, but you are welcome here."

Lola's face reflected her concern. "We can't afford this place."

"Baby, don't you worry your pretty little head about it. Your stay here is on the house, courtesy of Miss Lana and me. Like I told you, you're welcome here."

"Gracias," she said, hugging him.

"Come with me, and I'll get you checked in."

"I'm tired and going to the cabin," Lana said. "Can you handle things?"

"Gotcha covered," Clayton said. "KK and Sara are on their way."

"Go home, Don. That's an order," she said.

"Yes ma'am," he said, saluting.

She and Buck watched him disappear down the mountain road before heading for the cabin. Once inside the door, she kicked off her shoes and opened the wine chiller.

"I'm going to sit on the deck and drink a bottle of wine. Join me?"

"I could use a nip of Wild Turkey."

"You know where the liquor cabinet is. I'll be on the deck."

The curtains flapped in a warm summer breeze as he joined her on the deck. Sprawled with her bare feet propped on the railing, she sipped her wine with eyes half closed.

"Thank God Justin is such a stickler for backing up his work," she said. "Otherwise, we'd be toast."

Buck tapped her wine glass with his tumbler. "The evidence we have on Blade is enough to hang him. I'm happy with that, even if it's all we accomplish."

"We don't have to settle for that now."

Lana sat her glass on the side table and began rubbing the watch she'd purchased from Mr. Martino.

"I can see it means a lot to you. Tell me about your mom."

"She was my whole world. The man that fathered me was an abusive monster. He was a welder, and we were living in California. He made good money and spent most of it on whiskey, drugs, and whores. He was always angry when he finally made it home, and Mom usually took the brunt of the abuse. She got him off to work one morning and then took his car and drove us to Oklahoma. He followed us here on his 125 cc Honda. Grandmother met him at the door of her trailer with a hatchet."

"What happened to him?"

"He stabbed someone on a dance floor one night and went to prison for ten years. When they released him, he drank himself to death. What about your father?"

"Never had one, bad or otherwise."

"You're an orphan?" she said.

"I lived with more foster parents than I can count. My bad attitude always got in the way of adoption. Jim and Carol took me in when I was fourteen. Helped me straighten out my life. Otherwise, I might have wound up in prison."

Lana touched his glass again. "Sounds like we're kindred spirits," she said.

"At least you have a partner."

"It's not that I don't like men. I just don't know what I'd do without Sara."

"All men aren't monsters," he said.

"I know that. I'm even attracted to males, as you can attest. Though I know it's illogical, I just can't overcome my innate distrust of the opposite sex."

"Hey, I wouldn't change you for the world."

Lana finished her wine and poured more from the open bottle beside her.

"I was hoping you and Thorn would fall in love. She is so intelligent and beautiful, and you seem so compatible."

"She's every man's wet dream," he said. "Problem is it takes two to tango."

"You and KK went together."

"She recently tried to take a page out of your playbook and asked me to get her pregnant. Said her biological clock was ticking so loud it was about to drive her deaf."

"You're kidding me! What did you tell her?"

"I already have a son I rarely see," he said.

Lana squirmed in her chair, turning away from him.

"I'm so sorry you're bitter," she said.

"Not bitter. I just don't want to have two sons that don't know I'm their father."

She faced him again. "I told you things would change. Don't you believe me?"

"Sorry," he said.

"Let's get back to Thorn. Have you had her yet?"

"I'm not sure who had who," he said.

Lana's cell phone rang before she could comment.

"That was Clayton. He said Lola took over the kitchen and if we're hungry, we should join them. Would you like something to eat?"

"I'm starved," he said. "You bet I would."

Chapter 33

The aroma of enchiladas and refried beans met them as they opened the door to the lodge's main kitchen. Clayton sat at the table where the cook staff ate, Lola's oldest toddler bouncing on his knee.

The smallest boy occupied Sara's lap. KK was rocking the baby in her arms as Lola placed a steaming platter of tamales on the table. Justin sat beside Clayton, smiling for the first time since Lana had told him his father was dead. Lana and Buck pulled up chairs.

"Try the dip," Clayton said. "The best I ever tasted."

Lana touched Lola's arm. "We didn't intend to put you to work," she said.

"I love to cook," she said. "I could do it all day, every day. When Mr. Clayton told me we had no one to cook, I asked him to show me the kitchen."

"I'm glad you're happy," Lana said.

Lola was beaming. "If I had a kitchen like this, I would never leave."

"Your enchiladas are so good," Clayton said. "I may never let you."

Jake and Colley appeared, entering through the door Buck had left ajar.

"Man, we smelled the eats the minute we

walked through the front door," Colley said. "Got extra enchiladas for two hungry souls?"

"Sit," Clayton said. "Got enough eats here for a log rolling."

Jake grabbed the empty chair beside Buck. "We have problems," he said between bites.

"Like what?"

"Ezekiel's funeral is the day after tomorrow. I've known him and his family for years and would be remiss if I skipped it."

"Why is that a problem?" Buck asked.

"Another storm system is moving our way. Looks like lots of rain following the funeral. I need to finish the shoot by the end of the week, or else scrap it, and I don't know when I'll get back this way again."

"We can film in the rain."

"Establishing base camp won't be so easy."

"I'm not going to the funeral. Colley, a couple of men and I could transport the equipment to the valley. I could have the camp set up when you arrive."

"Colley, what do you think?"

"The equipment's packed and waiting on the pad. I could fly it to the valley now if you want. It's heavy, though. Even four strong backs will have a time moving it far from where we put it on the ground."

Clayton was listening to the conversation. "I got men that can help, and an ATV that's small but perfect for transporting packages too heavy to carry. Just say the word."

Jake and Colley walked out with Buck when they finished eating.

"If you're serious about setting up base camp for us, can you leave now?"

"Let me pack a few things. If Colley's ready to go I can meet him at the chopper in half an hour," he said.

"Make it three hours. Clayton's rounding up hands to help, and Colley needs to load the ATV."

They were soon winging toward the valley, Clayton's ATV dangling from the chopper. The sun was low on the horizon when Colley hovered above the valley opening and lowered the payload.

Clayton's ATV was little more than an engine attached to four wheels and a metal frame. There was no roof, only a front bench seat and a flatbed for stacking boxes. The little vehicle had surprising speed and power. It was growing dark as they unloaded the last box beside the pristine pool. Colley handed Buck an AK47 assault rifle before climbing up the rope ladder to the helicopter.

"I know Jake disapproves of weapons. Even so, you might just need this. There are thirty rounds in the banana clip. It's automatic. The ammo won't last long if you hold the trigger down."

"Where'd you get this?"

"Liberated it during one of my tours in Nam," Colley said. "I keep it in the chopper underneath my seat. Jake's never figured it out."

Buck handed it back to him. "I promised Jake there'd be no guns, and a promise is a promise."

"I understand," Colley said. "The tank on the ATV is full, and there are two 10-gallon gas tanks in case you need more."

"Thanks, Colley," Buck said, giving him a fist bump.

"See you in a couple of days," he said.

The chopper lifted off the escarpment, the sound of its motors fading in the distance. The ATV had knobby tires and enough power to climb a forty-five-degree grade. He could feel its power as he raced away along the flat surface back to camp.

Darkness comes late to Oklahoma in the summertime. Buck was still surprised by how much they'd accomplished. He'd strung miniature lights around the perimeter, powering them with a portable generator. After eating a can of beef stew, he doffed his clothes and lounged in the pool for almost an hour. It was dark when he got out of the water, and he was glad he'd strung the lights. He was almost ready to turn in for the night when his cell phone rang. It was Don, checking on him.

"I can't believe you're in the valley alone," he said.

"I'm fine. Colley offered to lend me his old AK47. I didn't take it. I think I'll be all right."

"Want me to join you?"

"I'm fine. Stay home and recuperate."

"I'll check on you tomorrow," Don said.

Exhausted from the toils of the day, he fell into a deep sleep. Something padding through camp awakened him before dawn. Unzipping the tent, he crawled across the moist grass that somehow grew in the constant shade. He'd turned off the generator before entering the tent. Now, it was almost like the inside of a cave, no star, or moonlight penetrating the thick canopy of vegetation. He stopped, hoping to hear something, even if he was unable to see it.

After hearing no more movement in the campsite, he decided to return to his tent. When he did, he realized he had a problem.

Though he attempted to retrace the path he'd taken from the tent, he couldn't find it. Finally giving up trying, he lay back, cradling his head in hands.

⌁⌁⌁

Disoriented when he awoke, Buck found himself only ten feet from his tent. When he scanned the campsite, he found several large footprints. Bigfoot had visited the camp. He wondered how the creature managed to see in the dark. Jake called him later that day.

"Colley said he got you situated. How did it go last night?"

"Dogged after helping move all the heavy equipment. I turned in early. When I got up this morning, I found I'd had a midnight visitor."

"Bigfoot?"

"It didn't disturb anything, though it left several footprints in the moist earth. Put some infrared game cameras on your list of things to bring. We might get some great photos."

"Will do," Jake said. "The funeral's shaping up to be quite a production. Governors and senators are attending, along with everyone in the county and half the state. I didn't realize just how many people Big Shoe knew."

"I won't be there, and I bet neither will Blade."

"I know you're raring to go. I'd appreciate it if you'd wait for the rest of the crew before making any important discoveries."

"No problem. I was only planning to do a little light exploring."

"Our show follows a standard script. We arrive at a spooky sight and then start seeing signs of paranormal activity. The finale is always the resolution, and the last big scene. You get my drift?"

"I guess," he said.

"It's not important that we actually film Bigfoot. What's essential is that our show builds real suspense and anticipation. It needs to keep the viewers flipping the channel our way to make our sponsors happy."

"But you told me it was your dream to document Bigfoot."

"Forget what I told you. What's imperative is the ratings. It wouldn't do to have the suspense dissipated before we ever start."

"Gotcha," Buck said. "You can count on me."

"I knew I could."

Buck had planned to drive the ATV up the valley to find out if Blade's City of Gold actually existed. Jake's ratings didn't factor into his decision. He was right about one thing, though. A storm was building to the west.

Distant thunder began rumbling before noon, the weather hot, and the air humid. He contained his curiosity by exploring the caverns above the falls. He'd made a discovery that would not make Jake happy. His phone rang before he had time to assess the situation. It was Don, checking in again.

"Everything okay?" he asked.

"From the thunder in the distance, I'd say the expedition's in for heavy rain."

"Come across anything interesting yet?"

"Last time here we found some caverns above the falls where we're camped. While nosing around just now, I learned they are more extensive than what we thought."

"How so?"

"Cavernous rooms connected by a network of trails lace the mountain. I followed one for more than a mile before turning around. There's evidence of human habitation everywhere."

"You have to be kidding me."

"Not recent signs. The ones I saw are hundreds, maybe thousands of years old."

"What's the plan?"

"Head west and see if Blade's City of Gold exists."

"Aren't you going to wait for Jake and the crew?"

"We had an interesting talk today. Despite what he told me earlier, he's more interested in ratings than results. Just as well for me, I guess."

"Good for you," Don said. "I talked with Lana earlier. Blade has dropped off the face of the earth."

"He'll be back."

"Like I said, call if you need me. I'll get there

one way or the other."

Thunder rumbled again, closer this time. Buck threw a few items he thought he might need on the back of the ATV and headed west. He soon realized the winding creek ran the entire length of the valley.

The lack of undergrowth made for a smooth path for the ATV he'd nicknamed the Mule. He began seeing wildlife: rabbits, an armadillo, and a small herd of deer. He had little doubt there were also predators lurking in the valley.

Instead of narrowing as he'd assumed, the valley widened the further he went. Though he was traveling no more than ten miles per hour, he knew he would soon reach the place where the canyon boxed. An abrupt change in topography stopped him before he reached it.

The flat valley floor had begun to roll. Small hills disrupted his path and giant boulders forced him to slow. He finally stopped, climbed to the top of a boulder, and took a long drink of water from his canteen. Something moving in the distance caused him to take notice.

He waited, not moving as he listened for the almost human sound he'd heard. Chalking it up as imagination, he slid off the boulder, returning to the Mule when he heard it again.

Because of the fallen boulders, the trail had narrowed, and he had to pick his way through the rocks carefully. A hawk startled him, swooping low over the Mule in pursuit of a field mouse. As the bird lifted its captive into the trees, he heard a woman crying. It wasn't his imagination.

Chapter 34

Glaring sunlight blinded him as he moved beneath a rare break in the trees. Hoisting his pack, he followed an ancient path to a clump of bushes. Whimpers of a woman in distress grew louder. When he parted the vegetation, he saw who was causing the disturbance.

Female she was, he could see by her pendulous breasts. All else was uncertain. She stood seven feet tall. Except for her breasts and face, grayish-brown hair covered every part of her body. Unlike animal fur, hers looked more like human hair.

She was rushing in hurried circles beside a pool of water, her arms in constant motion. When she saw him, she ran into the brush. She returned, afraid of Buck though too concerned to leave. It took him a moment to understand her cause of alarm.

The upper body of an even larger creature, flailing his arms, protruded from the water. A rapid bend in the creek had formed a stagnant pool, the creature sinking into the green mire. Quicksand, Buck realized. Slipping off his backpack, he grabbed his lariat hanging from a strap.

Except for thick beard and mustache, the face of the creature was bare of hair. Its head was huge, and Buck could only imagine how large he was. Twirling the lariat, he tossed it over the big fellow's outstretched arms. When he tugged on the rope, he realized a powerful suction had the creature trapped.

There was nothing except rapidly darkening sky overhead, the rough terrain making it impossible for trees to grow. Most trees, anyway. The gnarled branches of a stunted oak provided the lever he needed. Tossing the loose end of the rope over the lowest branch, he laid all his weight into it. The female drew close enough to brush past him, concern replacing her fear.

"Help me," he shouted.

She stopped in her tracks, staring at him. He knew a bit of Indian sign language and made the motion signaling he needed help. Reluctant at first, she drew closer, grabbing the rope and pulling.

The female was much stronger than he was. It didn't matter. Both of them pulling together couldn't keep the creature on the other end of the rope from sinking. Spotting a fallen branch, he picked it up as the female began sobbing again.

After pulling off his boots, he plunged into the water, dog paddling toward the panicked creature. When the big fellow began flailing its huge arms, Buck voiced a whispered prayer. Making matters worse, clouds had begun cloaking the sky. It began to rain, first as small drops, and then as a thunderous downpour.

A cloudburst peppered the stagnant water as he reached the creature and rammed the branch into the mud. He needed to break the quicksand's suction. If he failed, its grasp would soon drag the creature below water level. He laid his weight into the branch and began rotating it.

A bubble of air burst to the surface with a loud whoosh. As it did, the creature's lower extremities floated to the surface.

"Help me," Buck yelled to the female.

She was already tugging on the rope. When they reached the shore, he grabbed Bigfoot's shoulders. The massive creature weighed upwards of five hundred pounds. The female hurried to help, and they managed to pull him out of the water. It was then that he saw what had gotten him into the quicksand.

The jaws of a giant bear trap bit into the creature's leg, the wound caked with slimy mud and still oozing blood. He grabbed a first aid kit from his backpack. With its big eyes rolling in pain, Buck stuffed a rag in his mouth.

"Bite hard," he said, patting his chin.

When Buck began opening the trap, the creature's eyes closed and he clamped down on the rag. The jaws of the trap opened with a metallic clank and he slid it off the mangled leg. The big fellow emitted a moan that told Buck everything he needed to know about the depth of his pain.

After purging the wound with alcohol, he poured iodine on it and then wrapped it with a bandage. The bone wasn't broken, though the wound needed stitches. It was something Buck wasn't equipped to do. Finding a syringe and a vial of morphine, he injected the creature, hoping to ease its pain.

The broken chain attached to the bear trap attested to the strength of the creature. Weakened from the loss of blood, he must have stumbled into the stagnant water. Too weak to break the suction, the quicksand had begun pulling him under.

The female hadn't stopped crying. Holding the male's huge head, she continued chattering in some language unknown to Buck.

"Buck," he said, pointing to his chest and then at her. "Who are you?"

"Uligy," she said, her meaning unmistakable. She pointed to the big male. "Squamo."

"Help me, Uligy," he said, motioning toward the Mule.

Together, they managed to lift Squamo onto the back of the Mule. When Buck cranked the engine, Uligy grew animated, rushing in front of the vehicle as she waved her arms. When he changed directions, she nodded her head in the universal sign that she agreed.

"Hop on," he said, patting the seat beside him.

Though she was having no part of the noisy machine, she didn't try to stop him when he started away to the west.

He tooled ahead, following a narrow path through the boulders. The farther they traveled, the broader and wider the canyon became. The surrounding cliffs jutted into the sky. Rounding a bend, he saw something that caused him to disbelieve his own eyes.

A magnificent pyramid like ones he'd seen in the jungles of Yucatan, appeared before him. Worn limestone walls jutted almost to the top of the canyon's cliffs. He had to swerve to miss a fallen sculpture of a bird serpent threatening to block his path.

Heavy rain had morphed into slow drizzle. The rapid drop in temperature resulted in an eerie ground fog that snaked around broken columns, decimated buildings, and once ornate sculptures. Something else, high on the cliff walls, drew his attention.

Tens, if not hundreds of creatures like the one he'd rescued, stared at him from caves in the cliffs. They weren't just adults, but also adolescents and babies. None seemed brave enough to come down from their perches. When the female began calling for help, they approached the Mule.

After they'd lifted him off the vehicle, Buck followed them. They led him up a pathway worn by time to a cavern with an entrance so large that it gaped like a giant's open mouth. It was apropos because every creature in the cave towered over him. He'd not only found Jake's Bigfoot, he'd found dozens of them.

There was also someone else in the cave, and not as large, or as hairy. Though a woman stood with her back to Buck, he could see the rattlesnake tattoo on her shoulder. Thinking it was Esme, he almost gasped when she faced him and he realized she wasn't.

Dark hair draped the young woman's shoulders. Her eyes were the same color as the obsidian in the serpent's orbs littered around the pyramids. Turquoise draped the colorful dress reaching her knees. Her bare toes dug into the sandy floor of the cavern.

She watched as the creatures laid the big male Bigfoot on a bed of leaves. After putting her hand on his wound, she finally turned her attention to Buck.

"You saved Squamo's life. I am grateful, and so are the People of the Night."

"I'm Buck," he said.

"I know who you are. I am Delayne, daughter of Esme and Talako, and granddaughter of Chief Walking Wolf."

"Impossible," he said. "You're almost as old as I am, and I'm as old as your mother."

"And like me, you are also a spirit walker. You have yet to learn that time skews when you move across it."

She turned away, undoing the bandage on Squamo's leg. "What caused this?" she asked.

"Bear trap. He's lucky his leg isn't broken."

"These people have extra-large bones. It would take more than a bear trap to break it."

"Good thing for him or he'd be dead," he said.

She didn't comment as she applied a poultice to the wound. The creature opened his big eyes when she began bathing his forehead with an aromatic fluid.

"Why are you here?" he asked.

"Because you need help. Mother sent me to assist you. The evil one must have set the trap that snared Squamo. You are correct. He would be dead now if not for you."

"Is Uligy . . . ?"

"Squamo's female. She would never have left him."

"And these people?" he asked.

"Gentle souls with no hate in their hearts. This is their home, and they can't defend themselves. You must help me protect them."

"I'm confused. They are huge. Are they human?"

"As human as you or I," she said. "They feel both love and pain. I think you already realized as much."

"They don't smell bad," he said. "Shouldn't they be stinking to high heaven?"

Delayne laughed. "They have a scent bag like a skunk. They only release the foul odor when they are in danger."

"Blade was here?"

"The People watched him as he explored the ruins. It did not take him long to discover the trove of gold in the main pyramid. He must have set the trap before leaving the valley."

"That was several days ago," he said.

"He will return," she said.

One of the meek females brought him a gourd with water. She hurried back into the shadows as he touched the cool liquid to his lips. The view of the giant pyramid from the gaping mouth of the cave was like a picture postcard. A fantasy painting created by a color-happy artist. When he turned, he realized Delayne was smiling as she watched him. A tactile shock of pure pleasure pulsed through his arm when she touched his hand.

"You are even more beautiful than your mother," he said. "I didn't think that was possible."

"Esme told me not to believe a word you say," she said, dimples in her cheeks appearing as she smiled.

"I may have told lots of lies in my life. That wasn't one of them."

With the poultice beginning to work its magic, Squamo moved his big head as Uligy and several females fussed over him. Pulling loose from Buck's grasp, Delayne joined them, squeezing Squamo's thumb that was almost as big as her whole hand. Uligy lay draped across the big creature's chest, sobbing with joy that he was alive.

"Someone must stop Blade. Since I'm from another time, I can do little to help you."

"I understand," Buck said. "Please tell me about this ruined city."

"You already know it's Mayan."

"What happened to the people that built it?"

"The city grew until the valley could no longer support its thriving population. The Mayans moved, some of them assimilating with the Mississippians. The temples and pyramids became a holy place. The Mayans used them for a century or more for religious ceremonies and pilgrimages. The forest assimilated the ruins until it was populated only by the People of the Night."

"Where did the People come from?"

"The far corners of the earth. They live beyond the boundaries of civilization. They are a simple group and harm no one."

"The authorities are looking for Blade. If he returns to the valley, I'll try to deal with him. May be difficult because I have no weapon. What else do you need me to do?"

"You must promise me now that you will go to your grave without telling anyone about the ruins, or the People of the Night; a solemn vow that will surely haunt you for the rest of your life."

Chapter 35

Rain was peppering Buck's tent when he awoke the following morning. Only faint light illuminated a dull day as he hurried to the large canopy he'd erected. Firing up the stove, he began brewing coffee; glad the canvas roof had kept everything dry.

The aroma of bacon and eggs frying soon hung in the damp morning air. A lonesome coyote, its howls echoing in the distance, seemed miles away. He'd finished his last bite when his cell phone rang. It was Don.

"Got news for you," he said.

"Not bad, I hope."

"Blade's on his way into the valley."

"How do you know?" Buck asked.

"Been monitoring flight plans. A Fort Smith charter service filed a point-to-point yesterday. For a chopper flight to the edge of the national forest. I drove to Fort Smith and interviewed the pilot."

"And?"

"The customer paid in cash and used a fake I.D. When I showed the pilot a picture of Blade, he confirmed it was the man booking the flight. The pilot put him on the ground about thirty miles east of you."

"Wasn't he suspicious?"

"Blade told him he was a nature hiker. He had a document authorizing him to trek in the forest. He carried a backpack the pilot said must have weighed a hundred pounds or more."

"Thirty miles is a long hike, even for someone that's had special training."

"You know he's wanted for murder now?"

"Then the DNA on the glass checked out?"

"Like a charm. I notified the county, state, and even the U.S. Marshal's office of his whereabouts."

"And?"

"The Marshals were familiar with Blade. They said a platoon of Green Berets couldn't hunt him down if he wanted to remain out of sight. They advised me to get you the hell out of there, and they'd deal with him when he emerges."

"I'll call Jake and have him abort the expedition. Will you contact Colley and have him bring me a high-powered rifle with a scope, a pistol, and lots of ammo."

"You can't be serious."

"As a heart attack."

"You may be good, partner. When it comes to firefights, you're no match for Blade," Don said.

"I have to try."

"Can I ask why?"

"I don't want this valley opened up to treasure hunters when the story goes viral on social media."

"What difference does it make?"

"I have my reasons."

"My guess is Blade intends to kill everyone in your party and then take his time looting the City of Gold. If he kills you, no one will ever find your body."

"You're scaring me. Doesn't matter because I'm not leaving."

"Fine. I'll call Colley and get you that rifle. When he shows up, I'm gonna be with him."

"You stay put. I'll handle this."

"No way. Watch your back until I join you," Don said, signing off.

With words of doom still ringing in his ears, he called Jake.

"I know you don't want to hear this. You have to abort the expedition."

"Impossible," Jake said. "We're in the air, winging your way."

"I can't talk you into turning around?"

"Tell me what your problem is," Jake said.

"Blade is on his way into the valley. He's Big Shoe's murderer."

"Why would he want to return to the valley?"

"He thinks there's treasure here," Buck said.

"You know anything about a treasure?"

"Just rumors. Doesn't matter because he torched a building in McAlester, and then killed Big Shoe. If he believes there's treasure here, he'll pick us off one by one."

"This shoot sounds juicier every moment. And now I have an ace in the hole."

"What are you talking about?"

"Picked up a celebrity guest. The most eligible bachelor athlete in America. Our ratings will soar. The network executives are watering at the mouth. I couldn't back out now if I wanted to."

"I'm telling you, it's too dangerous. Please reconsider."

"Can't do it. I have Zeke Big Shoe, Ezekiel's son and the quarterback of the New Orleans Saints tagging along. With this treasure angle as a sidebar, we can't miss."

"Seems as if I remember your big shot quarterback knocking you into Clayton's spa. Did you kiss and make up?"

"Touché," Jake said. "Thorn got us together for a few drinks following Ezekiel's funeral. Zeke's mom loves Thorn."

"Oh?"

"The two love bugs were holding hands under the table. From what I saw, wedding bells are imminent."

"Just my luck," Buck said.

"Sorry I'm the one breaking the news to you. I know you and Thorn had a thing going."

"This may seem like the opportunity of a lifetime. It's not. Blade is a killer, and we don't even have a weapon."

"Journalists don't carry weapons. I've never backed away from a story in my life. I won't start now."

"If you aren't afraid, at least consider the others. You could be walking into a death trap."

"I'll talk to them about it. If they're frightened, I'll send them back on the chopper with Colley."

It was wet as he headed toward the cliff below the landing zone. Water misting from the high branches of the giant trees kept his nerves on edge. When he turned off the Mule's engine, he heard the approaching chopper. Zeke Big Shoe was the first person to descend the rope ladder tossed from the ledge.

"How's it going, McDivit? Jake says you're too scared to be part of this expedition."

His taunt was more than Buck could take. His straight right hand dropped the celebrity quarterback to his knees. Blood trickled down Zeke's chin as he glared at Buck, and then grabbed his knees, wrestling him to the ground. They were exchanging punches when Thorn reached the bottom of the ladder.

"Stop it, now!" she shouted.

When they didn't comply, she jumped on top of the fray. A punch nailed her with a glancing blow, knocking her backwards into the mud. Hearing her cries, Buck and Zeke stopped fighting immediately, their attention focused on Thorn.

"You okay?" Buck asked.

"No thanks to you. What the hell are you two doing?"

"That asshole punched me when I wasn't looking."

Thorn grabbed Buck's hand to keep him from punching Zeke again.

"Stop it!" she shouted. "I won't have this."

After helping Kristen descend the ladder, Jake turned his attention to Buck and Zeke.

"Knock it the hell off, and I mean right now," he said. "Who started this?"

"He did," they both said.

"I'm ending it. Leave now with Colley or else save your temper tantrums for when we get back to civilization."

"I'm good," Buck said, holding up his hands.

"Me too," Zeke said. "It's over, far as I'm concerned."

Kristen had a camera on her shoulder, filming the altercation. She managed to get a close-up of Jake's frown and the blood still trickling down Zeke's chin. Buck brushed himself off and walked to the Mule.

"What's going on down there?" Colley yelled from the top of the cliff.

"We're cool," Jake called. "Send down our stuff."

One by one, Colley began lowering their backpacks on a rope. Kristen climbed up the ladder, filming the chopper as it disappeared into angry clouds. Slipping as she descended, Zeke caught her. Thorn gave him a dirty look when he glanced to check her reaction.

Buck didn't bother helping them load their backpacks on the back of the Mule. Other than him, Jake was the only person present on the previous trip to the valley. The view astounded Thorn, Kristen, and Zeke. Heavy rain had returned, and they pulled their poncho hoods over their heads.

"You couldn't put two of those giant trees on a football field," Zeke said.

"They are so huge," Thorn said.

Kristen remained silent, her camera capturing their trip up the canyon. Her eyes grew larger when they reached the sculpted rock formation rising up from the valley floor. Buck remained in the Mule as Zeke followed Thorn and Kristen up the path to the top of the worn and eroded monolith.

"I named it Saddle Rock during our last visit," Jake said.

Thorn pointed to the cliff. "Oh my God!" she said. "What a beautiful waterfall."

Jake had already started down. "Let's go," he said. "You'll have plenty of time to check things out when it stops raining."

Thorn was grumbling as she joined Kristen and Zeke in the back of the Mule. Buck slowed to give them a better look as they drove past the waterfall pool. When they reached the canopy, he started a fresh pot of coffee as they unloaded their backpacks.

Thorn glanced up at the mouth of the cavern gaping behind them. "Is that our cave?" she asked.

"Let's have lunch, and then we'll explore it," Jake said. "Rain won't bother us there."

The gray day had only grown drearier as Buck served lunch.

"Grilled cheese sandwiches and tomato soup. Sorry I'm not a better cook."

"Just what I needed," Kristen said.

She'd finally put the camera down, a tear in her eye as she bit into her sandwich. Everyone was in a dark mood following Ezekiel Big Shoe's funeral. Buck tapped her shoulder.

"Sorry for your loss," he said.

"Thank you," she said.

Jake scowled at him for introducing a sore subject. No one else commented. When he finished eating, Jake stuck his hand out from the canopy. The rain showed no sign of abating as he slipped his poncho back over his shoulders.

"This isn't getting any better. Ready to check out the cave?"

Buck cleaned the dishes and tidied around the propane stove as the others started away to the cavern. Zeke stayed behind; slow to slip his own poncho over his shoulders.

"You didn't like my dad, did you?" he asked.

"I hardly knew him."

"What's going on here?"

"I'm not sure what you mean," Buck said.

"There's tension between you and Jake."

"He didn't tell you?"

"Tell me what?" Zeke said.

"The man that killed your dad is on his way into the valley. I told Jake he should abort this expedition. He said he'd give the three of you the option to leave with Colley."

"No one knows who murdered my dad."

"They do now. Haskel Doonkeen, your dad's business partner, killed him."

Zeke took a step in his direction, clinching his fist as if he were about to take a swing. Stopping short, he slammed it against the table instead. After taking a deep breath, he closed his eyes.

"Tell me what you know," he said.

"Doonkeen was stealing Indian artifacts. He and your dad had a company that sold them around the world."

"Not true," Zeke said.

"Doonkeen was getting inside information. Whenever Thorn and her group made a significant discovery, someone would steal it."

"What are you getting at?" Zeke asked.

"Pillow talk. You and Thorn were an item. She told you what was going on at the Archaeological Museum, and you let your father know what she said."

"I didn't," Zeke said.

Buck held up his palm. "I'm sure neither you nor Thorn had any idea you were tipping off the enemy. He'd quiz you, wouldn't he?"

"He was an honest man," Zeke said.

"You knew Kristen was his girlfriend. You saw them together."

"He wasn't perfect."

"Do you know that you have a brother?" Buck asked.

"What?"

"His name is Justin. He was at the funeral yesterday. His dad is your dad. He kept the books for Forbidden Treasures, the company Doonkeen and Ezekiel owned."

"This is too much information for me to handle right now," Zeke said.

"You have no choice. Doonkeen thinks there's treasure in this valley. He intends to kill us so he can keep the secret to himself. Colley will be returning with weapons for me. It may be too late."

"I don't believe you."

"Checked your cell phone lately?"

Zeke saw there was no signal when he pulled it from his pocket. "What the hell!" he said.

"Blade must have a jamming device he's employing to keep us from using our phones."

"That's crazy," Zeke said.

"We have no weapons. Blade does. If we do nothing, he'll kill us, take our scalps and leave our bodies to rot. Is that what you want?"

Zeke didn't answer. Rain poured even harder as thunder rumbled through the valley.

"What'll we do?" he finally asked.

"This valley goes pitch-black after dark. I'm not

trying to scare you. We need to stay in the cavern tonight.”

“Fuck you, McDivit! I’m blitzed by monster linemen intent on breaking every bone in my body every Sunday. I’m not afraid of Blade.”

“This ain’t football. It’s not a game at all. Blade’s as big as one of your linemen, and has a knife and a sniper rifle. If you don’t care about yourself, then at least think about Thorn.”

After a moment, Zeke said, “Got a plan?”

“We need weapons, and then we have to confront Jake before he gets us all killed.”

“I saw a canebrake at the base of the cliff. When I was a kid, we made bows, arrows, and spears using cane we’d cut.”

“And you think . . . ?”

“It’s the only idea I have,” he said.

“Then let’s do it. It’s a sorry plan, though better than anything I’ve come up with, and we may not have much time left.”

Chapter 36

They could hear Jake's voice echoing in the distance as they carried bundles of cane up the rope ladder to the cavern. After dropping their load near the entrance, they followed the sound into the darkness. They found Kristen filming and Jake watching as Thorn pointed to carvings in the wall.

"These glyphs are Mississippian," she said. "Probably carved a thousand years ago by a native point maker."

Kristen focused her camera on the cavern floor where piles of arrowheads and spear tips lay strewn.

"Where did they get the flint?" Jake asked. "The walls of this cavern are limestone."

"Not this wall," Thorn said. "It's chert, another name for flint." She picked up a beautifully serrated arrowhead. "Chert found in this region is perfect for creating points. Indians traveled thousands of miles, even from as far away as South America to trade for it. Mississippian artisans were the best point makers in the world."

Zeke picked up two spearheads and showed them to Buck.

"Put those back," Thorn said.

"We need them. Tell her, Buck."

Jake and Kristen waited to hear what he had

to say.

"What's he talking about?" Thorn asked.

"I gave Jake some important information earlier today. He apparently didn't see fit to tell you."

"Tell us what?" she said.

"Haskel Doonkeen killed Ezekiel. He thinks there's treasure in the valley. He's on his way here as we speak."

"That's bullshit, and you know it," Jake said.

"Do I? Tried your cell phone lately?"

Jake pulled it from his pocket, quickly realizing it had no signal.

"Blade's jamming our phones."

"Impossible," Jake said.

"Shut up and let him finish," Zeke said.

"Blade is armed and dangerous. We brought water and food from camp. We should stay here in the cavern until Colley returns with help."

"Kristen, I hope you caught this horseshit on camera," Jake said. "I'm going to debunk this whole charade right now."

He hurried to the mouth of the cave and started down the rope ladder.

"Don't do it," Buck said. "Even if he isn't here yet, he soon will be."

"Slosh around in bat guano if you like. I'm sleeping in my own tent tonight."

"What now?" Zeke asked.

"Make the spears," Buck said.

Hours passed, Jake strutting around the campsite below as if daring someone to shoot him. Buck kept an eye on him as he and Zeke crafted spears using twine, cane, and ancient Mississippian spearheads.

"Sure about this?" Thorn asked.

"When I talked with Don this morning he confirmed that Blade is in the valley. He's on foot and still a few hours away. Since his jamming technology is working already, I'd say he's close. I promise he's not here just to say hello."

"Whatever," she said. "Kristen, let's do more filming while we wait."

Rain continued pouring in sheets, keeping Jake confined to the dry space beneath the rectangular canopy. Buck watched him pace as Zeke added twine to the bow he'd made. Thorn and Kristen were returning when a shot rang through the valley.

A bullet wheeled Jake around. Dropping to his knees, he held his arm before collapsing to the ground beneath the canopy.

"Oh my God!" Thorn said, starting for the ladder.

Buck grabbed her arm. "Get down," he yelled. "Now!"

"Someone has to go for him," Kristen said.

"That's what Blade wants us to do. He could have killed Jake if he'd wanted to. He's using him as a decoy to draw us into the open."

When Jake tried to crawl to the end of the canopy, rifle shots pelted the ground around him.

"How deep is the pool?" Zeke asked.

"I couldn't touch bottom in the center," Buck said. "Why?"

"I'm fast enough to reach the ledge above the pool before Blade realizes I'm coming. There's a string of boulders almost all the way to the big tent from the water. I can pull Jake behind cover before Blade can get a shot off."

"This isn't the NFL," Buck said. "If you fail, you'll be permanently sacked."

"I'll take my chances."

"You'll still have to climb the ladder. Blade will never let you reach the top."

"Maybe he won't have to," Kristen said. "There's a maze of passageways in this cavern system. One of them probably leads to the pool."

"Then why not just go that way?" Buck asked.

"Because many of them are dead ends that get progressively smaller until they trap you," Thorn said. "Since we don't know which is which, we can't chance it."

"Once I have Jake, you can lead me up the correct passage by calling to me," Zeke said.

"Too risky," Buck said.

"A risk I'm willing to take."

The light beneath the canopy of vegetation had started to darken as Zeke stripped to his undershorts.

Thorn clutched his hand. "You don't always have to be the hero," she said.

Zeke kissed her, pulled away, sprinted out the mouth of the cavern and swan-dived into the pool as a bullet ricocheted off the rock wall behind him. After entering the pool headfirst, he swam underwater as Blade fired three more rounds. An explosion of sound echoed through the canyon, the last round dying away as Buck, Thorn, and Kristen held their cumulative breaths.

"He made it," Kristen said.

"So far, so good," Buck said. "Blade will be waiting for him to show himself."

As if he'd heard Buck's remark, Blade put two rounds through the door of the cavern.

"Shit," Kristen said. "Those were close."

Buck began searching through his pack, digging until he found his lariat. When he did, he stripped to his boxer shorts.

"I'm going down there. Blade probably has night vision equipment. Even if he has infrared, he won't be able to see the rope after dark.

"Then all three of you will die," Kristen said.

"No, we won't. Just make sure you help us find our way up the inside passage."

Without waiting for a reply, he raced toward the ledge above the pool, doing a cannonball into it, shots ringing out as he did. Zeke flinched when Buck touched his shoulder.

"I didn't need help," he said.

"Shut the hell up! I'll use this to pull Jake to us without the risk of getting shot."

"You can get that thing over him from here?"

"I was Oklahoma roping champ in high school. We need to wait till after dark."

Just before darkness swallowed the valley, Buck tossed the noose over one of Jake's outstretched arms.

"Got him," he said, pulling the noose tight. "He's dead weight. I need your help. Easy does it, or Blade will put another bullet in him."

Buck held his breath as they worked Jake ever closer to the shelter of the boulder covering him and Zeke. Fire suddenly flashed in the mouth of the cavern. As smoke wafted from the opening, Blade opened a volley toward it.

The ruse provided just enough time for Buck and Zeke to pull Jake behind the boulder. The mud and blood caking his shoulder wound had probably saved him from bleeding to death. They hurried him to the overhang beneath the opening of the cavern, immediately hearing Thorn's voice.

"Not that way," Zeke said when the path bifurcated.

"How do you know?" Buck asked.

"I'm feeling it. Just trust me on this one."

Ashes from the fire Thorn and Kristen had set flickered as they dragged Jake into a shielded room from the main part of the cavern. Thorn had spread a survival blanket on the cave floor as bats exited in waves from the hollows of the dark complex.

Buck and Zeke stood guard near the entrance as Thorn began cleaning Jake's wounds with water and rags. Kristen soon joined them.

"What now?" she said.

"Wait until morning. Blade has a position on Saddle Rock. If we try to move, he'll pick us off."

"How?" Zeke said.

"He'll have night vision goggles and scope. He can see us no matter how dark it gets."

"I didn't think night vision worked in complete darkness," Zeke said.

"Infrared senses changes in body heat. You stand up now, and he'll drop you, I promise."

Buck glanced at Zeke when he said, "He's a demon of darkness. You saved my life. I'm sorry about wrestling Thorn away from you. I know she was your . . ."

"Unanswered desire?" Buck said, finishing his question.

"Not exactly what I meant to say," Zeke said. "What now? We can't see in the dark."

"Yes you can," Kristen said.

"How?" Zeke asked.

"You're like me, almost full-blood. My grandma used to tell me she could see in the dark, a power only Indians have. I didn't believe her until my house caught fire. I found my baby daughter in a room filled with smoke."

"I'm happy you found her. You were lucky," Zeke said.

"No," she said. "Something guided me to her. My grandma had the power. So do I, and so do you."

"And if he doesn't?" Buck said.

"You have to trust yourself and the power of the Great Spirit," she said. "If you don't, you may as well dive headfirst off the cliff right now."

Zeke was silent for a moment. "How will I keep Blade from shooting me the minute I raise my head?"

"Mud," Buck said. "We'll coat ourselves with mud. Blade's infrared can't see through it."

"I don't need you," Zeke said. "I can toss a

football seventy yards with accuracy. If I get close enough, I'll crock that sorry asshole right through the heart."

"And I'll be there with you in case you miss, and we have to go into overtime," Buck said.

Thorn joined them. "I'm going with you," she said.

"No way," Zeke said. "Too risky."

"You'll never kill Blade with a spear, and no one can use a bow like me," she said.

"Someone has to stay to protect Kristen and Jake in case we fail," Buck said.

There were shallow pools of water with muddy bottoms throughout the cavern system. After stripping naked, Zeke and Buck caked their bodies with sticky goo until they looked like alien creatures. Buck half expected one of Blade's bullets to pierce his back as they descended the rope ladder.

The mud did its job, and they made it to the valley floor without alerting Blade. After connecting themselves with a length of twine, they started into the darkness. Buck yanked on the twine and drew close to Zeke.

"You know where you're going?" he whispered.

"Kristen was right. I'm a cat in the dark. I see the rock ahead of us. Blade is lying prone on it, not even looking our way."

"Maybe so," Buck said. "But the rain has already washed off most of our mud. He's going to spot us before you get close enough to clock him with your spear."

"Chance we'll have to take," Zeke said.

When a stick snapped beneath Buck's foot, Blade wheeled and fired. Too late for a surprise, Zeke broke the twine, released a blood-curdling war whoop, and then rushed the rock. Buck followed, relying on rapid flashes from Blade's rifle to guide him.

Zeke beat him to the rock, Buck right behind, following him up the path to Blade's vantage. Hearing them, he turned and fired from the hip. Hot lead whistled past them, muzzle flash illuminating the big sniper just long enough for Zeke to launch his spear. When it missed, he dived on him.

Buck could hear the sounds of battle as Zeke and Blade fought on the ledge above him. Total darkness had encompassed the valley, and he banged into solid rock after erring off the path to the top. He could also hear the clink of Blade's knife against the rock as he attempted to use it on Zeke. Unable to find his way up, he was about to panic when a dim glow illuminated the path. It was Inger, the forest spirit, floating above his head.

"Who am I?" she asked

"Sister of Fire," he yelled. "Bring the Arrow of Justice, and hurry."

Before her glow disappeared, he used it to rush up the path and join the fray, touching the sticky goo of oozing blood as he dived on top of the two men locked in the grip of death. Grabbing Blade's ponytail, he yanked hard, hoping to break his neck. His efforts earned him a slash from the bite of a knife.

When bright light lit the darkness, they found themselves staring at the big Indian, grinning like a demon as he prepared to shove his knife into Zeke's chest. He never got the chance.

Dropping the knife, Blade grabbed his neck as an arrow penetrated it. Blood gurgled from his lips as another pointed projectile penetrated his heart. Blade was already dead as he toppled off the monolith, landing with a thud on the ground below.

Thorn waited at the base of Saddle Rock, the makeshift bow still in her hands. Above her, Inger floated, her body radiating fluorescent light that began changing from flickering green to sparkling gold. Having no better response, Zeke dropped to his knees, raised his hands to the heavens, and began to pray.

Chapter 37

When Colley's chopper landed at dawn, he found the members of Jake's expedition waiting for him. Don was with him, moving well as he climbed down the rope ladder. He waved, looking relieved when he saw Buck sitting behind the wheel.

"Want us to break camp and retrieve the equipment?" Colley asked.

Jake was cognizant, lying on his back, his arm in a sling.

"Leave it. I'm sure this fiasco was my last shot with the network. All I want to do now is forget about it."

"You kidding?" Kristen said. "I captured the entire story on camera. I'm predicting there's an Emmy in your future."

"You okay?" Don asked.

"Nothing eight hours of sound sleep and a few band-aids won't cure," Buck said. "Thanks for coming. I'm glad we didn't need you."

"Me too."

The previous night's rain had moved east leaving behind a gorgeous blue sky. The chopper hovered a moment over the forest before turning and heading back to the lodge. Realizing he'd likely never see the glorious valley again, Buck took one last look.

Wearing a headset, Don occupied the co-pilot's seat next to Colley. Glancing into the passenger compartment, he winked at Buck, giving him a thumbs up. Buck mouthed a silent thank you.

Zeke had sustained several non-life threatening cuts from Blade's knife. With bandages on his chest and arms, he sat with his eyes closed as Kristen and Thorn cared for him and Jake. Thorn's look of concern told Buck everything he needed to know when she stopped what she was doing to talk to him.

"You okay?" she asked.

"One little cut on the chest. Nothing like Zeke's wounds."

"I'm sorry I haven't had a chance before now to tell you about Zeke and me," she said.

"That big hunk of ice on your ring finger already told me everything I needed to know. You saved our lives last night. I'm happy Inger reached you in time."

"Who is Inger?"

"Yellow Paint Woman's granddaughter," he said. "She lighted the way for you last night so you could find Zeke and me."

"I'm Indian. I found my way just like Zeke did by using my native perception."

"You don't remember the old woman's prophecy from the night we visited her?"

Her stern expression lightened into a grin for the first time.

"The only thing I remember is waking up naked in the grass with you groping me," she said. "I don't know what happened that night. I'd appreciate it if you'd keep it to yourself."

Buck started to say something and then thought better of it.

When they landed at the lodge, Thorn hugged him. Zeke clasped his hand before he could exit the chopper.

"I'm proud to know you," he said.

"Hope you two invite me to your wedding," Buck said.

"Wouldn't have it any other way, cowboy," Thorn said.

"I have tickets on the 50-yard line any time you have the urge to see a Saints game," Zeke said.

"Then I'm holding out for the Super Bowl," Buck said.

"One more thing," Zeke said. "You taught me a lot about life and my Indian heritage. I'm grateful. Tomorrow, I'm returning to the lodge to meet the little brother I never knew I had. Thanks for everything."

Jake got into the act. "I acted like a fool back there. Please understand, I'm forever appreciative of you and Zeke for saving my sorry life. Forgive me?"

"If you agree to let me tag along on one of your future expeditions," Buck said.

"Consider it done, pal."

Don removed his headset and climbed into the passenger compartment.

"I'm escorting Blade's body to McAlester," he said. "I'll file the police report, and wrap this case up with a pretty bow."

"Need me to come with you?"

"I'll take care of everything from here on out. You deserve a little R&R."

"Then it'll be awhile before I see you again," Buck said. "I'm heading home soon as I pack my things."

"Sooner than you think," Don said. "Josie's already picked out a house in Logan County. We'll be moving this weekend."

"Wonderful," Buck said. "I'll see you next week, help you move if you need me, and then we can tip a few cold ones to celebrate."

"You got it, good buddy," Don said as he

strapped his seatbelt and readjusted his headset."

Colley's chopper lifted into the air, banked to the west and headed toward McAlester. He watched until it disappeared. Clayton tapped his shoulder, shaking his hand when he turned around

He, Lana, and Justin were waiting to greet him. It felt like a homecoming as they exchanged handshakes and hugs.

"You're a hero," Clayton said.

"I'm glad Colley had a body bag onboard because I'm happy never to see Shampe Canyon again."

"What about the City of Gold?" Clayton asked.

"Only a pipedream; Blade's map the wishful thinking of some long dead conquistador," he said.

"And Jake's Bigfoot?" Lana asked.

"Oh, he's out there all right, though I doubt anyone will ever find him. How are you, Justin?"

The young man beamed when he said, "I have a job again."

"With Ezekiel gone, the lodge needed a new bookkeeper," Lana said.

"That's not all," Clayton said. "We're building a new Mexican restaurant here on the grounds. Lola will run it, and Justin will keep the books. Each of them will own a third. Lola and her kids will have their own house close by."

"And I have my own room at the lodge," Justin said. "With my cat, and a computer that is mine."

"Everyone on staff loves him," Lana said. "Oh, and Don is working for me now."

"That right? How does Clayton feel about you stealing away his best employee?" Buck asked.

"Don't you worry about old Clayton. Don will be around whenever we need him."

"You look so tired," Lana said. "Let's adjourn to the cabin, get you something to eat, and some sleep in a real bed."

"Thanks," he said. "But I have to pick up Pard and Lady from Thorn's ranch."

"You think they've missed you?" Clayton asked.

"Not as much as I've missed them," he said.

"Then we have a surprise for you," Lana said.

Pard met them at the door, jumping into Buck's open arms.

"Thorn's mom dropped them off earlier today. Lady's waiting down at the stables," Clayton said.

"Thank you," Buck said.

"Justin and I have some work to do at the lodge. Glad you didn't get yourself killed," Clayton said, slapping his shoulder.

"You look beat," Lana said, leading him into the kitchen. "I'll make a smoothie to boost your energy. I'm dying to hear what happened out there."

Listening to a whirring juicer, he watched as she blended fresh fruits and vegetables. He began feeling better after the first wonderful sip.

"Tastes great," he said. "What's in it?"

"Avocado, kale, spinach, coconut water, apple, and a few mint leaves. Works like a charm. Now tell me how you managed to survive out there."

"I had help."

"Who?" she asked.

Lana was the religious director of Lycaia, a town founded on Native American spiritual beliefs. They called the ancient sect the Southern Death Cult.

"You're one of the few people I can tell that would believe me. A forest spirit named Inger helped save us."

He waited for her reaction. Instead, she finished her smoothie, mixed a dry martini for herself and a Wild Turkey for him.

"Sounds as if you should recount your story while savoring an adult beverage. Now tell me about Inger."

"Several nights ago, Thorn and I visited an old Indian shaman named Yellow Paint Woman. A young woman there told us she was the old woman's granddaughter. Her name was Inger. Turns out, she wasn't quite human."

"I'm intrigued. Please continue."

"We became intoxicated during a tobacco ceremony performed by the old woman. During the ritual, she recited a prophetic riddle in the form of a poem. I didn't have a clue what it meant."

"But you do now?"

"The tobacco was hallucinogenic, Thorn and I both naked when we awoke the next morning."

Lana rested her elbows on the table and drew closer.

"Don't dare leave me in suspense. What happened?"

"There was a storm on the mountain, rain falling in buckets. Inger stripped off her clothes and led us to a pool of water she called the womb. She was beautiful, blond, and blue-eyed. Her golden skin glowed like the ring around an autumn moon. We didn't make love, though the warmth I felt was the most intimate moment of my life. It was like a dream."

"A wet dream," Lana said. "Keep that thought while I mix us another."

Buck sipped his fresh drink, enjoying the whiskey's burn as it touched his lips.

"Inger took our hands and flew us over Shampe Canyon. Thorn remembers nothing. Inger appeared to me twice after that night, both times reminding me of the riddle. The last time saved my life."

"Tell me the riddle," Lana said.

"Demon of Darkness, unanswered desire, mistaken judgment, Sister of Fire, Arrow of Justice, or death in the mire."

"What does it mean?" she said.

"Blade was the Demon of Darkness, Thorn my unanswered desire. Inger was the Sister of Fire, and Thorn the Arrow of Justice."

"And your mistaken judgment?"

"I thought I had all the answers to the riddle. Everything except for the identity of the person destined to kill Blade. Zeke and I were close to death when Inger appeared. When I saw her, the riddle's answer popped into my head. Thorn, an expert with a bow and arrow, was our salvation. Once Inger knew I had the answer, she bent time bringing her to save us."

"And Thorn doesn't remember Inger?"

Buck shook his head. "She thinks her Native American perception led her to us."

"Quite a story," Lana said, slugging her martini. "I feel I know Inger, the Goddess of Light, and I can't remember feeling quite so hot. Clayton's in for a pleasant surprise when he returns home tonight."

Chapter 38

Buck was loading the Jeep the next morning when Lana and Clayton exited the cabin. Holding hands, they were both beaming.

"Remind me to give you a raise when we get back home," Clayton said.

"Have a good time last night?" Buck asked.

"You can't even imagine," Clayton said. "Lana is one fantastic woman. Getting ready to leave?"

"Quick as I can load Lady and head down the mountain."

"You're in for a surprise," Lana said.

"Oh? A pleasant one, I hope," he said.

"I think it'll make you happy," she said. "I talked with Jim and Carol earlier this morning. Little Adam is spending the rest of the summer with them. They've already picked him up."

"That's wonderful news," he said. "You two sticking around here for awhile?"

"KK and Sara are on their way to join us. Meanwhile, Clay and I are planning to take an evening walk down one of the forest trails. See if we can find that forest spirit you told me about."

"Good luck," he said, waving out the window as he backed out of the drive.

Pard's head poked out the passenger window after heading down the mountain.

"We're going home, Pard. First, we're stopping to see Jim, Carol, Coco, and Adam."

Pard barked as if he understood.

"What then, you say? I haven't forgotten that pretty Guthrie photographer named Laura. Maybe I can talk her into line dancing and a few cold one's Saturday night."

As Pard barked his approval, a flickering light appeared in the sky. Inger's image flashed for a moment, then burst into an exploding climax of fiery colors and disappeared.

Buck smiled and blew her a kiss.

END

Book Notes

Southeast Oklahoma is a beautiful and mysterious place of which few people outside the state are aware. The Mounds at Spiro are real; the Heavener Runestones are real; The Black Cup is real; the ancient Ouachita Mountain Range is real.

Is Bigfoot real? Hundreds of sightings of the giant, nocturnal creature in southeast Oklahoma are hard to explain away. There's even a yearly Bigfoot festival in the tiny town of Honobia, Oklahoma.

I had a blast writing Blink of an Eye, my third novel featuring Buck Mcdivit, my flawed and horny P.I. with a heart of gold, that loves animals and doesn't have an ounce of quit in his body.

If you liked *Blink of an Eye*, please check out *Ghost of a Chance* and *Bones of Skeleton Creek*, Books 1 and 2 of the Paranormal Cowboy series. If you love mystery, thrills, and suspense with a touch of romance, you might also like my French Quarter Mystery series set in New Orleans.

Thanks for being a fan. Without wonderful readers like you, my stories would be little more than morning fog wafting across a forgotten lawn before disappearing forever into the Great Unknown.

About the Author

Born on a Louisiana bayou, Halloween night, beneath a full moon, Eric Wilder grew up escaping snakes and alligators and listening to his grandmothers' tales of ghosts, voodoo, and political corruption.

The author of ten novels, four cookbooks, many short stories, and *Murder Etouffee* that defies classification, he now lives in Oklahoma, about a mile from historic Route 66, with his wife Marilyn, three dogs, one coyote, a cat, but not a single alligator.

www.ingramcontent.com/pod-product-compliance
Lightning Source LLC
Chambersburg PA
CBHW050547190726
48283CB00007B/2042